Gaylene B Corben is a compliance specialist living on the beautiful South Coast of NSW. She has a Science degree majoring in Biology, a post graduate Compliance degree, a Diploma of Education and has completed courses at the Australian Writers' Centre. Gaylene has transitioned from teaching high school students to writing policy documents and training guides in the financial services industry to writing her debut novel.

A DATE TO

Die For

Gaylene B Corben

AIA PUBLISHING

A Date to Die For
Gaylene B Corben
Copyright © 2022
Published by AIA Publishing, Australia
ABN: 32736122056
http://www.aiapublishing.com

ISBN: 978-1-922329-28-8

*To my mother who introduced me to the
world of creative writing.*

*To my father who taught me the value of hard
work and perseverance.*

*To my husband for his unending encouragement, support
and most importantly love, throughout this journey.*

*To our police, past, present and future, male, female
and K9, for their commitment, courage and diligent
service to the community.*

1

The devil whispered in my ear, 'You're not strong enough to withstand the storm.' I whispered back, 'I am the storm.'
—Unknown.

The scene held no hint of the violent act that took a young woman's life the night before. The ocean's salty scent, drifting on the early morning breeze, added to the freshness and tranquillity of the morning. Tiny diamonds sparkled in the silver-blue ocean under the rising sun. A golden retriever chased the white foam of breaking waves, barked at squawking seagulls, and played on the cool, wet sand with the spirit and energy only a young pup can have.

A surfer in the distance, board under arm, whistled and called the dog. 'C'mon girl, you'll get left behind.'

The dog sprinted towards the young man to catch up. Ten metres … twenty metres … then she slowed … and then she stopped. She sniffed the air and cocked her head as she looked towards where the beach meets the spinifex-covered sand dunes. She looked at the surfer, looked back to the sand dunes, looked at the surfer again and whimpered. The dog's two-hundred-million-plus scent receptors had separated the familiar smells of the salt air, seaweed, seagull droppings and surfboard wax, from an unfamiliar, but ominously metallic, slightly sweet odour.

The surfer strolled over to the dog and knelt beside her. 'What is it, girl?'

The dog ran to where the pale gold sand meets the silvery spinifex reflecting the morning sun. The surfer followed. Then he slowed ... and then he stopped, just like the dog had. What the dog had sniffed moments before, the surfer now saw. He fell to his knees and vomited. He vomited where the beach meets the sand dunes. Just a metre from the mutilated body, concealed in the blood-splattered spinifex.

***

Detective Joseph Paterson could hear John Lennon singing 'Imagine' faintly in the distance. The music grew louder and closer, more persistent. Where was it coming from? Eventually, he half woke from a restless sleep and fumbled for his iPhone to turn off the alarm. With gritty eyes and lids that didn't want to open, Joe yawned, stretched, and put his feet on the cool timber floor. He stood, and still bleary-eyed, shuffled to the bathroom.

Refreshed after a short, but hot shower, Joe towel dried his thick brown hair and dressed in dark grey suit pants and a white shirt. He paused at the mirror and ran his fingers across the small, jagged scar under his left eye, a more recent scar than the red, round bullet wound on his right shoulder.

Joe checked his watch. Enough time for breakfast. Coffee and toast, maybe an egg. He walked down the long hallway, past the study and the guest room, to the kitchen. Joe stopped, put his hand on his hips, and shook his head. A smoky grey ball of fur with yellow-green eyes greeted him from the middle of the grey granite kitchen bench. 'Banjo, how many times have I told you—benches are out of bounds for cats?' Banjo sprung from the bench with a loud 'meow.'

'You think because you're the same colour as the bench that I won't notice you. I should have named you Macavity— Macavity the master criminal who defies the law.' Banjo weaved and rubbed his way back and forth around Joe's legs, stopped at the fridge and looked up at Joe with big round expectant eyes. 'Okay, okay, I know—you're hungry. Let's find Bonnie first?'

A light tan greyhound sat on her bed in a corner of the living room, her brown eyes watchful. Joe knelt beside her and rubbed behind her ears. 'Hey, Bonnie,' he said gently. 'How's my favourite girl? Time for breakfast.' Bonnie wagged her tail ever so slightly.

Bonnie and Banjo fed, Joe reached for the coffee jar just as his mobile buzzed with a text from Detective Tessa Rose Mariani. 'Can you drop by my place—need a lift?'

'Okay, there in forty-five,' he replied.

He reached for the coffee again. His mobile rang the theme from *Law and Order*.

'Who? … Where? … On my way.'

He put the coffee jar back and turned it, so the label faced forward. Too early for breakfast anyway, he thought.

Joe sent another text to Tessa. 'Be there in twenty-five. A body at the beach.'

***

Tessa was locking the security door of her town house when Joe arrived. Her conservative black pants, white shirt, black jacket, and low-heeled black boots—disguised a bubbly, extravert personality.

Tessa opened the back door of Joe's car and tossed her backpack on the floor. She hopped in the front, clicked her seatbelt, and brushed a strand of wavy brown hair from her dark brown eyes. Joe heaved a silent sigh of relief when she didn't slam the door of his black Holden Monaro like she had the first time she rode in his pride and joy.

'Thanks for picking me up. Any details about the body?'

'Young, female.' Joe checked the rear-view mirror, looked over his right shoulder, and pulled out from the curb. 'A teenage boy found her early this morning. Well, his dog did really.'

Tessa said, 'Is it ...'

'I don't know.'

'Okay, I guess we'll know more soon enough.'

***

Fifty-five minutes after he got the call, Joe parked behind a police patrol car flashing red and blue lights. The general duties officer had set up the control centre on the beach and secured the scene, keeping back the usual inquisitive onlookers. Some of them, Joe knew, would be eager for ghoulish gossip fodder to munch over with friends at the coffee shop later that day. The sketch artist, wearing protective gear to prevent contaminating the evidence, recorded the scene. Joe saw Olivia Chatfield, the police photographer, talking to an officer and wondered if she'd finished filming the scene. As if reading his mind, she pointed to her camera and gave him the thumbs up.

The forensic pathologist arrived a few minutes after Joe and Tessa, and the three made their way to the body in silence.

Joe closed his eyes and felt the sun's warmth on the back of his neck and a cool sea breeze on his cheeks. A perfect spring morning—no, wrong—not perfect. Not perfect for the victim's

4

family. Only they don't know it yet. Joe imagined that the family would be at this moment carrying on with their normal daily routine, unaware of the devastating news they were about to receive. He took a deep breath, as if to renew his emotional energy. Then he opened his eyes. Opened his eyes to see the unseeing blue eyes of the mutilated corpse. Joe felt for the button in his pocket. The button he always carried with him when he was on duty. The one from his late father's police uniform. He massaged the button between his thumb and index finger, a gesture that was his silent commitment to the victim.

The victim's blood-stained midnight blue cocktail dress, black bra and matching panties were shredded. The mangled flesh of her chest and abdomen, bloodied from multiple stab wounds, left little doubt about how she died. A thorny white rose protruded from between her legs, and a note pinned to her left breast fluttered quietly in the gentle morning breeze.

Fists clenched, shaking her head, Tessa said, 'Just like the others.'

Almost to himself, Joe murmured, 'Yeah ... number three.'

'Roses used to be my favourite flower. Not anymore,' Tessa said.

'I'll know more after I've examined her,' said the forensic pathologist. 'But it looks like she wasn't alive when he, assuming *he* put the thorny end of the rose inside her—thankfully.'

There's nothing here to be thankful for, Joe thought.

The victim's face was slashed and disfigured. Her short hair matted with blood and sand.

'She's blonde, like the others,' Tessa said. 'I wonder if she was pretty, like the others?'

Joe shook his head. 'Impossible to tell.'

Tessa took a step closer to the young woman's body. 'The note ...'

Joe breathed deeply and nodded. 'Looks the same as the other two.'

'When I get my hands on the son of a ...'

Joe interrupted Tessa's outburst. 'What time?' he asked the forensic pathologist. *When did her heart stop pumping blood?* Joe thought, feeling his own heart pounding in his chest. He stared at the body, discoloured a purplish red in the lower regions, due to gravity causing the blood to pool there.

'Judging by her temperature and rigor mortis, I'd say between ten and fifteen hours ago. So probably sometime last night between seven and midnight.'

'Here, or was she moved?' From the amount of blood that had transformed patches of the surrounding sand from gold to dark red, Joe knew the answer.

'Here. There's no indication she's been moved.'

'Who was first on scene?' Joe called out.

An officer, who looked to be around forty, stepped forward.

Joe recognised him. 'Still hanging in there, Tom?'

'Yeah, nineteen bloody years on the job, but this ...' he pointed to the body, 'you never get used to it.'

'Have we found the murder weapon?' Joe asked.

'Not yet,' Tom said.

'We'll need to sift the sand in the area,' Joe said. 'Who found her?'

'He did.' Tom pointed to a young man patting his dog's head while talking to an officer near the control centre. 'I told him to wait till you got here.'

A couple in their mid to late forties, who Joe assumed was the young man's parents, stood next to him.

'He knows nothing,' Tom said. 'The first he suspected something odd was when his dog started acting a bit weird like. The only other thing he mentioned was the car. He saw it parked up on the street when he first got here.' Tom pointed. 'It's up there, near the restaurant. The blue Corolla—it's the victim's car. We checked. The registration matches the name on her licence. We found her bag near her body. It contains a wallet with cash and credit cards, brush, lipstick, the usual. And her mobile. There doesn't appear to be anything missing.'

'Where's the driver's licence?' Joe asked.

An officer from the evidence collection team handed Joe a clear evidence bag that contained the licence.

The photo of Phoebe Anne Duncan on the licence resembled the victim closely enough they knew it was her. Joe examined the photo and thought, *Yes, she was pretty like the others. And only twenty-three.*

Joe handed the evidence bag containing the licence back to the officer and then looked in the surfer's direction. 'What's his name, the surfer?'

Tom checked his notes. 'Liam Gilmore. His father dropped him off at the beach just before dawn. He, Liam that is, thought it was unusual to see another car here without surfboard racks so early in the morning. And he didn't see anybody fishing. But he forgot about it when he started waxing his board. Thought no more of it.'

'I wonder if anybody up there saw anything last night,' Tessa said, pointing to the restaurant on the hill overlooking the beach.

Joe looked towards the restaurant. 'Yeah, it's closed now, but we can check with the staff later.'

'The Sandpiper,' Tessa said. 'It's new, but becoming quite popular, I hear. Though probably quiet on a Sunday, so maybe not so many patrons last night. The staff might have contact details from the bookings.'

When Joe and Tessa finished speaking with Tom and the evidence collection team, they made their way to the control centre where a man, who Joe had assumed was Liam's father, stood with a protective arm around Liam.

'Hello, Liam. My name is Detective Joseph Paterson, and this is Detective Tessa Mariani.'

Joe looked at the couple. 'Are you Liam's parents?'

The mother folded her arms across her chest and nodded. 'Yes, we are. And we need to take him home now. The officer over there.' She pointed to Tom. 'He told us to wait for you. But we've been here for …'

'We understand,' Joe said. 'But we need to ask Liam some questions, while the details are still fresh in his mind.'

'I don't think I'll ever forget.' Tears streamed down Liam's face. He ran shaking hands through his sun-streaked hair. His father held Liam closer.

Joe turned to Liam. 'We're very sorry for what you've been through. But if you're up to it, just a few questions and then you can go home.'

'Dude … Sorry, I mean detective … sir, I already told the other cop everything I know.'

'Just a few more questions. We promise,' Tessa said. 'And then you can go home.'

Liam recounted the details of his morning. He was waiting for his friend so they could surf together. He confirmed he knew nothing was wrong until his dog picked up on the scent.

'Did you touch or move anything?' Joe asked.

'No, no.' More tears. 'I puked—in the sand. And then I just ran … as fast as I could. I just wanted to get away.'

'That's enough,' Liam's mother said. 'He's obviously distressed. We need to take him home. Now.'

'Yes, of course,' Joe said. 'Just a couple more questions.'

After confirming the details of who Liam called and how long after he found the victim he'd called, Tessa and Joe gave

Liam and his parents their cards. 'Thank you for your time,' Tessa said. 'Contact us if you think of anything else. Anything at all, the smallest detail, even if you're not sure if it's relevant.'

Joe patted the dog. 'She looks like she's a great friend. She'll help you through this tough time. But contact me if you think you need further support. We know groups who can help.'

When Liam and his parents left, Joe and Tessa collected more information from Tom and the evidence team. Then gave final instructions to the officers before heading back to Joe's car. Before they reached the car, a pack of reporters assaulted them like a flock of hungry squawking seagulls at a beach picnic fighting over the last potato chip. The reporters shouted questions at them, shoving microphones in their faces. 'Who's the victim?' 'Is it a woman?' 'Any clues?' 'Is it connected with the others?' 'Is it a serial killer?'

'You know we can't release any information at this stage,' Joe said. 'I expect the superintendent will give a media statement in due course.'

'How do you sleep at night … facing horror and tragedy every day?' asked a journalist who Tessa had introduced to Joe only a few months ago. A journalist Joe now knew well and respected. A journalist who had a gift of asking questions Joe couldn't ignore.

'Sleep?' Joe bit his bottom lip, closed his eyes, and shook his head. He then opened his eyes and looked directly at the journalist. 'Sleep doesn't come easy, Alex. A lot of nights I don't.'

2

Joe parked outside a modest, but neat, blonde brick two-storey home, separated from the footpath by a freshly mowed lawn enclosed by a Lilly Pilly hedge. Joe's stomach churned and his legs felt like rubber as he and Tessa climbed the three steps that led to the front door of the house that Phoebe would never enter again. Joe closed his eyes, took a deep breath, and slowly exhaled before ringing the doorbell.

Mr Duncan's face paled when Joe and Tessa introduced themselves. Joe recognised the dread in Phoebe's father's eyes. *The family always knows something's wrong when they see us at the door.*

Joe heard Mrs Duncan call out to her husband, asking who was at the door. He reached out and touched Mr Duncan gently on the shoulder. 'Can we come inside? It's best if you sit down.'

When Joe and Tessa told Phoebe's parents what had happened to their daughter, Mrs Duncan was too distraught to speak. Mr Duncan was equally distressed but composed himself long enough to give Joe and Tessa Phoebe's older sister, Sally's mobile number before showing them to his daughter's bedroom.

'Anything that will help you find who did this to our precious daughter,' Phoebe's grief-stricken father had said, as he led Joe and Tessa up the stairs to Phoebe's room.

He stopped just before the bedroom door and slumped to the floor. 'I can't … I can't,' he sobbed.

Tessa squatted next to him and placed her hand on his shoulder. 'It's all right,' she said softly. 'We can go in … if it's okay with you.'

Mr Duncan nodded. 'Anything,' he sobbed. 'Anything you have to do.'

The bedroom looked more like it belonged to the adolescent Phoebe who had slept, played, and kept her precious possessions in the room, rather than the twenty-three-year-old Phoebe that now lay dead in the morgue. A rose-pink bedspread matched paler pink walls, and an ice blue bedframe complemented a navy-blue bookshelf that housed a young girl's treasured classics such as *Black Beauty* and *Heidi*. There was even a copy of *'Twas the Night Before Christmas*, that Joe remembered well from when he was a child. The only clues that a young adult woman had slept in this, what now felt like an abandoned room, was a black desk that held a laptop sitting on a stand, a large, curved monitor and a keyboard and mouse. A real estate agent's course information booklet and application form sat next to Phoebe's mouse pad. And a copy of *To Kill a Mockingbird*, with a bookmark at the beginning of chapter ten, sat on her bedside table. *It's a sin to kill a mockingbird,* Joe thought, … *it's a sin.*

Joe and Tessa opened and examined every drawer and door in Phoebe's room. They found nothing that provided any clue about why anybody would want to murder her. They would talk to friends, work colleagues, and Sally, Phoebe's sister, to delve more deeply into her life. But on the surface, everything indicated that Phoebe was a normal, intelligent young woman, very much loved by her family.

When Joe and Tessa finished examining Phoebe's room and ensuring the Duncans were being taken care of, they left with Phoebe's laptop.

***

Tessa and Joe didn't talk initially as they drove back to the station. Joe knew each of them was dealing in their own way with the emotional burden of delivering news that caused so much grief for the Duncans. Shattering news that broke their hearts and would change their lives forever. The Duncans would move on sooner or later. But they would never fully heal.

John Lennon's *Double Fantasy* played in the background.

Joe broke the silence after about fifteen minutes. 'So, what's wrong with your car?'

'Nothing. It's having a sleepover at the pub. My brother dropped me home last night.'

'Not like you to be out on a Sunday night. Especially without Alex.'

Joe caught just a few of Tessa's words. His mind drifted to the past when John Lennon sang '...*and your daddy's here ...*' *But you're not here, are you Dad? You're not here to chase away my monsters.*

Distracted by his thoughts, Joe only caught snippets of Tessa's chit-chat. '... article ... band ... planned a barbeque ... are you ...?'

'Sad really,' Joe said. 'He didn't see Sean come of age.' *At least Dad saw me come of age. Just,* he thought.

'Who, what, what are you talking about?'

'John and Sean Lennon. John died before Sean came of age. You know, the words to the song. Where John sings that he can hardly wait to see Sean come of age.' Joe turned the blinker to signal left. 'What were you saying before? Something about a barbeque?'

Tessa took a packet of cigarettes and lighter out of her pocket.

'Don't even think about lighting that,' Joe said.

'Shit, sorry,' Tessa said. 'Flashbacks of being in the car with Damien. He smokes more than I used to.'

Stopped at a set of traffic lights, Joe glanced at Tessa. 'Used to? How can you say "used to" when you're sitting there with a packet of cigarettes?'

'Yes. Used to,' Tessa said. 'I can't believe you haven't noticed. I gave up when Damien and I split, and I started seeing Alex— not easy—but worth it. I keep a pack for emergencies.'

Joe turned when the arrow changed to green. 'Keeping a pack for emergencies isn't giving up. You should …'

'I don't need how-to-quit lectures from you,' Tessa said. 'I'm doing fine. Anyway, as I was saying, Alex was writing a magazine article last night, you know—tight deadline, so I went to watch my brother's band play at the pub. They're talented, you've heard them play. It was a good night, late but good. Then I said, speaking of weekends, which we weren't, it's Papa's birthday and we're having a barbeque. I told you—weeks ago. Are you still free?'

'Did you sing?' Joe asked.

'What? Jesus Joe,' Tessa said through clenched teeth. 'You're so frustrating. You either don't listen or you change the topic.'

'Did you sing? Last night. With your brother.'

Tessa sighed. 'When have you known me to resist getting up on stage to belt out a tune? You should bring your guitar along one night. Anyway, are you free for Papa's birthday bash?'

'You guys would outplay me. I can't remember the last time I picked up my guitar.'

'It's not a competition. It's letting your hair down, chillaxing, getting away from the day-to-day shit. And don't forget, I've heard you sing. You're good. And from memory, you've even penned a few numbers. You should pick up your guitar more often. Anyway, are you coming to Papa's birthday?' Tessa asked again. 'Or do you have to polish the Monaro? It must be two weeks since you've done it.'

'I'm free—um … I think I'm free—I'll check.'

'Who are you trying to kid, genius? You don't have to check. With your photographic memory, you could probably recite the time and place of all your appointments for the next six months. And probably for the last six months.'

'No such thing as a photographic memory. Well, the jury is still out about it. So, who's going to your Papa's birthday? Jesus!' Joe slammed on the brakes as a car changed lanes in front of him, little room to spare.

Tessa laughed. 'No, Jesus isn't coming. Alex is coming, and Mamma, of course is making her famous Panzanella. And Papa will share his famous homemade wine. And his famous homemade salami, of course.'

Joe wrinkled his nose.

'Well, anyway, your Mum loves his salami. She said she'd come. And Nonna Bella and Nonna Bernadetta will be there.' Tessa let out a long, heavy sigh. 'And shit, double shit, quadruple shit even. I just remembered. Damien's coming. He sent me a text to tell me he'll be there. He gets on well with Mamma and Papa, and the nonnas adore him. Probably wants to show off his latest. I don't know how he even found out about the barbeque.'

Amused and a little envious of Tessa's ability to carry on a conversation, Joe grinned as he slowed for another red light. She was always fun, never boring. And beautiful. With long thick brown hair pulled back in a tight ponytail, and deep brown eyes, Tessa looked as Italian and stunning as a Ferrari—in stark contrast to her Aussie as an FJ Holden accent.

'What are you grinning at?' Tessa said.

'Facebook.'

'Facebook what?'

'I bet that's how Damien found out about the barbeque. I'm surprised you haven't unfriended him. Anyway, it might be good to catch up with Damien. I haven't seen him for months. Not since he took on the rape case.'

'Bloody, filthy, scum of the earth cockroach.'

'Damien?'

'No, the scum he's defending, Johnson.' Tessa punched a clenched fist into her palm. 'What I would do if I got hold of him.'

'This will be interesting.' The lights turned green. Joe grinned. 'Entertain me. Tell me, what would you do if you got hold of Johnson?'

Tessa made a twisting motion with her right hand. 'I'd rip his cock off, put it in a blender and when the blood and flesh are thoroughly mashed, I'd spoon feed it to him.'

Joe squirmed in his seat. 'So Tess, how's your anger management going?'

'I'm not having anger management.'

'If you don't learn to keep you cool, you soon will be.'

'Okay, Mr Iceman.'

'I might appear cool, but you know me. I get sick to the stomach when I think about the rapes and the violence, and every other shitty thing we have to deal with. But losing control of your emotions doesn't help catch the bad guys. It's counterproductive. You know that.' Joe paused, then added, 'All we can do is keep control and follow the process.'

Tessa pulled the passenger sun visa down. 'Well, we caught

this particular bad guy, Johnson, that is. I just hope the process puts him away. And, by the way, keeping your emotions to yourself isn't good for you either.'

'My emotions and I are fine.' Joe thought about the way he handled the reporters this morning. He wondered if he could have handled Alex's question better. *Sometimes I don't sleep at night. But it's true, I don't,* he thought.

Tessa looked at Joe. 'It's okay,' she said softly. 'It's okay to show your emotions—when it's just you and me. I understand you.'

Joe took his left hand off the steering wheel, reached over, and squeezed Tessa's. 'I'm fine. Enough of me. How are things going with you and Alex?'

'Early days, very early—we're taking it slow. And ... well, um ... do you remember that feeling you got in your tummy when you were a teenager? That tingling feeling, butterflies in your tummy feeling, but in a good way, not a bad way feeling ... I never thought I would ever have that feeling again.' Tessa shrugged. 'But there it is.'

Joe checked the traffic in the rear vision mirror. He knew the feeling. *Yeah, I remember that feeling ... every time I look at Olivia.* Then quickly dismissed the thought, as if afraid Tessa could read his mind. Joe had concealed his feelings for Olivia Chatfield, the police photographer, since he met her nine months ago when she was new to the station. His mind drifted again. He remembered the first day she arrived. Olivia had no nonsense shoulder-length, shiny brown hair and *that smile*, a wonderful smile that made her fringe-framed hazel eyes sparkle and her nose crinkle. Not short, not tall, Joe imagined her head resting on his shoulder as they embraced.

Joe slowed for a pedestrian crossing and came back to the moment. 'How do your parents feel about you and Alex ... you know, being in a relationship?'

'They don't know.'

'They don't know?' Joe took his eyes off the road for a split second to look at Tessa. 'What do you mean, they don't know? How long has it been? Six months? Or more?'

'Well, they know Alex. They've met Alex, but they think we're just friends. They thought Damien was perfect for me. Not Italian, but nice looking, successful, always charming. But I knew from the beginning he wasn't right … not what I wanted. Well, that's obvious now, isn't it? So not what I wanted.' Tessa emphasised 'so.' 'I just didn't have confidence in myself until Alex. No, not confidence. I guess I've denied myself all these years, haven't been able to let go. You might get as lucky one day if …'

'You're not planning a blind date for me at the barbeque, are you?' Joe interrupted. 'The other night, when I had dinner with Paul and Trudi, Paul's cousin was there. It was awkward. I spent the first ten minutes trying to remember her name and the last two hours trying to invent a reason to leave early.'

'You had dinner with Paul? How's he going? Was he drinking? I haven't had a chance to catch up with him since he came back—well, not in any really meaningful way. I've seen him around, but I've been so focussed on finding this murdering arsehole psycho. How's he handling being back on the job?'

'Your interview technique with suspects and witnesses is way better than it is with me.' Joe grinned. 'So, Detective Mariani, in response to your interrogation, Paul had one glass of wine, no spirits. And how is he? He appears to be fine. I'm not sure he could have recovered without Trudi's support. She's been as good, if not better, for him than the psychologist. As far as back on the job is concerned—so far, so good. He's working with the team on rape cases, including the Johnson case.'

'You're piggy in the middle.' Tessa smirked. 'You've got

17

two friends pitting against each other. Damien trying to keep Johnson out of prison and Paul trying to put him away. I wonder who will come out on top with that one.'

Joe shrugged. 'Anyway, back to you and …'

'Where are you going?' Tessa interrupted. 'You missed the turn off—again. Genius with no sense of direction. Sometimes I wonder how you find your way to work.'

Joe laughed. 'Sometimes it takes me two or three attempts. But it's good thinking time. So, back to you and Alex. You have to tell your parents. Choices have consequences. Not telling them is a choice. Think of the consequences if you don't tell them.'

'Another bloody lecture. How to quit smoking, tell my parents about Alex, blah, blah, blah. Forget Alex. We were talking about Paul.'

'And before that you were telling me about how you're going to tell you parents about Alex.'

'It's beyond me why somebody hasn't snatched you up by now.'

'You're changing the subject. Tell your parents,' Joe said, emphasising each word. He repeated: 'Tell your parents. And your brother. Keeping secrets from them isn't fair. It will only hurt them if they find out from somebody other than you. Oh, what a tangled web we weave when we keep secrets.' Joe smiled as he thought how his English teacher mother would squirm at his misquote of Sir Walter Scott.

'No, I'm not changing the subject. Stop interrupting me. I'm saying nice stuff about you. As I was saying, I don't know why you're not attached by now. You're the cliché of clichés of what women want. Tall, good-looking, great smile, hair that looks like Vidal Sassoon himself had fashioned it.'

Joe slowed as he approached a roundabout. 'Not Vidal. He's dead.'

Tessa ignored his interruption. 'Even that scar adds to the appeal of your killer blue eyes. Not Ted Bundy killer blue eyes. More Mark Harmon, I'd follow you to the ends of the earth, blue eyes.'

Joe shook his head and grinned.

'What's so funny?'

'You know Mark Harmon played Ted Bundy in a movie.'

'That was Zac Efron.'

'I'm talking about the nineteen-eighty something version.'

'Okay, whatever, but anyway I'd go for you if I wasn't ...' Tessa's mobile cut her off in mid-sentence.

'Hi Olivia ... yep, I'm with Joe. We'll be at the station in about two minutes.'

'Olivia?' Joe hoped his face wasn't as flushed as it felt. 'What did she say?'

'The crime scene photos are ready.'

3

Joe and Tessa arrived at the Southside police station a few minutes after one. The long rectangular building located five kilometres southwest of the beach, where the surfer and his dog found Phoebe's body, stretched almost the full length of the block. Joe felt the familiar sense of belonging when he drove into the station's car park. He spent most of his waking hours, working, collaborating, and socialising with his second family— in the nineteen-sixties' two-story building in need of a face-lift. The builders had used recycled brown bricks from the original station built in the late nineteenth century to construct the first story of the twentieth century police station. Function and economics won the battle over aesthetics. So they used common red bricks to construct the second story. Six sandstone steps led to the double glass door entrance. The station was almost at capacity, accommodating over three-hundred employees. The building appeared tired on the outside; however, the station's occupants gave life and energy to the inside. The officers, detectives, technicians, analysts, IT specialists and support staff, each had different roles and functions. But in the same way the organs, tissues and cells of a living body synchronise as one to maintain the body, the station's occupants co-ordinated and worked together to achieve a common goal—catching the bad guy.

'I'll drop this off to Des,' Tessa said as she took Phoebe's laptop out of her backpack. 'Hopefully, it won't take him long to crack the password. Then I'll grab a sandwich. Do you want anything from the café?'

'No, I'm fine,' Joe said. Then remembered he hadn't eaten since the night before. 'No wait, can you get me a curried egg sandwich? I'll get a coffee from the kitchen. Thanks.' He handed her twenty dollars. 'My shout today.'

'Do you want to come for a walk?'

'No, thanks. I'll go over our notes from this morning. And maybe check social media to see what I can learn about Phoebe before her sister, Sally McKay, comes in. See if I can find any connection between Phoebe and the first two victims.'

Ten minutes later, when Joe returned from the kitchen, he straightened his mouse pad, which wasn't crooked, and placed the coffee on his desk—the only desk in the squad room that had a coaster. He didn't need to revisit the medical reports to recall the details of how the first two victims, Amber Thompson and Isabel Reinhard, had died. They were brutally bashed, strangled, and stabbed. Each had multiple stab wounds on their chests and abdomens. There was no evidence of rape, so the crimes didn't appear to be sexually motivated. In fact, Isabel Reinhard was still a virgin. The toxicology report for both victims showed no evidence of drugs or alcohol.

A thorough search of both crime scenes yielded nothing. Based on the wounds on both victims, the weapon appeared to be a ten-inch double-edged knife. The only physical evidence at the scenes was the rose and the note. Each victim had the same note pinned to her breast.

Trust not too much to appearances. The beauty hides the thorns.

Joe recalled the afternoon they arrived at the scene where the killer left Amber's body, the first victim, partially hidden in the Royal National Park. Just metres from where the second victim, Isabel Reinhard, was found three months later. He remembered the scent of the Eucalyptus and the magpie songs in the distance. The black silhouette of trees in the setting sun signalled the end of a day of picnicking, swimming, and boating. A scene of peace and tranquillity, reminiscent of the serenity that morning at the beach where the surfer and his dog found Phoebe Duncan's body. Scenes in stark contrast to the sadistic, brutal acts that resulted in the mutilated bodies of three young women.

Joe walked to the murder board. Despite the large open workplace, he was unaware of the noise around him as he examined the photos of the victims. He didn't hear the phones ringing, the discussions and debates between the other detectives and officers in the squad room, even the sudden outbursts of laughter.

Olivia had put Phoebe Duncan's photos next to Amber Thompson and Isabel Reinhard's photos. He studied Amber, Isabel, and Phoebe's photos on the board. *Olivia is exceptionally good at her job,* he thought. Joe admired her skill as a photographer. He appreciated but was equally disturbed at how she captured every detail with her camera, the stark reality of the violence that occurred. *It's like you're still at the scene. Yeah, Olivia, you're good, too good.*

Joe turned from the photos. He'd seen enough atrocity. He closed his eyes, but he could still see the bloodshed and carnage. He opened and closed his eyes, again and again, but the visions stayed. They always did—they were etched in his brain. He didn't know how much more repeated exposure to violence and depravity he could take without losing control. But he had to keep control to do the job. Joe started to feel himself breathing too rapidly, exhaling more air than he was inhaling. Then the familiar nausea and the waves of light-headiness threatened to overtake his control. He grabbed his mobile and strode towards the squad room door, almost bumping into Tessa on his way out as she was coming in.

'Where are you going?' she asked. 'I've got your sandwich.'

'Just for a walk … I mean, um, I remembered I have to pick up my dry cleaning. Back soon.'

Outside, Joe inhaled deeply until his breathing returned to normal. He bought a coffee and walked to the park on the next block. Calmed by the solitude and serenity of the park, Joe smiled at the sound of the fallen leaves from an old Moreton Bay fig crackling under his shoes as he approached a park bench. He sat, closed his eyes, and inhaled the minty fragrance of the eucalyptus trees. He breathed deeply again, welcoming the peace and the quiet. The distant traffic noise was muffled by tall, leafy trees, chirping galahs and magpies singing and bathing in the nearby water fountain. Joe sat for ten minutes, wanting to move, willing himself to go back to the station, but he was frozen, couldn't move. A passer-by might think he was sleeping. He didn't want to leave this small part of the world that knew no violence, no hate or madness. Then the words to a song he'd written years ago came back to him. *I can't help you if I can't help me.* He opened his eyes and thought, *But it's not about me, it's about them.* He felt in his pocket for his father's button, and with renewed commitment, made his way back to the station.

Tessa looked up from Isabel Reinhard, the second victim's file, when Joe returned to his desk twenty-five minutes later. 'You've been gone for nearly half an hour. Where's your dry cleaning?'

'Dry cleaning … oh right, it's not ready yet,' Joe said as he sat at his desk which faced Tessa's and was separated only by a low partition. 'I got my days wrong.'

'Rubbish, sometimes you get lost when you're driving, but you don't get your days wrong. Where did you go?'

'I just needed to stretch my legs. Thanks for the sandwich. I'll make a coffee. Do you want me to make one for you?'

'No thanks. I'm trying to cut back. Drink more water.'

'Giving up smoking, cutting back on coffee. Alex is a healthy influence on you,' Joe said as he stood to go to the kitchen.

Five minutes later back at his desk Joe sipped his coffee, ready to revisit the details about the first two victims, and then check social media for any information about Phoebe Anne Duncan. He hadn't checked social media, had no background information about Phoebe, or read past the first paragraph in the first file when the front desk rang to tell him that Phoebe's sister, Sally, was waiting in reception. She arrived sooner than he expected.

4

Sally, eyes smeared with mascara, puffy and red from crying, sat next to her husband Simon, across the table from Joe and Tessa in the small meeting room opposite reception. She controlled her emotions well enough to give Joe and Tessa information about Phoebe's friends, where she worked, and her ex-boyfriend Sebastian Sanders.

'No, she wasn't seeing anybody in particular at the moment, as far as I know,' Sally said. 'But Phebes doesn't discuss her dates much. Actually, she never discusses her dates. She keeps ... kept that part of her life pretty much to herself. Except Sebastian. He was the first.' Sally paused, took a deep breath, and shook her head. And almost to herself, she said, 'And the last.'

'How long did she date Sebastian Sanders?' Tessa asked.

'Just a few months. Her company sold him a penthouse at Bondi Beach. Rich doesn't describe how much money he has. I guess that might have been the initial attraction.' Sally paused, wiped away tears with the mangled tissues in her hand. 'Oh God, Phebes. Why ... why did this happen to you?' She sobbed, burying her head in her husband's shoulder. 'I'm sorry, I can't believe it, this isn't real.'

'It's okay, Sally,' Tessa said, sliding a box of tissues to her. 'Take your time.'

'I know I have to be strong. I don't know how Mum and Dad will get through this. You have to get the bastard who did this to my sister.'

'You're right, Sally,' Joe said. 'You do have to be strong. We need you to be strong and we need you to tell us everything you can think of. No matter how insignificant you might think it is, it might be a lead for us. Tell us more about Sanders. Did you meet him?'

Sally composed herself and sat straight. 'We, Simon and I, met him twice. He bought dinner for all of us to celebrate the first and second month he and Phoebe had been dating. He took us to Aria the first month and Tetsuya's the second month.'

'Why did they stop seeing each other?' Joe asked.

'Phoebe said he was possessive and controlling. He smothered her. Even after Phoebe told him she'd had enough, he rang her every day, sent a dozen roses every other day to the real estate where she works … worked.'

Joe leaned forward. 'What colour roses?'

'I don't …' Sally began to cry again. 'I don't know. What difference does the colour make?'

Joe sat back. 'Every detail, no matter how small, might be important.'

'I don't know,' Sally repeated.

'Maybe we should have a break. Would you like a tea, coffee?' Joe asked.

Sally nodded. 'Um … yeah … tea, thanks. Do you have peppermint?'

'We do,' Joe said. 'Simon?'

'Water is fine. Thanks.'

26

When Joe returned with the tea and water, Tessa said, 'Would you like a few minutes alone?'

Both Sally and Simon shook their heads. 'No, we're fine,' Sally said. 'Let's go on.'

'What can you tell us about Sebastian Sanders?' Joe asked. 'What were your impressions, Sally? Your first impressions?'

Sally hesitated, and Simon put an arm around his wife's shoulder.

'I guess he was charming,' Sally said. 'But it was a sort of superficial charm.'

Joe frowned. 'Superficial charm?'

'I mean, he knew all the right things to say, and all the right things to do,' Sally said. 'Polite. Over polite. Opened the car door for me, pulled out my chair at the restaurant. Paid attention when anybody was talking. Didn't interrupt. But I got the feeling it was all show, rehearsed graciousness, not natural. Some would say he's charismatic. And I guess you'd say he's nice looking, except ...except ...'

'Except what?' Tessa asked.

Sally bit her bottom lip. 'Well, he has a pleasant smile, perfect teeth ...'

'I bet those teeth cost thousands,' Simon interrupted.

'Anyway,' Sally continued, 'his smile looked almost genuine. That is ...' She paused, bit her bottom lip. 'That is, until you looked into his eyes,' she whispered.

Joe said in a voice almost as quiet, 'What about his eyes, Sally?'

'They were cold, dark. I ... well, I don't know if I imagined it, but it felt as though he looked right through you, as though he could read your thoughts. I didn't like him. He ...' Sally hesitated again.

Simon removed his arm from Sally's shoulder and sat forward. 'He likes to show off how rich he is. Talked about how many boats and cars he has, his BMW, his Porsche SVU—a car and of course, a boat, for all occasions. Even though he couldn't smoke in the restaurant, he had his gold Dupont cigarette lighter on the table. I took notice of the brand because it looked expensive. I Googled it. They sell for hundreds of dollars, some of them two thousand. I thought at the time that it was a lot of money to pay to give yourself lung cancer.'

'And he ordered Phoebe's meals for her,' Sally added.

'Do you know how he accumulated so much wealth?' Joe asked.

'Well, he's a stockbroker,' Simon said. 'But I'm not sure why he has a day job. He inherited companies from his grandfather. And his parents are stinking rich too.'

'He has offices in Brisbane, Sydney, and Melbourne,' Sally said.

'And Singapore and London too,' Simon added. 'He's always jetting off somewhere.'

'I thought he was too old for her,' Sally said. 'Phebes is only … was only twenty-three. Sanders is in his thirties.'

Sally had stopped crying, and Joe thought she was ready now to talk more about Phoebe. 'Okay, Sally, you've told us a lot about Sanders. Now, can you tell us more about Phoebe? What sort of person she was? Anything you can think of that may help us. The smallest detail.'

Tears rolled down Sally's cheeks again.

Simon stood and took Sally by the shoulders to lift her from the chair. 'This is too much for her. I'm taking her home.'

'Just…'

Simon cut Tessa off before she could say any more. 'Shouldn't you be out there finding who did this? Shouldn't you be arresting Sebastian Sanders? He did this.'

'We need evidence,' Joe said. 'And the more we know about

the victim…'

'The victim,' Sally said, barely audible. 'The victim's name is Phoebe.'

'I'm sorry,' Joe said. 'Yes, you're absolutely right. We're doing this for Phoebe. And the more we know about Phoebe, the better chance we have of finding who took her life.'

Sally sat again and coaxed Simon back into his chair.

'She was sweet, outgoing, kind. She was the …' Sally paused, took a deep breath. 'She was the … the baby of the family, so I guess a little spoilt.'

Joe and Tessa spent the next hour gathering information about Phoebe, her personality, what she enjoyed doing, what she liked, didn't like, what she did on weekends, hobbies, friends, social media. Simon filled in details that Sally missed.

At the end of the interview Joe said, 'Thank you, both. We'll keep in touch. And I promise, as soon as we know something, we'll contact you.'

'And call us if you think of anything else. Even the smallest detail might help us,' Tessa reminded them.

'I didn't get to tell her …' Sally bit her lower lip. Tears flowed down her cheeks. She put her arm around Simon. 'I didn't get to tell my sister … I'm pregnant. She didn't know she was going to be an aunt in seven months.'

5

Joe was updating his notes from their interview with Sally and Simon McKay when he felt a tap on his shoulder. He looked up to see Detective Paul Shipway staring down at him and shaking his head.

'I've been talking to you for the last fifteen seconds,' Paul said. 'Where are you?'

'Sorry, Paul, in the zone, focussed—you know how it is. What's up?'

'I just asked if you want to grab a coffee. You haven't touched that one. It looks like it's been sitting there overnight, along with the half-eaten sandwich.'

'It's okay. I can make a fresh cup,' Joe said.

'I, ah... I need to talk to you about something,' Paul said.

'Okay. Tess, do you want...?' Joe noticed Paul slowly shaking his head, and understanding the silent message, said '... us to bring a coffee back for you?'

'No thanks, I'm good,' Tessa said. 'Wait,' Tessa called out just as they reached the door. 'Cappuccino and a muffin. Blueberry. Thanks.'

'What is it,' Joe said when they left the building. 'Why didn't you want Tessa to come with us?'

'I want to talk to you about something, sort of personal. Man to man. My shout for coffee.'

***

Café Athena, where Nik the owner enjoyed playing his traditional Greek dance music in the afternoon, and romantic Greek ballads in the morning, was busy. It was always busy in the afternoon. The usual coffee crowd downed their caffeine fix to get them through the rest of the day. A couple occupied Joe's favourite table near the window, so he settled for a table at the other end of the café opposite the window while Paul ordered the coffee.

Joe spotted Olivia sitting in a corner under a print of the Parthenon. She didn't look up, didn't appear to have noticed Joe come in. A book sat on the table next to her laptop. Joe contemplated the book. *Some kind of reference or textbook. Too big to be a novel.* Olivia alternated between studying the book and making notes on her laptop, apparently unaware of any noise or activity around her. Joe wondered what was so interesting about the book that Olivia didn't even appear to notice when the man on the table next to her cursed loudly when he knocked over a bottle of water. He was reminded of his university days as he watched Olivia absorbed in her notetaking. He thought of the hours he and Damien spent in the campus coffee shop debating the best way to answer an assignment question. The days before, no years before, Joe introduced Damien and Tessa, and they became an item. Joe grinned when he remembered how his father grumbled about the cost of his textbooks that Joe rarely opened. And his father's grumbles turning to praise when Joe always passed his exams and assignments with at least a credit grade, and more often than not, a distinction. Joe's grin faded. Those days are now gone when his father was around to grumble and praise. *Yes, those days are gone.*

Distracted from his reverie when Paul sat, Joe said, 'What's on your mind?'

'What's on *your* mind?' Paul asked. 'Focused? In the zone again?'

'No.' Joe sipped his coffee. 'Just wondering what's on your mind.'

'How's your coffee?'

'Coffee's good. So, stop stalling and tell me what's going on?'

Paul bit his bottom lip and ran fingers through his sandy red hair, making it stand up like echidna spines.

Joe waved his hand in a 'Come on. Out with it,' motion.

Paul wriggled in his seat. 'Trudi and I have been living together for about a year now.'

'Ri-i-ght?' Joe nodded slowly. 'And…?'

Paul picked up the salt grinder, turned it, examined it from all angles.

Joe took the salt grinder from Paul and placed it next to the pepper grinder, making sure they were perfectly aligned. 'Out with it, what's up?'

Paul sipped his coffee, sat straight, and took a deep breath. 'Okay. You know Trudi is the very, very best thing in my life. She's the most wonderful person I've ever met. I can't imagine life without her. You know she…' He looked down, hesitated a moment then looked up, looked Joe in the eyes. 'She stuck right by me through the whole PTSD thing, the counselling. She's the one who got me through all the post-traumatic stress stuff. I couldn't have done it without her. And you too Joe. You were there for me the entire time.'

'I know,' Joe said. 'She's a wonderful person. One of the best. And…?' Joe waited for Paul to elaborate.

Paul toyed with the froth on his cappuccino.

Joe shifted in his chair and started tapping his fingers on the table. 'Do you think you'll get to the point before Christmas?'

'Okay, right. Trudi's so beautiful, on the inside and the outside,' Paul continued. 'God knows what she sees in me.' He wasn't male model material. But Paul had impish good looks and a cheeky glint in his eyes that matched his sense of humour.

'Jesus, Paul. Out with it. What are you trying to tell me?'

Paul sipped his coffee, put the cup down, looked around the coffee shop and leaned in a little closer to Joe and whispered, 'I want…' Two men at a table near them burst into laughter as they stood and scraped their chairs on the polished concrete floor.

'What? I didn't hear you.'

'I want to ask Trudi to marry me,' Paul said, not quite a shout, but more loudly than his normal volume.

Two young women at a nearby table clapped their hands and called out 'Congratulations' to him.

Paul blushed and slumped in his chair. Then leaned in closer to Joe and spoke in a loud whisper. 'Did you hear me? I want to marry Trudi.'

'And…?' Joe said.

'Well, what do you think?' Paul asked.

This isn't a normal conversation between two men, Joe thought. He shifted in his chair again and said, 'Why are you asking me, the least likely to have a meaningful relationship with the opposite sex?'

'Next to Trudi, you're my best friend, Joe. You know Trudi. You know how we are together. Is it too soon? Will she want us to spend the rest of our lives together—grow old together?'

Joe saw Olivia's reflection in the large ornate mirror on the back wall. She was at the counter paying for her coffee. Joe looked at Paul. 'Trudi loves you. Grab any chance you have for happiness with both hands.' Joe glanced at Olivia again in the mirror. 'Only a fool lets happiness slip away.'

6

'Thanks, we'll see you there in about an hour.' Tessa was ending a call when Joe and Paul returned.

'That was the restaurant on the beach. The manager and two of the staff who worked last night will be there tonight. We can call by before we pick up my car.'

Paul handed Tessa her coffee and blueberry muffin. 'Is what happened last night related to the other murders?'

Joe leaned against his desk and crossed his arms. 'We think so.' He nodded. 'Pretty certain.'

Paul sat on a spare chair near Tessa's desk. 'Any leads yet?'

'No,' Joe said. 'We've got two or three suspects, but nothing concrete yet. The first victim, Amber—we've all but ruled out her flatmate, friends, and relatives. A jealous colleague is a contender, with a question mark. He has an alibi. We did some digging there but found nothing yet to reject it. And Amber's manager, well—he's married, and we suspect he may have been having an affair with her. Or trying to. He has no alibi, but we have no evidence either way, so…' Joe shrugged. 'Who knows?'

'The second victim, Isabel—her ex-boyfriend is on our

suspect list,' Tessa said. 'The background check on the primary suspects brought up one or two minor speeding and parking tickets. Nothing major.'

'Our third victim.' Joe walked to the board and pointed to Phoebe Duncan's photo. 'We know very little about Phoebe. It's too soon. All we know is what we learned from her sister and her sister's husband this afternoon. And what we saw this morning.' Joe noticed Paul grimace and look away from the board.

'Have you found any links between the victims?' Paul asked.

'No, but ...' Joe rubbed the back of his neck. 'The white rose, the note, the similar physical characteristics of the victims ... It's not random. There has to be a link.'

Paul nodded. 'Agree. Any witnesses last night? Any clues about motive?'

'We've ruled out robbery. Phoebe's bag was still at the scene, and there didn't appear to be anything missing out of it. A preliminary door-knock around the beach area has uncovered nothing so far,' Joe said. 'Based on the last report, nobody that the team has interviewed so far saw or heard anything unusual last night or early this morning. A helicopter and grid search of the beach and surrounding areas found nothing. We didn't find the murder weapon.' Joe pointed to the timeline on the board. 'We have to move on this before there's a fourth. Three months elapsed between Amber and Isabel, and two months between Isabel and Phoebe. The attack on Isabel was even more brutal than on Amber. He might be escalating.'

'We know that's what happens,' Paul said. 'The killer grows in confidence. Gets an insatiable taste for whatever sick pleasure he gets out of it—power, sexual gratification.'

Joe returned to his desk. 'Isabel was still a virgin, and there was no evidence that he raped Amber. We'll have to wait for the medical examiner's report to find out if he raped Phoebe.'

Paul glanced at the photos briefly and turned away again. 'Was there any sign of masturbation?'

'Not that we found,' Tessa said.

'The attack looks angry, and the way he left the bodies— there's no remorse,' Paul said. 'The killer isn't thinking about the victim as an individual. He's just thinking about the kill.'

'If it's anger,' Tessa said. 'Could the attacks be a spur of the moment? Something sets him off during the date, assuming it's a date.' Tessa shrugged. 'But I'd say it's definitely a date, judging by the "Meet me near the surf club—we'll go for a walk before dinner," text. And we know Amber left in a taxi to go on a date.'

'The killer sent a text?' Paul said. 'So I assume you weren't able to trace the number.'

'We traced it, no problem,' Tessa said. 'It was a pre-paid mobile. And because the victims wouldn't have recognised the mobile number, it was probably a blind date, possibly arranged on an online dating site. Online dating is trending upward. I know at least two married couples who met online.'

'It's hard to buy a prepaid without identification these days,' Joe said. 'We traced it to a first-year university student.'

'I assume you've ruled out the student as the killer,' Paul said. 'Did he or she have a driver's licence as proof of identity to buy the mobile?'

Joe nodded.

'So how did the killer end up with the mobile?'

'She said he paid her to buy it. Imagine what an eighteen-year-old university student can do with five-hundred dollars.'

'What did she say he looked like?'

'He wore dark sunglasses and had a fake looking beard and moustache,' Tessa said. 'She said his jeans were frayed, but not in a fashionable way, more in an old, grubby way. He looked creepy, but she wasn't going to let five hundred dollars get away.

She thought there was something hinky about the deal. But …' Tessa shrugged. 'Well, student, five-hundred dollars. And they were in a busy Westfield shopping complex, so she didn't feel threatened.'

'Disguised himself behind fake facial hair,' Paul said. 'And no way to see the colour of his eyes behind the sunglasses. Did she notice the colour of his hair?'

Joe shook his head. 'He wore a cap, and she didn't take that much notice.'

'So, no way to match him with the suspects,' Paul concluded. 'He was wearing shabby jeans, but he could afford to throw away five-hundred dollars to get a pre-paid.'

'Yep, it's an easy guess he was disguised,' Joe said. 'Our killer is probably clean shaven and well dressed.'

'Back to whether it could have been a spur-of-the-moment attack,' Tessa said. 'If the date doesn't go as planned, does he become angry, go into a rage?'

'No, I don't think it's spur-of-the-moment,' Paul said. 'He's got away with it three times that we know of. He's cold, calculating. He's angry. But he can control his anger long enough to plan and engineer the time, the victim, and the setting. When you said about the dates not going as planned. I don't think that would be the case. The dates will almost certainly go as planned. He plans down to the last meticulous detail. The planning—it's foreplay for him. And the final release, the climax comes during the kill. That's when his anger explodes, and he goes into a rage. That's his climax.' Paul looked at the photos, closed his eyes as he turned away again. 'How many times did he stab Phoebe?'

'We're not sure yet,' Joe said. 'It looks like seven. The same as Amber and Isabel. We'll know for sure when we get the medical report.'

'As I said,' Paul continued. 'The anger explodes from him

during the kill, but he still has control.'

Joe studied his friend. Paul was in control. Not timid or shy now. There was no hesitation in his words. He didn't run his fingers through his hair, the way he did when he's nervous. The way he did in the coffee shop when he was talking about asking Trudi to marry him. Paul was confident in his own ability to read a crime scene, see the violence happening. The ability his years of experience had given him. But there was pain in Paul's eyes. Joe knew Paul was not only reading the killer's intent and emotions. He was also feeling the fear, terror and pain the victims suffered for who knows how long before their death.

Paul was the most gentle and caring person Joe knew, apart from his father. Joe's thoughts drifted to his father again. He thought about the times his father nursed injured animals back to health. And the tears that filled his father's eyes when he couldn't save an animal. Was it the memory of his father's gentleness that drew Joe to Paul? Was gentleness the foundation of his friendship with Paul? Was it the gentleness he sees in Olivia's eyes that draws him to her?

'He stabs them seven times, not six times or eight times. Why?' Paul said, bringing Joe back to the present.

Tessa shrugged. 'Seven. Everybody's favourite number.'

Paul's turn to shrug. 'You're right. Not everything a killer does has premeditated intent. Any other similar cases elsewhere?'

'A search of our databases found nothing here or in any other state,' Tessa said. 'And nothing that links our victims to each other or any other victims.'

'What about work, social, Facebook?' Paul asked.

'Isabel was at university full time, studying veterinary science,' Joe said. 'So, there's no work connection there. Amber was a compliance analyst, studied law part time but at a different university from Isabel. No work connections, no university connections, and it appears no social connections.'

'It's possible Amber and Isabel were just practice runs,' Tessa said. 'And Phoebe was the actual target. Or Amber, the first victim was the target, and he got a taste for the kill and kept going, selecting victims at random. Or is there a connection between Amber, Isabel, and Phoebe and we just need to dig deeper?' Tessa paused, shook her head. 'Or there's no connection. And we're going around in circles.'

'He maybe selecting victims that resemble somebody he knows,' Paul said. 'Like Bundy did.' Paul huffed and shook his head. 'I just did the very thing that makes me angry. Just like everyone does, I used Bundy as the serial killer benchmark.'

'Are you talking about Zac Efron or Mark Harmon?' Tessa smirked. 'Hollywood certainly has glorified serial killers.'

'Especially Bundy. Because he was handsome and charming,' Joe said. 'A charismatic psychopath. Or was he a narcissist?'

'I'll settle for just plain evil,' Paul said.

Joe walked back to the board. 'He left the same note pinned to Phoebe that he left pinned to Amber and Isabel. *Trust not too much to appearances. The beauty hides the thorns.* Obviously a message. But who for?'

'He met both Amber and Isabel near the surf club, maybe lured them into his car, and then... well, we know the rest,' Tessa said. 'He took Amber and Isabel to the National Park. The question is, why did he take Phoebe to the beach, breaking the pattern? Not that two makes a pattern, but... maybe there is no pattern. Maybe there's no connection. Maybe he selects the victims randomly. Shit, maybe, maybe, maybe ...'

'No maybes.' Joe stood in front of the board with his hands on his hips. 'There *is* a connection between the victims.' He inhaled deeply and breathed out slowly. In a calmer voice he said, 'And we'll find it. Hopefully, we'll know more when we examine Phoebe's background.'

'This is what we think we know about him so far.' Joe pointed to each of the photos. 'The major stab wounds were on the left side of the bodies. So we think he's right-handed. But so is ninety percent of the population.'

Joe continued. 'There were no wounds in the back. And the bruising pattern on the necks shows he choked them front on. He wants to watch the fear on their faces.'

'Yeah,' Paul said with a hard edge to his voice. 'And he wants to watch their last moments as the life fades from their eyes.'

Paul spoke quietly, but Joe sensed the anger and rage in his voice.

Tessa stood and walked to the board. 'Based on the age of the victims and assuming they were on a date with him, we estimate he's in his late twenties, early thirties, possibly late thirties.'

'Late twenties to mid-thirties would fit the serial killer stereotype,' Paul said. He looked briefly at the photos again. 'What about the rose? That has to be a message.'

'Agree.' Joe returned to his desk. 'Based on Google articles, roses are ancient—they've been around for about thirty-five million years. And the oldest living rose is about one thousand years. The history's probably not relevant. But the colour, white, I think that's key. The white rose traditionally symbolises love, innocence, and purity,' Joe said. 'And some sources say it can symbolise new beginnings.'

'I know we've been over and over this,' Tessa said. 'But the way he left the bodies—in an obscene pose. That's in direct contrast to what the white rose symbolises.'

'And I think this is where the note comes into play.' Joe handed a copy to Paul.

There was nothing distinguishing about the note. It was computer generated, so there were no handwriting clues. The font was Calibri, size fourteen, italics, with expanded spacing between the letters. There were four lines on the note, each of them centre aligned, and each line started with an uppercase letter. The first line was *'Trust not too much.'* The second line read *'To appearances.'* The third line *'The beauty,'* and the fourth *'Hides the thorns.'*

'There are no fingerprints on the note,' Joe said. 'The killer isn't dumb enough to leave prints. Which doesn't necessarily mean he's a genius.'

'But he's smart,' Paul said. 'So, do you have any theories about the note? Agree, it's a message. But what does it mean?'

'The first bit, *Trust not too much to appearances,* is a quote from Virgil.'

Paul frowned. 'Virgil Donati. The drummer?'

'I admire your knowledge of Australian music,' Joe said. 'But no—not Donati. Virgil. The ancient Roman poet.'

Joe looked at the note again. *'Trust not too much to appearances.* Is he saying these women appeared to be pure and innocent? But in his mind, they weren't. Or maybe it's not about them specifically. Do they symbolise somebody whose appearances deceived him—somebody who betrayed him?'

'What about the second part of the note?' Paul asked.

'The beauty hides the thorns. I don't think this is a quote from anyone famous. I've Googled it, checked with my mother and her other teacher friends. I'm pretty sure it's the killer's own words. So what's he telling us? Maybe something beautiful is hiding something evil on the inside.'

'He hid the thorns inside their vaginas.' Tessa studied the photos on the board. 'Is he saying that part of the woman's body is the beautiful part of a woman?'

'Maybe.' Paul said. 'Or maybe the woman's entire body is hiding the thorn—hiding an evil soul. This could tie in with the new-beginnings symbolism. Maybe by killing them he's giving them a chance at a new beginning. A chance for an existence of innocence and purity.'

'The obscene pose symbolises their existence when they're alive and the rose their new beginnings in death,' Tessa said.

'Or should we not trust the appearance of the body or the rose? Maybe none of it means anything. The only reality is the first part of the note,' Joe said. '*Trust not too much to appearances.*'

'Are we dealing with extremist religious motives?' Tessa said. 'But if he's a religious nut, wouldn't he be leaving Bible quotes?'

'The rose might be the religious connection. New Testament. Mary is often linked with the white rose. Maybe that's why he's hiding the thorns. He might be making a garland of roses, like a string of rosary beads,' Joe said. 'And he's adding to the garland with each victim. Which means there's no end in sight for him.'

'Or his motive might be as simple as revenge?' Paul said.

'Or a combination of religion and vengeance,' Joe said. 'We're going around in circles, again. But what we know for sure is we have to stop this psychopath before he kills again. Time is not on our side. It's not a matter of if he kills again, it's a matter of when.'

7

Joe and Tessa left the station around five-thirty and headed to the Sandpiper restaurant at the beach before picking up Tessa's car. It was early, and a Monday evening, so there were only a few patrons and cars at the restaurant. Joe didn't have to drive too far from the restaurant to find a park away from the ever-present danger of cars with careless drivers and passengers who didn't care about denting other cars when they opened their doors.

Joe and Tessa walked up the wooden ramp that led to the restaurant which had the words Sandpiper Restaurant and the outline of a bird etched on the glass door. Inside, six couples and two tables of four clinked glasses and solved the problems of the world over plates of prawns, scallops, and other assortments of seafood in a restaurant that holds fifty diners on a busy night.

After interviewing the staff and the manager, Joe and Tessa took the names and contact numbers of the other staff and details of the contactable patrons who dined at the restaurant the previous night. The manager confirmed that most of the patrons were walk-ins, which was usual for a Sunday night. Only one of the staff, a waiter, noticed anything unusual the night before. He saw a young woman waiting outside the restaurant entry for about five minutes. He described her as blonde and petite.

'Is this her?' Tessa handed him a photograph of Phoebe that her sister, Sally had given them.

'Could be her. She had her back to me, so I'm not sure if I'd recognise her.' The waiter handed the photo back to Tessa. 'I can't say it wasn't her. She was there when I went down to the cellar to get a bottle of Moët champagne for a couple celebrating their wedding anniversary. I noticed she was still there when I came out of the cellar.'

'What time was this?' Joe asked.

'Around seven-thirty. When I saw her the second time, I think she was sending a text message. And then she left.'

'Did you notice which way she went?' Tessa asked.

'No, it was dark outside, and I really wasn't taking any notice. I was concentrating on not falling up the stairs and dropping the champagne.'

'Did you see anybody else by themselves, a man?' Joe asked.

'No, nobody. Just the blonde chick.'

Joe handed the waiter a card. 'Okay, thanks. Contact us if you think of anything else.'

Joe and Tessa walked towards the door.

'Hang on,' the waiter called after them. 'I just thought of something. I'm not sure if it has anything to do with it.'

'Anything you can tell us. The smallest detail might be relevant,' Joe said.

'Well, it wasn't last night. It was last Thursday. There was a man sitting at a table by the window. He was alone all evening.'

Joe walked towards the window. 'Which table?' He could hear the pounding roar of the surf breaking on the shore below. It was as though the calm of the morning ocean never existed.

The waiter, shifting from one foot to the other, looked towards the diners. 'I really should get back ...'

'Just a couple more minutes,' Joe said. 'Which table was he sitting at?'

The waiter walked to the corner table near the window. 'I thought it was strange he was alone, because it's one of our best tables and he would have booked well in advance to secure it. But then I thought because it was a Thursday night, maybe he was from another state, you know—travelling for work. We get that here at times.'

'What did he eat?' Tessa asked.

'I'm not sure, I didn't look after that table, but I noticed he had the lobster. But I don't know what or if he had an entrée or dessert. Stefan looked after that table. But it's his night off.'

'This is all very helpful information,' Joe said. 'Can you describe him, what did he look like, what was he wearing?'

The waiter described a man about six feet, in his thirties, and fair hair. 'You know, not blonde hair, but not brown,' he said. 'I imagine women might say he's not bad looking.' The waiter added, 'And some guys too, I guess.'

Joe showed him a photo of Sebastian Sanders that Sally McKay had found on Facebook for them. 'Is this the man?'

'Could be.' The waiter shrugged. 'Can't say for sure. I really took more notice of his clothes. He wore blue jeans, a white shirt, grey jacket and black shoes with multi-coloured socks.'

'You've got an excellent memory,' Tessa said.

'I'm studying fashion design, so I notice what people are wearing. You should wear burgundy. It would accentuate your dark brown eyes.'

The waiter looked at Joe. 'And you should wear ...'

'How long did he stay?' Joe interrupted. 'What time did he leave?'

'Sorry, I'm not sure. I didn't see him come in, so I'm not sure how long he stayed. And I didn't take notice of what time he left.'

'Anything else?' Tessa asked.

'No.' He took a step towards a diner who was waving for his attention. 'Sorry, I really have to …' He stopped. 'Oh yes, one thing. Ben, the other waiter, you spoke to him before, told me the guy paid in cash and left a twenty-dollar tip. And you, detective,' the waiter said over his shoulder to Joe as he walked towards the impatient diner. 'You would look good in any shade of pink.'

They re-interviewed Ben. 'Yeah, I remember that guy,' he said. 'Not friendly. Sort of abrupt. Not interested in chitchat. I was surprised he left a tip.'

'Did you notice the car he drove?'

'No, I didn't take any notice.'

'Do you remember anything else?' Joe asked.

'Not really, except he went outside two or three times for a smoke. Spoils the taste of good food if you ask me. I have to get back to my tables.' Ben turned to leave then stopped. 'Wait. I just remembered. He left his glasses case on the table. They're in lost property.'

'Can you get it for us? Thanks, Ben,' Joe said.

'Expensive brand,' Tessa said as they walked back to Joe's car. 'Could be sunglasses. Hard to say if the case is for reading glasses or sunglasses.'

'The waiter said it was a dark night. But the guy may have been there before dark. So could be sunglasses. But if they're reading glasses,' Joe added, 'that would make him at least age forty.'

'Not in his thirties, like the waiter said. What do you think?' Tessa said as they walked back to the car. 'Could it have been him checking out the scene?'

'Don't know. Could be nothing. But if he's our guy, at least we have fingerprints now.'

Tessa opened the case. 'And his email.'

8

'Are you okay?' Tessa said.
       'I'm fine.'

'Sure you are,' Tessa said in a tone that made it impossible to miss her scepticism. 'You're gripping the steering wheel so tightly all the blood has drained from your knuckles.'

'I'm fine. Let it go.'

'It's still early,' Tessa said as they approached her car. 'Do you want to have a bite to eat with Alex and me tonight? We've got some leftover something in the freezer. Take your mind off the case for a few hours.'

'I thought you only stayed at Alex's place on weekends.'

'Mostly ... anyway do you want to ...'

'Thanks, but ...'

'But—I know—you've got a hot date. Is this one a one-night or two-night stand?'

Joe said nothing.

'Well?'

'Yes, I've got plans for tonight.'

'Who is she? What's she like? So, is she a one or a two

nighter? Dating on a Monday night—it must be serious. Could be even a three nighter. Works out well. She's gone by Thursday. So, you can rest up for your weekend one-night stands.'

'Are you done?'

'Pretty much. Tell me, who is she?'

'Sorry to disappoint you. I've got a date with Paul. He texted when we were at the restaurant. He's dropping by home tonight. We're going over Amber and Isabel's files together. You know, fresh eyes. Paul might have some fresh insight. He's got some more ideas after our discussion about the case this afternoon.'

'So not what I had planned for you tonight,' Tessa laughed. 'Anyway, back to Paul. After three months away from the action, it'll be good for him too, to get back on the bike.'

Joe parked behind Tessa's car. She opened the door to get out, put one foot on the road, then put it back in the car, turned to face Joe. 'Do you have anything to eat at your place? Of course you do. Silly question.'

'Eggs,' Joe said. 'My girls are laying almost every day. More than I can eat.'

Tessa took her mobile out of her pocket. 'Hi sweetie ... yep, I'll be late. I'm heading back to Joe's. We're going over our case files with Paul ... No, don't worry about dinner. Joe's making an omelette ... Okay, I'll call when I'm leaving.' She put her hand over the phone and whispered, 'Love you too.'

'How did you know I'm an omelette-making guru?' Joe laughed. 'Alex doesn't mind?'

'No, not a problem, all good. Don't forget, Alex is a journalist. They work odd hours too.'

'An excellent journalist. A journalist who can write sensational articles, without sensationalising, if that makes sense,' Joe said. 'And based on fact, too. Relevant fact.'

Tessa got all the way out of the car this time. 'Race you

back there,' she said as she closed the door, careful not to slam it. She'd learned to treat the car that Joe had inherited from his father with kid gloves very early on in the piece. It was old, but it looked like it had just come brand new off the showroom floor.

***

Tessa pulled into Joe's circular driveway and parked next to his car in the garage. The first time Tessa saw Joe's garage, she was confused because it only contained a car, a motorbike, and a large, framed print of a floodlit Adelaide cricket ground. It was a triple garage that had so much space in it you could open the car door all the way to get in and out of the car without scratching it on whatever might stick out from bowed shelving that looked like it would break and spew its contents at any time. Not that Joe had bowed shelving. Joe had no shelving to be bowed. Garages were supposed to be full of junk, old tools you never use, vinyl records you'll never listen to, a Christmas tree and decorations that you might use every other year. And sometimes, like her father's garage, it contained so much junk there wasn't any room for the car. So her father's car always sits solemnly on the driveway, in front of the garage door that should be the entrance to its home.

Just twenty kilometres and twenty minutes south down the highway, Joe's house, built by his great grandfather eighty years ago, on three acres overlooking the ocean, was as different from Tessa's two-bedroom town house as a cricket match was from a rugby match.

When Joe opened the door, Banjo, sitting on the table in the foyer, greeted them with a loud, demanding meow. 'Hey Banjo boy, how's my grey furry ball of mischief?' Joe said as he rubbed Banjo behind the ears. 'I bet you're hungry. Let's find Bonnie, she'll be hungry too.' Banjo jumped from the table and ran in front of Joe, meowing all the way to the kitchen.

Tessa followed Joe and Banjo. 'He's very verbal.'

'Yeah, he's good company. Fun to be around.'

While Joe fed Bonnie and Banjo, Tessa surveyed the kitchen, hoping to find something out of place. No luck. The polished stone benches sparkled, not even one dirty spoon in the white farmhouse kitchen sink. She inspected the pantry. Yes, all the labels pointed forwards. All the tins stacked facing the same direction.

Then Tessa heard sounds of classical music emanating from the front door. 'That'll be Paul. I'll get it. Who's your doorbell playing these days?'

'Mozart. What do you think?'

'Different. Nice,' Tessa said over her shoulder. She walked from the kitchen to the front door, glancing sideways into each of the rooms. 'Yep, spotless as usual,' she muttered to herself. *Why does a single man need four bedrooms and a study*, she wondered? 'Hey Joe,' she called behind her, 'I think there's a speck of dust near the front door. Should I get the mop out?'

When she opened the front door to let Paul in, she put her index finger against pursed lips and ran into Joe's study, turned a book on a shelf above his computer monitor upside down, and moved his keyboard to an awkward angle. She dared not touch Joe's treasured photo of Bradman's nineteen forty-eight Invincibles or the indigenous cricket team that toured England eighty years before the Invincibles. She turned to leave, then stopped briefly to admire the even more treasured photos of Joe's father in his police uniform and his parents' and grandparents' wedding photos.

She gave the keyboard an extra turn and satisfied that she'd disrupted Joe's very ordered life in a small way, Tessa darted out of the room—straight into Joe.

'You are so, so predictable, Tess,' Joe laughed. 'I'd be disappointed if you didn't play one of your little tricks. Last time she was here,' he told Paul, 'she put the coffee on the peanut butter and vegemite shelf, and she turned the toilet roll around the wrong way.'

'I didn't know there was a right or wrong way for toilet rolls,' Paul said as he followed them to the kitchen.

'If your name is Joseph Paterson, there's a right and a wrong way for everything in the house,' Tessa said.

'And the garden,' Joe added. 'And…'

'There's my girl,' Paul interrupted as he bent down to give Bonnie a rub.

Tessa saw Joe, stopped mid-sentence, biting his bottom lip as he watched Paul and Bonnie. She knew what Joe was thinking. *Paul and Bonnie—two tortured souls.*

9

Joe watched Paul and Bonnie. *Would Bonnie find the strength to overcome her past? Mistreated, drugged, malnourished.* He wondered. *Would Paul find the strength to deal with what he can't control—the brutality and depravity he faces day after day. That we all face day after day. The horrors and the darkness that will never go away. Never.*

Tessa, with a voice soft but firm, broke Joe's pondering. 'Maybe we should start ...'

Joe turned his attention away from Paul and Bonnie. 'Yep, right, I'll start dinner.'

He sliced mushrooms, crumbled ricotta, crushed garlic and chopped fresh herbs from his garden. Forty-five minutes later they'd eaten and were ready for work. 'Coffee or tea,' Joe asked as he cleared the dishes from the dining table.

'That omelette was the best, thanks,' Tessa said. 'Tea would be good.'

'I've got chocolate,' Joe said.

'Mm ... in that case, coffee. Thanks.' Tessa surrendered to the temptation of, what Joe knew was for her, a match made in heaven. Chocolate and coffee.

'Paul?'

'I can't let you two drink alone,' Paul said. 'Coffee, thanks.'

Joe placed a box of chocolates and coffee on the dining table where they had set up their laptops and notes—ready to go over the files again, share information with Paul, hoping for some fresh insights.

'Where do we start?' Joe said. Since the first murder, he and Tessa and the task force had interviewed over a hundred people. From those interviews Joe and Tessa had two main suspects— Edward Kowalski, Amber's manager. And Aaron Thompson, Isabel's ex-boyfriend.

'Okay, let's start from the beginning. Amber Thompson was the first victim.'

***

Joe opened Amber's file and summarised for Paul, details about Amber and their interviews conducted since April with friends and colleagues.

Amber was twenty-six, five feet two with medium length blonde hair. A group of bushwalkers found her body on a Monday afternoon, early April.

Joe and Tessa notified Amber's parents Monday evening. Amber's father, seated on the lounge with his arm around his wife, sobbed as he described his daughter as loving, generous, studious, and loyal to her friends. Everybody loved her. Nobody would want to harm her. No reason to.

A collage of framed photos on the living room wall of four children, Amber, a sister and two older brothers, from babies to teens and young adults, appeared to be a testament to a happy, normal family. Photos on another wall showed the two brothers with their wives and children. Amber's father gave what details he knew of Amber's friends and where she worked.

The first person they interviewed was Jayden, Amber's flatmate. As far as Joe and Tessa could determine, he was the last person who knew Amber to see her alive—the night before she was found. He said she was excited about her date and was dressed in her favourite going-to-a-bar outfit. Jayden broke down when he told them he didn't worry when she didn't come home that night. He had assumed the date went well, or she was staying with a friend. It wasn't the first time Amber didn't come home after a night out. Jayden didn't recall Amber mentioning her date's name or where they were meeting. She left in a taxi around seven, maybe a bit before.

Jayden knew Amber for about twelve months before she moved in with him six months ago. He echoed what Amber's parents had said about her. He described her as smart with a good sense of humour, not the tidiest person around the apartment, and a workaholic—started work early and finished late. It's no wonder she didn't socialise much, he'd commented. She spent most of her weekends catching up on work, visiting her family or studying—she was in her last year of a law degree. Jayden hadn't met any of her dates and she never talked about them. Joe and Tessa later confirmed that Jayden had cooked dinner for his parents at his unit the night Amber left for the last time.

***

Joe sat straight in his chair and stretched. 'We've got Jayden at the bottom of the suspect list. Just about off the list.'

'There doesn't seem to be any romantic involvement there,' Tessa said. 'He's two or three years younger than Amber. Not the studious type. And judging by the posters on his walls he's into football, motorbikes and ... um ... can I say, well-endowed girls. I don't think he would have been anything but a friend and flatmate for Amber—not her type, I wouldn't think. Amber was petite, so judging by the curvy girlie posters I don't think she was his type either.' Tessa chuckled, 'I wonder if he took the girlies down when Mummy and Daddy visited.'

'I wonder,' Joe agreed.

'What about Amber's colleagues?' Paul said. 'Who's this Kowalski suspect?'

'We'll get to Kowalski shortly. The first person we interviewed at Amber's company was Harvey Cosgrove,' Tessa said. 'He came across as a jealous colleague.'

Joe continued with his summary, highlighting the main points. The interview with Amber's colleagues at her company told a somewhat different story from her parents and Jayden. Yes, Amber was a conscientious and smart girl. But she was a loner, kept her private life to herself and declined lunch invitations and Friday night drinks. Harvey said he didn't like to 'speak ill of the dead,' but Amber got promotions because she, in his words, 'sucked up to the bosses.' Harvey was in his late twenties, early thirties, average height, with chubby features and a pudgy build. He looked like he took the lifts between floors more often than the stairs. Joe remembered how Harvey's lips pressed together to form a thin, tight line at the first mention of Amber's name. Was it because he didn't like her or didn't want to answer questions about her, or both?

'Time for a break,' Paul said. 'I'll make another coffee. Tess? Joe?'

'Water, thanks,' Tessa said. 'Coffee at this hour, you won't sleep tonight.'

'Who sleeps anyway, in this job?' Paul said.

'I need a stretch too,' Tessa said. 'I'll get the water. Water or coffee, Joe?'

'I'm fine for now, thanks.'

***

While Paul and Tessa stretched, Joe replayed the interview with Harvey over in his mind.

'She never came to lunch or coffee breaks with us,' Harvey said. 'But I saw her at least two or three times recently in the coffee shop with Ed, Edward Kowalski. He hates being called Ed. He's the senior lead for all our compliance projects.'

Tessa asked Harvey where he was on Sunday night.

'I had a quiet night in with my girlfriend.'

'Her place or yours?' Tessa asked.

'Mine.'

'Did she spend the night?' Joe asked.

'That's none of your business. I have to get back to work.' Harvey pushed his chair back to leave.

'Well, Harvey, I admire your conscientiousness, but murder is our business,' Tessa said, 'so that makes your business our business. Did you spend the night with your girlfriend?'

'No.'

Joe asked Harvey what time his girlfriend left.

'I don't know, about ten, I guess.' Harvey stood. 'I have to get back to work,' he said again.

'Give us your girlfriend's details, then you can get back to work,' Joe had said in a tone that made it clear to Harvey it would be in his best interest to co-operate.

Joe and Tessa confirmed the next day that Harvey's girlfriend was at his place until around nine-thirty. They had only been dating for a few weeks, so Joe and Tessa thought it was unlikely she'd lie to protect him. Particularly when murder was involved.

***

Paul and Tessa returned with coffee, water, and a tray of cupcakes. Tessa shook Joe on the shoulder. 'Are you sleeping?'

Joe opened his eyes. 'No, just thinking about the interview with Harvey Cosgrove.'

Tessa reached for a cupcake. 'I found these in the fridge. Looks like you've been baking again.'

'Mum,' Joe said.

'So where are we with Harvey Cosgrove?' Paul asked.

'Harvey came across as a jealous colleague, but we've got him near the bottom of the list. The timeframe doesn't work. Amber left home at seven. Harvey's girlfriend left his apartment sometime between nine-thirty and ten. She was there about three hours. He wouldn't have had time to meet with Amber.'

'Mostly agree,' Tessa said. 'But there was something hinky about her. Maybe we should do more digging there.'

'Hinky? You watch too much American TV,' Joe laughed. 'My mother would agree with Sam Gerard—don't use words that have no meaning.'

'Sam who?'

'Sam Gerard. From *The Fugitive*, one of my all-time favourite movies,' Joe said.

'You love your nineteen-eighty something movies, don't you,' Tessa said.

'This one was nineteen-ninety something. And yes, I love my old movies.'

Joe took a sip of water. The bottle was empty. He debated about making a coffee, looked at his watch and decided it was too late for coffee and settled for another bottle of water.

'So that brings us to one of our main suspects,' Joe said. 'Edward Kowalski.'

10

Joe passed his laptop to Paul. 'These are the notes from our first interview with Kowalski.'

While Paul read the notes Joe closed his eyes and as he did with Harvey replayed the interview with Edward Kowalski.

Kowalski was tall, about the same height as Joe, in his mid-thirties, with fair to light brown hair and dark brown eyes. Joe and Tessa interviewed him in a meeting room situated in the corner of a large, open-planned office. Despite the room's glass walls, the fifty or more staff scattered around the office appeared oblivious to the meeting, apparently used to the comings and goings of people they didn't recognise. The meeting room, on level twenty-five, had extensive views of Sydney Harbour, its ferries, the Opera House, and Luna Park in the distance. Joe, Tessa, and Kowalski occupied three of the available twelve chairs around an oval conference table. A sixty-inch wall mounted monitor watched over the meeting room, and a teleconference phone resembling a flying saucer sat in the middle of the table.

Kowalski said he was chairing a meeting in ten minutes and could only afford to spend two or three minutes. He was shocked of course to hear the news about Amber—yes, she was a clever, ambitious employee with a promising career ahead of her. Throughout the interview, he jiggled and twisted his wedding ring.

Joe recalled Edward Kowalski's reactions to their questions. His face flushed when Tessa asked him about having coffee with Amber. 'Oh yes, well, um … I was helping her with her assignment for her law degree. As I said, she was smart and had a promising career.' Another twist of the wedding ring.

'Are you a lawyer, Ed?' Tessa asked.

'Edward,' he corrected Tessa.

'Are you a lawyer, Mr Kowalski?' Joe asked.

Kowalski reached for a tissue from the box at the end of the table, removed his glasses and started to polish them. 'I studied law about ten years ago.'

Joe leaned in closer. 'Are you a lawyer, Mr Kowalski?'

'No, I didn't finish my law degree. I have a diploma in …'

'Where were you on Sunday night?' Joe interrupted.

'Sunday, my wife and I were at a restaurant with my wife's sister and her husband. We were celebrating my sister-in-law's birthday.'

'What time were you there?' Tessa asked.

'We had a late lunch. We left around three, three-thirty.'

'So where were you Sunday night?' Joe asked again.

'At home.'

'All night? Can your wife vouch for that?' Tessa asked.

'Well, not all night. My wife watches one of those annoying lifestyle home renovation shows on Sunday nights, and I went for a run.' Kowalski's mobile played the default iPhone ringtone. 'Give my apologies, I'll be there in a few minutes. Start the meeting.' He stood to leave. 'If that's all, I have to go to my meeting. It's important.'

'Sit down, Ed,' Tessa said. 'We haven't finished. So, you went for a run on a full stomach after a boozy lunch?'

'My name is Edward. And I didn't drink. I was designated driver and I'm in training for a half marathon. I really have to go.'

Joe remembered the tobacco smell he noticed when they first met Kowalski and wondered how that affected his marathon performance. 'We're sorry for delaying you, Mr Kowalski, but we're trying to find out who murdered Amber, a colleague and friend of yours. We'd appreciate any help you can give us. What time did you go for your run?' Joe asked.

Kowalski twisted his wedding ring, again. 'She wasn't a friend. She was a direct report.'

'What time did you go for your run?' Joe repeated.

'Around seven, seven thirty.'

'A little more detail,' Joe said. 'Where did you run? How long did you run?'

Kowalski stood. 'I'm getting a little tired of all these questions. I told you, I have an important meeting.' He walked to the meeting room door.

'Sit down, Mr Kowalski.' Slowly articulating each word, Joe said, 'We understand you are a busy man, and you have important meetings to attend. But as I said, we are investigating the murder of a young woman. A young woman who you worked with. I think a murder investigation trumps your meeting.'

'Am I a suspect?'

'We have to investigate all avenues, Ed,' Tessa said. 'Where did you run and what time did you get home?'

'It's Edward. And I drove to the local park where I run most times and came home around ten.'

'Two and a half to three-hour run—late at night? Do you do that often?' Joe asked.

'I told you, I'm in training.'

'Was there anybody else there? Can anybody vouch for you?' Tessa asked.

'There may have been one or two people walking their dogs, I don't know, there often is. But maybe not at that time of night.'

Joe asked, 'Can your wife confirm what time you got home from your run?'

'She was asleep.'

'We'll need to speak with your wife,' Tessa said. 'What's her mobile number?'

'There's no need for you to speak with her. I've helped you all I can. She knows nothing.'

'We'll decide that,' Joe said. 'Now, can we have her contact details—please?'

'That's all for now. Thank you for your co-operation, Mr Kowalski,' Joe said after Kowalski wrote his wife's mobile number on a business card.

Joe handed Kowalski his card. 'And please contact us if you think of anything that will help us with our investigation into the murder of your colleague.'

'Thanks, Ed,' Tessa said as she handed him her card. 'You better run along to your very important meeting now.' Joe smirked as he gave Tessa a sideways glance. He always pretended to disapprove but was always secretly amused at her sarcastic sense of humour when she didn't like somebody. And he had to admit, most times she had good reasons for not liking somebody. Tessa was the best he knew at reading people.

Joe opened the meeting room door but stopped before exiting. 'One more question, Mr Kowalski. Did you have romantic feelings for Amber?'

Kowalski's face flushed. 'That's absurd. I'm a married man.'

***

'Ed Kowalski's at the top of the list,' Joe said when Paul finished reading the notes. 'When we interviewed his wife, she said she was probably asleep when he came home—she was in a separate room because he snores when he's been drinking. She agreed he was the designated driver at lunch, but he had a few drinks when they came home. And she thought it was odd that he would want to run with alcohol in his system. But he runs at strange hours, so she didn't think any more of it. When we re-interviewed Kowalski, he admitted he may have had one or two drinks, but he was fit, and a bit of alcohol didn't stop him from jogging. He said he'd forgotten about having a drink when we interviewed him the first time.'

'And he denied his feelings for Amber,' Tessa added. 'I'm betting that's a lie too. The way he kept twisting his wedding ring every time we mentioned Amber's name during the first interview.'

'And the increased blood flow to his face when we asked if he had romantic feelings about Amber was a bit of a giveaway,' Joe said.

Paul leaned on the table, steepled his hands. 'I wonder what else our Ed Kowalski lied about.'

'Mind your manners. Don't you mean Edward?' Tessa said. 'Yep, there's definitely something, can I say hinky, about our friend Ed. He's right-handed. We confirmed that when he wrote his wife's contact details on the card. And he doesn't have an alibi he can prove. Ed is high on our current list of suspects, and I think Aaron Thompson is up there too.'

Paul looked at his watch. 'It's still early. Tell me about Aaron Thompson.'

11

Aaron Thompson knew the second victim Isabel Reinhard. So Joe and Tessa spent the next fifteen minutes summarising Isabel Reinhard's file for Paul.

Isabel was age twenty-two, lived at home with her mother and stepfather. She had one older sister, single, also living at home. Isabel was close to her biological father and stayed with him at least once a month sometimes twice. Issy, as her friends called her, was in her third year of a veterinary science degree. She was petite, with long streaked blonde hair.

Interviews with friends and relatives revealed similar attributes as Amber Thompson, victim number one. There was no reason anybody would want to harm her. Isabel was smart, studious, and good natured. But, unlike Amber who was outgoing and confident, friends described Isabel as a shy, private person. Joe and Tessa agreed that Isabel's apparent reserved nature might explain her lack of social media presence.

She had a few close girlfriends with whom she went to clubs or movies, mainly on Friday nights, because she dedicated her weekends to her studies. Isabel wasn't in a serious romantic relationship, although she dated Aaron Thompson on and off for a few months until, according to her sister, she broke it off. Joe noted at the time that Aaron's surname was the same as Amber's, the first victim. Both had the initials A.T. Was Aaron related to Amber? Was he the link between the two girls? Or was the same surname just a coincidence?

Aaron was interstate for a concert when Joe first contacted him. Joe and Tessa interviewed Aaron at his unit the following week. Research prior to the interview revealed that he reported directly to the head of sales and marketing at the same company as Amber.

'So, tell me about the interview with Aaron Thompson,' Paul said. 'How did he react?'

***

Tessa's narration of the interview for Paul played like a movie in Joe's mind.

'Thank you for making the time to speak to us, Aaron,' Tessa said as they entered the tiny, almost claustrophobic living area of Aaron's unit. 'We understand you went to Brisbane for a concert. That's a long way to go to see a band.'

'I couldn't get tickets for Sydney. The concert was sold out and the band probably won't be back in Australia for a year or two. And I was able to combine the trip with a business meeting.'

'Handy,' Tessa said. 'A leisure trip paid for by the company.'

'Lurks and perks,' Aaron said. 'You take 'em when you can.'

'Is that the band playing on your iPad?' Tessa said. 'Do you mind turning it down?'

'No, not down. Off.' Joe walked to the small round dining table. A laptop sat on the table with a beer on a coaster to the right of it and a mouse to the left on a mouse pad with his company's logo. 'Take a seat Aaron, we have some questions.'

Joe and Tessa sat with their backs to the balcony, which was just metres away from the next tall block of units obstructing any potential views of Sydney.

'We don't want to hold you up any longer than necessary, so we'll get to the point,' Joe said. 'As you know, Issy was murdered last Sunday week. It must be hard for you. We understand you were close for a while.'

'I'm not sure why you want to talk to me,' Aaron said. 'I don't know anything. I haven't seen Isabel for weeks.'

'We're talking to everyone who knew Issy, friends, relatives, even casual acquaintances,' Joe said. 'We need all the information about her we can gather so we can apprehend the person who murdered her. You were close to Issy. I'm sure you want us to find and arrest the person who did this to her. So we really appreciate your time and cooperation. Can you tell us more about your relationship with Issy?'

'You're wrong. We weren't close. We were hanging out for a while, but I broke it off.'

'When did you last see Issy?' Tessa asked.

'I saw Isabel at a coffee shop one morning, about eight, maybe ten weeks ago. That's when we agreed to go our separate ways.'

'You said you broke it off. Was it your decision or a mutual agreement?' Joe asked Aaron.

'Yes, mutual, I said I think we need a break. She agreed. We agreed.'

'We understood it was Issy's decision to break up,' Tessa said.

'No, you're wrong, it was mutual. The relationship wasn't going anywhere and she ... I mean, we wanted to get on with our lives.'

'You must have known Issy well. Do you know of any reason why anybody would want to harm her?' Joe asked.

Aaron slouched in his chair—his neck turtled into his shoulders. He bit his bottom lip and didn't answer.

'Sorry Aaron, I know this must be hard for you. But do you know why anybody would want to harm Issy?' Joe repeated.

Aaron sat up, hesitated, said 'No, I can't think of any reason.'

Not wanting to discuss Isabel's virginity with Aaron, Joe simply asked Aaron, 'How close were you and Issy?'

'We dated for a bit, that's all. I told you, the relationship was, well, nothing was happening.'

'So, you lost the bet,' Tessa said.

'What bet?' Aaron's face flushed. 'What bet, what are you talking about?'

'You know exactly what we're talking about,' Tessa said. 'We've been talking to your and Issy's mutual friends. According to them, you had a bet with your mates that you could get Issy into bed. And you'd video it as proof.'

'No, that was a joke. A stupid joke. I wouldn't do that.'

'Where were you that Sunday night?' Joe asked.

'I, um … I'll have to check my diary.'

Aaron opened his laptop, checked the diary, and closed the laptop. 'There's nothing in my diary. Sunday nights I mostly stay in, watch TV, you know, some Netflix bingeing. There's nothing in my diary, so I was home.'

'Can anybody vouch for you?' Tessa asked.

'This is a secure building. There'll be a video recording showing that my car didn't leave the building.'

'Did you leave the building?' Joe asked.

'No, I don't go anywhere without my car. Check the videos.'

'You don't go out for the occasional walk?' Tessa said.

'No, not in this neighbourhood.'

'We'll check the videos,' Joe said. 'How well did you know Amber Thompson? We noticed she had the same last name and the same initials as you?'

Aaron shook his head. 'I ... I don't know her. Was she one of Isabel's friends? I thought I knew them all.'

'Where were you the first Sunday in April?' Tessa asked.

'Are you serious? You know, that always amuses me when the cops ask the same type of ridiculous question on TV. Where were you six months ago? Now I've got cops asking me the same silly question in real life.' Aaron pointed at Tessa. 'Do you know where you were on the first Sunday in April?'

'If you value your index finger, you'll stop pointing it at me.' Tessa reached over and opened Aaron's laptop. 'Now, maybe if you check your diary again, you might find an answer to our silly question.'

'Okay, okay. Keep your pants on.' Aaron accessed his diary with not so gentle keystrokes. 'There's nothing in my diary for that day. Again, I probably stayed in. That's my Sunday routine.'

'You're close to the city here, bars, restaurants. You didn't go out for a drink or a meal?' Tessa persisted.

'No, no. How many times do I have to tell you? I ...'

Joe noticed Aaron's knuckles turning white from clenched fists. 'We just need to make sure we get our facts right. And as I said before, we really appreciate your co-operation, Aaron.' Joe said in his quiet, liquid-gold voice. 'You know what it's like. You have to get your reports right for the boss, don't you? Well, we do too. So, think carefully back to April. Around Easter. You might have altered your routine.'

Aaron unclenched his fists. 'No, I start work early, high-pressure job. I always stay in on Sunday nights. Like you said. I have reports, deadlines.'

'Amber Thompson,' Joe said. 'You work at the same company as she did.'

'More than three thousand people work there. I have a team

of six reporting to me, and she's not one of them.' He shrugged. 'So I'm not interested.'

'Okay, thank you, Aaron,' Joe said. 'That's all for now. Contact us if you think of anything that would help our investigations.' Joe and Tessa handed him their cards.

***

Tessa finished summarising the Aaron Thompson interview for Paul. 'That's it, not much to go on there.'

'How old is he?' Paul asked

Tessa checked her notes. 'Twenty-nine.'

'Right age for our profile,' Paul said. 'Young to have a team reporting to him.'

Tessa studied the names of the chocolates on the box and chose a dark chocolate with strawberry cream. 'Smart, workaholic, knows how to play office politics.'

'So, how did he react to your questioning?' Paul repeated the question he'd asked before Tessa summarised the interview. 'Was he co-operative, reserved, hiding information?'

'We had to drag information out of him,' Tessa said. 'And he appeared to be quite angry at one point, sort of like a controlled anger.'

'Controlled anger,' Paul said. 'Interesting.'

'Yeah, but you know Joe. Mr Iceman can be Mr McSmooth when he needs to be. He can calm a hurricane. But we still didn't get much out of Aaron.'

'We checked the video footage.' Joe reached for a chocolate. 'And confirmed that Aaron didn't leave the building in his car in the relevant timeframe. An alibi, but not strong. We don't have any proof that Aaron didn't leave the building on foot. He could've been wearing a hoodie, so he could leave without being recognised. He'd know where the cameras are located.'

Without warning Banjo sprang onto the dining table and plopped himself on Tessa's keyboard. 'What is it with cats and keyboards?' she laughed. 'Frankie, my cheeky feline, does the same thing. I think they like the warmth.'

'And attention seeking.' Joe picked up Banjo and put him on the floor near his food bowl. 'I'm having trouble convincing him he's not allowed on benches and tables.' Joe laughed as he poured treats into Banjo's bowl. 'Maybe because I always reward his unacceptable behaviour with his favourite nibbles.' He looked over at Bonnie asleep in her bed. 'She's much better behaved,' he said with a soft smile and warmth in his voice.

'She's adorable,' Paul said. He sat for a few moments quietly watching Bonnie. Then he shifted in his chair and sat straight as if bringing himself back to the moment. 'So you have no evidence against Aaron Thompson? And he didn't leave his apartment in his car, but you're not convinced that he didn't leave on foot?'

'Correct,' Joe said.

'Then how would he have got to where he had to go?' Paul asked.

'He could have hired a car,' Tessa said.

'Tess, you mentioned that everybody called her Issy,' Paul said. 'And Aaron called her Isabel.'

'That's right. He always referred to her as Isabel.'

'Distancing himself maybe,' Paul said. 'It's obvious he had no affection for her, slime bag that he is.'

'Slime bag is too generous a description about Aaron Thompson,' Tessa said. 'I'd call him a ...'

'Hey Tess,' Joe interrupted, 'when we asked Aaron if he knew why anybody would want to harm Issy, I'm sure I noticed a slight nod of his head before he said "No". I don't know, maybe

I imagined it.'

'You didn't imagine it. I saw it too. You're getting good at reading body language.'

'He used his mouse with his left hand,' Joe said. 'We think the killer is right-handed, but we can't rule out Aaron. He might be ambidextrous.' Joe shrugged. 'But unlikely. Only about one percent of the population is.'

***

Joe yawned, stood, and stretched. 'I need a coffee.'

'I'll join you,' Paul said.

'Drinking coffee this late,' Tessa said. 'No wonder you're not sleeping.'

'Yeah, yeah, you keep reminding me,' Joe said. 'But most of the time they go cold before I finish. Anyway, I'll cut back when we're done with this case.'

Tessa sighed, 'If we're ever done with it.'

'We'll get him, Tess.' Joe pointed to the sticker on his laptop, with a quote from the *Apollo 13* movie. '*Failure is not an option.*'

'Amber, Isabel, Kowalski, Aaron Thompson,' Paul said. 'How do they connect?'

'And now Phoebe. We're missing something,' Tessa said. 'There has to be a link. Amber, Issy, Phoebe ... they're connected somehow. They have to be.'

So far Joe and Tessa found no personal connections between Amber and Isabel. They had no mutual friends, went to different schools and different universities. When Isabel, the second victim was murdered, Joe and Tessa re-interviewed Amber's flatmate Jayden and her work colleagues, Harvey Cosgrove, and Edward Kowalski. They found nothing to connect Isabel with Amber. Kowalski claimed he stayed in all night and watched

TV. His wife couldn't confirm it because she and their son were visiting her parents in Canberra that weekend.

However, there were similarities between Amber and Isabel. They were both well educated, and liked by friends and relatives, except Amber by her work colleagues. And like Phoebe, they had blonde hair, were slim, short to medium height, and killed on a Sunday night. Amber and Isabel received the same text message, 'Beautiful evening. Meet me near the surf club, south end of the boardwalk—we'll go for a walk before dinner.' They both said yes.

'I wonder if he sent the same text to Phoebe, suggesting they go for a walk before dinner,' Joe said.

Tessa cut a cupcake in half. 'We should have the transcript from her mobile in the morning. I wonder why he left the mobiles behind. I guess he knows we can retrieve the text messages with or without the mobiles.'

'He's no dummy.' Joe said. 'No fingerprints. No DNA. No fibre.'

'I guess he didn't know about Locard's exchange theory,' Paul said. 'The perpetrator always leaves something behind, DNA, fibre. And always takes something away from the scene. It doesn't seem possible that he didn't leave a trace of himself behind.'

Joe perused the chocolates, looking for a dark one. 'There were shoe prints in the sand near Phoebe's body, but with the wind and the boy and dog disturbing the scene, they weren't clear enough to find any distinguishing features about them.'

'Size?' Paul asked.

'About my size,' Joe said. 'So the guy is probably as tall, if not a little taller than me.'

'He's clever, and he's arrogant,' Paul said. 'Clever enough not to leave any physical evidence, but arrogant. He's playing a catch me if you can game, by leaving clues—the roses and the notes. His arrogance will be his downfall.'

'Agree,' Joe said. 'He thinks we're not clever enough to follow the clues, but he's underestimated us.'

'I hope you're right,' Tessa said. 'How many cryptic letters did the Zodiac killer send the San Francisco police department? They never found him.' Tessa crossed and uncrossed her arms over her chest stretching her back and shoulders. 'Sorry, I'm tired and feeling a little negative. I feel like we're just going around in circles.' Tessa shrugged. 'You're right. He has underestimated us. So let's keep going around in circles till something gives. Because it will. Right?'

Joe stood, walked over to Bonnie, and bent to give her a rub behind the ears. 'Right. So what have we got? Three victims and two suspects so far—Kowalski and Aaron Thompson. Both have the smarts, based on their job profiles. Kowalski is a senior project lead and Thompson reports to the head of sales and marketing and is two down from the CEO. So both should be well organised with good time management skills. I imagine Kowalski would be the more calculating type and Thompson, I guess more creative. Is our killer calculating or creative?'

'Or both calculating and creative,' Tessa said.

'Agreed,' Paul said. 'And neither sound like the caring type. Their ages fit the profile, late twenties to mid-thirties. But what's the motive?'

'And what's the connection with Amber, Issy and now Phoebe?' Joe stretched. 'I don't know what it is, but I do know there is a connection. When we find the connection, we might find the motive.'

Joe closed his eyes and saw the note pinned to the victims' breasts. Another macabre vision to haunt his dreams.

Trust not too much to appearances. The beauty hides the thorns.
How did the words connect the victims? What was the message? Who was the message for—the victims, the police, society? he wondered.

12

Early the next morning Joe walked to Tessa's desk carrying two coffees. 'I saw your car when I drove into the car park. It's early. I thought you might need this,' he said, handing her a coffee.

'Thanks. All that coffee at your place last night, I couldn't sleep. I've been here since seven.'

'Don't forget the chocolate. We polished off more than half the box.'

Tessa sipped her coffee. 'I did need this. Thanks.'

Joe's mobile rang. 'Okay. Tell them we'll be two minutes.'

'What is it?' Tessa asked.

'It's Amber's parents. At the front desk.'

'It's very early. Were we expecting them?'

Joe shook his head.

When Joe greeted Mr and Mrs Thompson in the reception, he was shocked but not surprised at their changed appearance since the first day he met them. The day he broke the news to them about their daughter, Amber. He'd seen too many times, far too many times, he thought, how the internal emotions of grief and loss can transform the external physical appearance.

Less than six months ago, Mr Thompson, a man in his early sixties, stood straight and tall. His thick grey hair accentuated his clear blue eyes, which sparkled with vitality despite his age. Mrs Thompson was an attractive lady with caramel-highlighted, soft brown hair cut in a jaw-length bob. She wore makeup, natural, not heavy. Manicured nails. Fast forward to the present. They'd both lost weight. Their red-rimmed eyes were puffy with dark circles from crying and lack of sleep. Mr Thompson no longer stood tall. His posture was more of an arthritic ninety-year-old man. Mrs Thompson's nails were chipped, and her hair was stringy with streaks of grey roots appearing. Mr Thompson held his wife close. Joe wasn't sure if it was to support himself or his wife.

Joe and Tessa led Amber's parents to the meeting room opposite reception. Joe's mobile vibrated in his coat pocket. He ignored it.

'We found out, a few hours ago,' Mr Thompson sobbed and choked on his words. He closed his eyes and composed himself. 'We found out. It's happened again to another young woman. What are you doing to catch this beast who took our little girl from us?'

'We're following every lead and looking for new ones,' Tessa said. 'I'm sorry, we understand how you …'

'You don't understand,' Mr Thompson snapped. 'Do you have children? Do you know what it's like to lose a child? It's destroying my wife.' He held his wife even more closely. 'And our family. Amber's sister and brothers. I can't …' he wept, then continued, his voice weakened, 'I can't tell you … I can't find the words to describe what this is doing to us. The wound, it's a festering scab, that will never, never heal.'

Joe held his own emotions in check. 'We're doing everything

we can to find him.'

'It's been nearly six months,' Mr Thompson said. 'What have you done in all that time?'

'We will find him,' Joe said. 'We promise.'

Joe noticed Tessa glance in his direction, open her mouth to say something, but didn't. Mrs Thompson moved away from her husband's protective arms, held his hand instead, and sat straight in her chair. 'When you find him, you make sure he stays alive, don't kill him. Death is too good for him. Even Hell is too good for him. We want him to suffer and rot in prison for the rest of his miserable life. Don't kill him. We pray he gets what he deserves in prison. Do that for us.'

Joe nodded and said in a soft voice, 'We will, we'll do that for you, and for Amber.'

'I'm sorry to ask you again,' Tessa said. 'But is there anything you might have recalled that might be important? Any little detail.'

'There is one thing … another reason we came today,' Mr Thompson said. 'The last weekend Amber spent with us, it was the Easter break …' he stopped to put his arms around Mrs Thompson, who had started to sob again.

'Take your time,' Joe said.

'We had a wonderful weekend … walks, picnics, lots of laughs,' Mrs Thompson said as she regained her composure. 'Thank God for happy memories.' She paused, didn't wipe away the tears that dampened her cheeks. 'I don't know.' She shook her head. 'Sometimes I wonder … I wonder if the happy memories make the loss worse?'

'We spent the last weekend with our baby at our holiday house in Ulladulla,' Mr Thompson continued. 'We probably already told you. Anyway, we haven't been back there since, but her brother was there last week and found her iPad.

We thought because you wanted her laptop, you might want the iPad too.' He handed Joe an iPad protected in a deep red cover with a white and yellow daisy pattern.

13

On the way back to their desks Joe remembered his mobile had vibrated earlier. He took it out, but before he could check his messages, Tessa grabbed his elbow. 'Wait, before you do. The Thompsons, you promised them we'd catch the killer.'

'I noticed that glare you gave me. What's wrong?'

'What if we don't find the killer? What if we fail them? You've given them hope when all we might give them is disappointment. That's not fair.'

Joe stared at Tessa, not speaking.

'Joe?'

'How can you not believe we'll get him? He's made a mistake. I don't know what it is yet, but we'll find it.'

Tessa shook her head. 'I can't be certain about such an uncertainty. But I pray for the Thompsons you're right.'

'Not just the Thompsons. Pray we stop him before there's another victim.' Joe held up his mobile. 'If we're done here, I have to check my messages.'

Des, the IT tech had left a message. 'Call me. Found something interesting on Phoebe Duncan's laptop.'

Five minutes later, Des connected the laptop to a monitor on Joe's desk.

Des explained what they were looking at. 'Phoebe is a frequent, I mean, was a frequent visitor to this dating site. This is a transcript from her more recent visits.'

'I've never heard of this,' Joe said.

'What? The dating site? I'm not surprised you haven't heard of it. It's a gay dating site,' Des said. 'Actually, a bisexual dating site. There's monthly charges on her bank statement that correspond.'

Joe leaned forward. 'You're right, this is interesting. I wonder if this could be our connection.'

'It has to be our connection. And we were right about the blind date.' Tessa pointed at the transcript. 'Look at the dates, the timeframe is right.'

'Look at the name, PartyGirl. And the photo,' Joe said. 'If this is the killer, he's pretending to be a woman.'

Tessa nodded. 'A very beautiful woman with long dark hair.'

'Hi guys.' It was the police photographer, Olivia Chatfield. 'What have we got here?'

Joe felt his face flush when he heard Olivia's voice and hoped no one noticed. 'Um, it might be a connection between Amber, Isabel and Phoebe,' Joe said, not looking at her. 'But we don't know yet. We might be jumping to conclusions.'

'So, what is it?' Olivia asked again.

'It's a transcript from Phoebe's laptop, from a gay dating site,' Tessa said.

'Bisexual,' Des reminded Tessa.

Olivia grabbed a spare chair. Tessa sat between Olivia and Joe as the three of them read the transcript together.

***

Phoebe11

I'm bubbly, outgoing, love to party and love the outdoors. I'm 23 and 160 cm. Genuinely looking for someone to love. As you can see from my photo, I'm kinda cute.

PartyGirl011

Hello Phoebe.

Yes, you are very, very cute.

Let me introduce myself.

I love to party too.

You look and sound like a person I'd enjoy spending time with.

I'd love to know more about you.

Do you work or study?

I love to surf in the summer and ski in the winter.

I'm 28 and 168 cm.

As you can see from my photo, I'm okay looking too.

Phoebe11

Hi PartyGirl. I'm a receptionist for a real estate agent. I'm enjoying it, but I hope to get my licence soon. I plan to enrol in the course after Christmas. I'll have my own business one day.

PartyGirl011

OMG what a coincidence.

I'm a conveyancer.

I liaise with the local real estate agents.

We really do have a lot in common.

Maybe we could meet for coffee.

Phoebe11

Sure, would love to meet for coffee. Get to know more about you. But first things first. What's your name? BTW you've got gorgeous long brown hair.

PartyGirl011

Thank you.

Are you free for coffee on Sunday afternoon?

We could meet outside the QVB, near the Queen Victoria statue.

Say around three.

Phoebe11

Okay, but what's your name?

PartyGirl011

Perfect.

See you then.

And BTW my name is Zoe.

Ciao.

PartyGirl011

Something has come up.

Can't make coffee.

Can I buy you dinner tonight to make up for it?

Say 7:30 at the new restaurant near the beach.

The Sandpiper.

It's had excellent reviews.

We should swap mobile numbers.

I'll text you the address.

And we can text when we get there.

Phoebe11

Okay, but I've got work tomorrow. So it can't be a late night.

PartyGirl011

That's fine.

It most definitely won't be a late night for you.

I promise.

Looking forward to my evening with you.

Ciao.

***

'We're looking for a killer pretending to be a woman on the dating site,' Tessa said when they finished reading the transcript. 'We're looking for Zoe.'

Joe nodded. 'We're looking for a killer pretending to be a bisexual woman.' He looked at the transcript again. 'And a killer who inserts a hard return after every sentence. How long will it take to trace PartyGirl, Des?'

'Depends.' Des started to explain virtual private networks and other technical details that could slow the process.

Joe interrupted. 'Work your magic, okay, as soon as possible.'

Tessa asked Des if he'd found anything similar on Amber and Isabel's laptops. She already knew the answer but asked anyway.

Des shook his head. 'No, I didn't. Nothing.' He confirmed what was already recorded in Amber's file. 'Amber used her laptop for work,' he said. 'The stuff on it is mostly work stuff, some personal emails back and forth from her parents, most from her mother. And she saved her university notes and assignments to OneDrive.'

Joe and Tessa had also read Amber's emails and concluded the same as Des. They were mainly work emails. Nothing in her personal emails stood out as being anything other than normal correspondence between family and friends.

Joe had asked Amber's roommate Jayden why Amber didn't have her own personal laptop. He explained that she only used a work laptop because she didn't want to carry around two laptops when she had lectures at night. She always carried her laptop with her in case she needed to work from home the next day. And she could work on her law assignments during lunch and quiet times at work. So everything was in one place.

The situation was much the same for Isabel. She used her laptop mainly for her university studies and personal emails.

Her browsing history was clear except for veterinary and animal science searches related to her studies.

'There's got to be something there. We've missed something,' Tessa said.

'Let's go back over the emails with fresh eyes. With this additional information, we might pick up on something we missed before.' Joe saw doubt in Des's eyes. 'I know ... it might be a stretch. If there's a connection with this dating site, you would have found it on their laptops, I know.'

'Not necessarily,' Tessa said. 'If Amber and Issy were using the dating site, they might not have used their personal laptops, or work laptop in Amber's case. If you were smart, you definitely wouldn't use a work laptop to browse dating sites. Amber was smart, we know that. And Issy may not have wanted to risk her family finding out what may have been a secret part of her life.'

Joe thought, *Yeah, Tess, you know about keeping secrets from your family, don't you?*

'What about Amber's iPad? There might be something on that,' Joe said.

'What iPad?' Des asked.

Tessa handed Des Amber's iPad.

'Jesus, Tess. Why didn't you give me this before now?'

'We just got it,' Joe said. 'Amber's parents brought it in just this morning. I can understand why they didn't remember it before now. They're devastated. Anyway, how soon can you get back to us, Des?'

'I've got an urgent job for Rob C and now tracing this PartyGirl on the dating site. I'll look at the iPad when I'm done there.'

'I can get you seats in the Members' Stand for the first cricket match this season,' Olivia said. 'My father has a lifetime membership.'

Joe rolled his eyes. *Of course her father has a lifetime membership*, he thought. Olivia came from a wealthy family. Her wealth made Joe think their relationship couldn't be anything other than purely professional. He didn't want to be seen as a money grabber. A 'can't-commit one-night stander' was okay, but not a money grabber. He wondered why Olivia worked anyway. She didn't have to. Especially not in the police force as a photographer. But he never asked. He didn't want to appear to be interested in anything about Olivia, even though he was interested in *everything* about her.

Joe knew he was kidding himself. It wasn't just Olivia's wealth that was a barrier to their relationship. It wasn't even a barrier. It was an excuse. The barrier was Joe himself. He thought back to his conversation with Paul at the restaurant. He remembered looking at Olivia's reflection in the mirror and telling Paul only a fool lets happiness slip away. *Am I a fool?*

Conscious of his eye-roll reaction to Olivia's offer of tickets for the Member's Stand, he looked at the others to see if anybody had noticed and was relieved their attention was on Des and the iPad.

'You serious, Livy? First cricket match? Members' Stand? Can we make it an international game?' Des said.

'Of course.'

Des puffed out his chest. 'Did I tell you about the Ashes match we went to at Lord's?'

Joe scratched his head. 'Let me think. Do you mean the one where the pommies sang *You all live in a convict colony* to the tune of 'Yellow Submarine?' No, tell us ... again.'

'Smart arse.' Des snatched the iPad. 'I might get to this next week,' he said over his shoulder.

'How many seats do you want?' Olivia called after him.

Des turned. 'Four?'

'Done.'

'I'll start now. I love you, Liv,' Des said. 'If I wasn't married with children …'

Tessa laughed. 'Not to mention your children have children of their own, Grandpa.'

Des winked at Olivia. 'I started young.'

Come back with something for us, Des, Joe thought as he headed to the kitchen for coffee.

***

When Joe returned, Olivia was still at his desk. She stared at the monitor, shaking her head. 'What's wrong?' he asked. 'Besides the fact we have another dead girl.'

Olivia looked at him and shrugged. 'Oh … I don't know. Just wondering if Phoebe's outgoing personality meant she was too trusting, maybe a little naïve of …. Okay, let's call it what it is, "stranger danger."'

'Maybe, whatever, I don't know. All I know is, she didn't deserve what happened.' Joe sat next to Olivia. Close enough to inhale her fragrance. It wasn't an overpowering fly spray smell like the perfume a lot of women wear. It was soft, slightly musky, with a hint of vanilla. An almost familiar scent, like his favourite ice cream when he was a boy. Joe looked into Olivia's hazel eyes and for the first time since he met her, felt a calm settle over him. A calm after the tension this morning with Amber's parents. 'Um, I ah, I need a short break. I'm going for a coffee. Do you want to come along? My shout.'

'You've just made a fresh cup.'

'It would be good to get out for a few minutes. Can I buy you a coffee?'

Olivia hesitated for a micro-moment and then with a slight nod and a shy smile that didn't crinkle her nose this time, she said in almost a whisper, 'Yeah, a coffee, that would be nice.'

14

Café Athena was a bouquet of coffee aroma and freshly baked pastries. The ten o'clock morning coffee rush was over, so Joe had his choice of tables. He led Olivia to his favourite table near the window where a couple had just left, and the waiter was replacing the tablecloth with a freshly laundered blue and white check cloth. Nik's Greek romantic ballads were a mellow backdrop for comfortable conversation.

'Sorry, I've known you for nearly a year and don't know how you like your coffee,' Joe said.

'Full cream latte, no sugar, and very hot. Thanks.'

Joe came back with two coffees and a muffin. 'Hope you like blueberry. They're big, so I bought one to share. But I can get another one,' he added, thinking *shit is sharing a muffin, too intimate.*

'No, no. It's way too big.' Olivia cut the muffin in two, a third for her and two-thirds for Joe. 'Sharing is fine. Thanks.'

They sat in silence for a minute or two, sipping their coffees, nibbling the muffin, and looking out the window. *Thank God for the window seat and things happening outside,* Joe thought. *What have I done? Don't be stupid, it's not a date. It's just coffee. Relax.*

Olivia placed her coffee mug on the table. 'The coffee's good here'.

'Yeah, I was here yesterday. I noticed you, I mean, I was here with Paul. Sorry, I mean I saw you. With a book. Looked like a big book.' *Oh God, how old am I, fourteen?*

'I saw you too. I didn't say anything. You and Paul looked like you were having a deep and meaningful.'

'Yeah, I guess we were. Anyway, I noticed the size of your book, big and heavy. It reminded me of my uni books.'

Olivia grinned and winked at him. 'Yeah, that's my little secret.'

Joe felt the tension easing from his shoulders. 'Do you want to share your little secret?'

'Okay, as long as you don't mind being bored.'

Elbows on the table, Joe rested his chin on his hands and said, 'I'm all ears.'

'Okay, I'll kiss it.'

Joe's arms dropped onto the table. 'What?'

Olivia laughed her infectious laugh. This time her nose crinkled. 'My version of kiss. I'll keep it short and simple.'

'Take as long as you like, I've got ten minutes.' They both laughed.

'I love working here,' Olivia continued. 'I love photography. But I don't love them together.' She leaned forward in a come closer pose, almost conspiratorial. 'When I toured France last year, I was overwhelmed by the art.' Her eyes glistened as she stared into the past and described her art adventures in Paris. 'A whole new world opened for me. I studied art in school, but I never had the emotional connection until I visited the Louvre, the Musée d'Orsay, Monet's Garden and ...' Then she refocused, came back to the present. 'Sorry, I'm rambling. It must sound like I'm bragging about where I've been.'

Joe was silent.

'I've stopped rambling.' Olivia nodded an invitation. 'Your turn.'

Joe realised he was staring at her, transfixed. He shifted in his chair, sipped his coffee. 'So, you're studying art? You're going to be an artist?'

'Yes and no.'

'Sports people say that all the time,' Joe said. '"Yes and no". What does it even mean?'

'Yes, I'm studying. No, I'm not studying art. I'm studying law. And yes, I want to become an artist, an artist with my camera. I don't want to spend the rest of my career taking photos of dead people. I want to spend the rest of my life photographing people who are alive, photographing landscapes, insects, flowers.'

'You're a talented photographer,' Joe said. 'This way you get the best of both worlds. You stay in law enforcement, and you get to make beautiful photos. Art.'

Olivia looked at Joe. 'You understand.' She reached over and touched his hand, almost caressed it. 'Thank you.' A bolt of electricity surged through his body at her touch. He took a slow deep breath, trying to counteract the hot blush he felt colouring his cheeks.

'And thanks for the coffee,' Olivia said, apparently not aware of the effect she had on Joe. 'Enough about me. What's your secret dream?'

To drench myself in your alluring, liquid hazel eyes, every day— in Nik's café Athena, on a Greek island. Joe looked at his watch. 'My turn another day over another coffee and muffin. My dream now is to catch this bastard.'

'I wonder if Damien will defend him when you catch him. I know it's his job, but I just don't get it. How he defends the low life that he does. I couldn't do it. When—if I get my law degree, I'll be on the other side—trying to put them away.'

'Damien only defends the low life who can afford him. If you can't afford him, he wouldn't defend you, no matter if he was one hundred percent sure that you're innocent. He's in it for the money.'

'And he's successful,' Olivia said. 'I have to get there yet, pass my exams.'

Joe crossed his arms on the table, leaned forward and looked directly into Olivia's eyes. 'Don't doubt yourself. You will pass your exams.' He emphasised 'will.' 'You will get your degree.'

'Thank you. I'll keep reminding myself.' Olivia stood. 'My shout next time.'

Next time? There's going to be a next time. Had they connected? Joe wondered as they walked back to the station.

Olivia hesitated at the top of the steps that led to the double glass door entrance to the station. 'Tessa's barbeque, you know, her dad's birthday. Are you going? Maybe we could ...'

'I don't know. I mean, yes I'm going ...' *It's too soon,* Joe thought. *I can't commit to a date ... too soon.* Joe looked over her shoulder, at something in the distance, something not there, something not Olivia. 'I don't know ...'

'Never mind, sorry, I should've known, you've got plans. Forget I mentioned it. Thank you for the coffee.'

'I ...' Joe watched Olivia stride away. *Whatever connection we might have made, I just broke it. Broke it into a million shitty little unfixable pieces.*

15

Joe's mobile vibrated as he stood frozen at the entrance to the station, watching Olivia. 'Yeah, Tess.'

'Sanders?' He watched Olivia stop and talk to the receptionist. 'Sanders who?' Olivia didn't look back. She laughed at something the receptionist said and then disappeared through the stairwell door.

'Yes, of course, Sebastian Sanders, Phoebe Duncan's ex-boyfriend. Sorry, Tess. Just a bit distracted… No, nothing's wrong… What time did you tell him?'

Happy to distance himself from what just happened with Olivia, he said, 'Let's leave now.'

'Lunch? Just grab a couple of muesli bars. They're in my top drawer. Meet me at the car.'

'I noticed you walking out with Olivia,' Tessa said as she buckled her seat belt. 'Where did you go?'

'Coffee.'

'Ah, a coffee date.'

'Not date. Just coffee,' Joe said through clenched teeth.

'Just coffee. So, when are you going to have a real date?'

'We're not.'

'Yes, you are. It's obvious you two have feelings for each other. It's just a matter of time.'

Joe's knuckles turned white as he gripped the steering wheel. The last thing he needed was to be reminded that he had just screwed any chance he had with Olivia. 'Drop it, Tess.'

'You haven't had a proper date, let alone a relationship since Olivia came on the scene.'

'Number one. What makes you such an expert on my dating habits? Number two. Olivia isn't on the scene. We're colleagues. She takes photos. I solve crimes.' Joe turned left, sharply. 'So drop it.'

'But ...'

'If you don't drop it, I'll pull over and you can hitch a ride.' The car slowed as Joe eased his foot from the accelerator.

'Okay, okay. Chillax. You're Mr Iceman, remember.'

They drove in silence for ten minutes, then Joe pulled over.

'What are you doing? I didn't say the Olivia word.'

'I just realised we're going to Bondi,' Joe said as he set his GPS. 'And who knows their way around Bondi?'

'With your non-existent sense of direction, not you, that's for sure. Bondi ... who knows their way around? Mm, let me think ... I don't know, maybe tourists and backpackers.'

Joe couldn't help but grin. Tessa had a talent for breaking the ice.

'Thank God, Joe's back,' Tessa said. 'Mr McShitty-Head has left the building.'

After forty-five minutes and a few wrong turns, they found a secure car park.

'This is miles from where Sanders lives,' Tessa said. 'Can't we find a closer park in the street?'

'There are no car parks in the street. Even if there was, I'm not parking my car in a street around here.'

'I told you we should take the station car.'

'No, you didn't. But even if you did, I would've ignored you. Besides Sanders is only about a kilometre from here.'

***

After not quite a fifteen-minute walk past terrace houses, pubs, busy outdoor cafes and boutique shops, Joe and Tessa arrived at a modern white cement render and glass apartment complex opposite the beach. They caught an elevator to Sebastian Sanders' apartment on the top floor.

'Not a bad shack you have here,' Tessa said as they entered Sanders's apartment. Her boots clicked on the stark white, almost slippery, shiny tiles.

'It's a penthouse, and yes, I'm rather partial to it.' Sanders pointed to Tessa's boots. 'And you'll remove those.'

Eyebrows raised, Tessa obediently took off her boots.

'And you ...' Sanders looked at Joe's already removed shoes. 'Oh.'

Joe shrugged. 'Habit.'

Sanders glided into the living area. 'You'll note the expansive uninterrupted views of the world-famous Bondi Beach.' He drew out every syllable in 'expansive', in an almost upper-class British accent. 'Can I offer you a refreshment? It's afternoon. A French Chardonnay? I brought a dozen bottles back from Reims on my last trip to Europe. I don't think you'd find this one in Australia. Very boutique.'

'Do you have any horses doovers to go with the chardy?' Tessa said with an eye roll.

Sanders frowned 'Horses what?'

'Hors-d'oeuvres,' Joe said. 'And we'll pass on the wine.

Thank you.'

'Please take a seat.' Sanders pointed to a white-as-the-tiles, two-seater lounge. 'I'll pour you a water then,' he said as he walked to the kitchen.

'Seriously.' Tessa shook her head. 'Expansive uninterrupted views of the world-famous Bondi Beach. Sounds like a property ad.'

Joe noticed a packet of cigarettes and the Dupont lighter, Sally's husband, Simon, had mentioned, next to a white vase with one blood-red rose on the glass coffee table.

Sanders returned and placed three glasses of sparkling mineral water, each with a slice of lemon and a mint leaf, on the table. He returned to the kitchen once more and came back with a tray of cheese, crackers, and fresh strawberries. He sat opposite in the matching two-seater lounge.

Joe eyed the refreshments. 'This isn't a party, Mr Sanders. We're here to ask you some questions about ...'

'Well, it's not the Spanish Inquisition, I hope. There's absolutely no reason we can't be civilised. And you may call me Sebastian. Now, you said on the phone you wanted to talk to me about Phoebe, poor thing. What a tragedy. She was such a pretty little thing. I didn't know her well. So I'm not sure how I can help.'

'We understand you've been away,' Tessa said. 'Where were you?'

'I'm not sure why that's any of your business.'

'You were associated with a murder victim, Mr Sanders. Everything about you is our business,' Tessa said.

'Well, if you insist ...'

'We do,' Tessa said.

'If you want me to answer your questions, don't interrupt.'

'You've got the floor,' Tessa said. 'The shiny, slippery floor.'

Joe noticed the colour rising in Sanders' cheeks. He remembered the colour rising in his own cheeks when Olivia touched his hand in the restaurant a short time ago. Then quickly came back to the present. 'Continue please, Mr Sanders.'

Sanders turned and focussed his attention on Joe. 'I have business interests in several places. My most recent trip was to Singapore.'

'When did you come back to Sydney?' Joe said.

'I flew in last Wednesday.'

'Where were you Sunday evening?' Joe asked.

'Let's see. When I'm in town, I go to the gym Sunday afternoons and pick up supplies for the week on the way home. There's a market close by that has the most divine fresh produce. Strawberries are coming into ...'

'Sunday night,' Tessa said.

'You're testing my patience, missy; let me finish.'

'Detective Mariani,' Tessa said.

'Well, Miss Mariani ...'

'Detective, Detective Mariani,' Tessa repeated. 'Continue. Where were you Sunday night?'

'Yes, well, as I said, I picked up supplies for the week. Came home, showered, dined, and then went to a local bar for one, maybe two hours.'

'Can anybody vouch for you?' Joe asked.

'I arranged to meet a friend, but he couldn't make it.' Sanders shrugged, 'So, I only stayed for one drink and then came home. I ...'

Joe interrupted. 'You said you were there for two hours.'

'Well, when you're drinking by yourself it feels like two hours.'

'So, you can't verify where you were and what you did on Sunday night,' Tessa said.

'I don't need to.' Sanders reached for his cigarettes. 'I have nothing to hide.'

'If you can verify your movements on Sunday night, then we might know you have nothing to hide,' Tessa said.

'You have my word. That should be enough.' He lit the cigarette and blew a cloud of smoke in Tessa's direction. 'I am a stockbroker, after all.'

'What sort of car do you drive?' Joe asked.

'I don't see how that's relevant.'

'Everything is relevant in a murder investigation, Sanders,' Tessa said.

'Mr Sanders to you.'

Joe leaned forward. 'Do I need to repeat the question, Mr Sanders?'

'Your rude colleague needs to learn some manners. She must call me Mr Sanders. But you're quite amenable. You can call me Sebastian.'

Joe stared silently at Sanders.

'The car I drive depends on the circumstances. I zip around the city in my Audi TT, and long drives in the country demand my BMW.'

'What's the name of your friend who stood you up?' Tessa asked.

'He didn't stand me up. I don't get stood up. I told you, he couldn't make it. Something came up, and he had to change his plans.'

'What's his name?' Tessa repeated.

'There's no point in talking to him.' Sanders placed his cigarette in the ashtray and reached for his drink. 'He has nothing to do with anything.'

Tessa stood. 'Stand up, Sanders.'

'Stand up? Why? And, as I said, it's Mr Sanders to you.'

'Stand up, Sanders. I'm charging you with the crime of

perverting the course of justice. This is a serious offence with a maximum…'

'Wait, wait …' Sanders put up both hands in a stop gesture as he stood, dropping his Waterford glass that shattered into hundreds of sparkling crystal shards on his tile floor.

'Pity. That's the trouble with tiles,' Tessa said. 'You could jack hammer them up. They're so—well—seventies.'

Sanders put his hands on his hips. 'They're Italian.'

'You're still under arrest, Sanders.'

Joe sat back and covered his mouth to stifle a laugh. He turned away so Sanders couldn't see the amusement in his eyes. He had to hand it to Tess—she knows how to pick the pathetic, weak ones.

Joe gathered himself. 'What is your friend's name and his contact details, Mr Sanders?'

'Okay, okay.' Sanders wrote the details on the back of his business card. Joe noted that he was right-handed.

'Now, tell us about your relationship with Phoebe,' Joe said.

'Well, as I said, I didn't know her well.' He knelt to clear the broken glass. 'I met her when I bought this penthouse through the real estate she worked for.'

'When was that?' Joe asked.

'Let's see, I bought the penthouse late October, in time for the summer season here. I had just come back from a European river cruise and intended going back for the ski season in Austria, Lech of course. The dining there is amazing. Five-star hotels. But a friend told me about this penthouse. It was too good to miss.'

So far Sanders is living up to Sally McKay's description of an egotistical show off, Joe thought.

'Yeah, okay, all very interesting,' Tessa said. 'But we're not here to talk about your overseas jaunts. Back to your relationship with Phoebe. How long did she and you date?'

'We didn't exactly date,' Sanders said over his shoulder as he left the room to dispose of the broken glass.

'Sit, Sanders,' Tessa said when he returned. 'I'll ask one more time—how long did you and Phoebe date?'

'We didn't date. We had dinner together once or twice. We ...'

'Mr Sanders,' Joe leaned forward, his blue eyes stared directly into Sanders' dark brown eyes. 'We don't have time for your bullshit. Think about it. You must realise that we spoke to Sally. You know Sally, Phoebe's sister. You spent quite a lot of money on dinner for her and Simon, her husband. Not once, but twice.'

'And as I recall,' Tessa said, 'they were celebration dinners. Anniversary dinners for you and Phoebe. And the Facebook photos Phoebe posted showed more than just a casual dinner together.'

'So, Mr Sanders, would you like to re-consider your account of your relationship with Phoebe?' Joe said.

Sanders stubbed out his cigarette and lit another one. 'It sounds like I'm a witness in a court of law.'

'Well, if it turns out you had anything to do with Phoebe's murder, this is good practice for you,' Tessa said.

Joe looked at the ashtray full of cigarette butts and wondered how Sanders kept his perfect teeth so white. 'Your relationship with Phoebe. Please continue.'

'Okay, okay. I'll just get another drink first. Can I interest you in a lemon, lime and bitters?'

Joe leaned in even closer. 'Get your drink. Return. Sit. Take one last puff of your cigarette. And then tell us about your relationship with Phoebe.'

'You took my line,' Tessa said when Sanders left.

'What do you mean?'

'"We don't have time for your bullshit". That's my line. You took my line. You're the nice guy during interviews. I'm the bitch. You took my line,' Tessa chuckled. 'But I loved it.'

'So full of himself.' Joe sat back. 'Pity arrogance isn't a crime.'

'You're under arrest, Sebastian Shithead Sanders, for the annoying crime of arrogance,' Tessa said.

'How about you,' Joe said with pretend annoyance. 'Charging him with perverting the course of justice.'

'Don't think I didn't see your amusement. Anyway, I might end up charging him if he gets his friend to provide a false alibi. Did he seriously mean it when he said, "You have my word. I'm a stockbroker." He might as well say "Trust me, I'm a lawyer."' Tessa reached for a cube of cheese. 'Yum. Nice cheese. I'm getting this for the barbeque. I wonder what Phoebe saw in him—other than his money.'

'Whatever it was, it didn't take her long to get over it. Sally and her husband were right about him. Egotistical bastard.'

'And those eyes,' Tessa whispered. 'Those dark piercing eyes.'

'Just like Sally described. Cold, dark eyes that look right through you.'

Tessa reached for a cracker. 'Did you notice he said Phoebe worked for the real estate? He didn't say works for like her sister said?'

'Yep. He's already processed and accepts that she's dead. He doesn't have the normal feeling of denial like Sally has.'

Sanders returned with his drink and a coaster made of polished brass encircling a green stone in the centre.

'I got a set of coasters just like that one from Kmart last week.' Tessa bit into the cracker spilling crumbs on the tiles. 'They were on special. Though mine's more of a limey green. Did you get yours on special from Kmart?'

Sanders winced. 'Hardly. I've never set foot in Kmart. I bought them in Harrods the last time I was in London. The stone is jade.'

Joe didn't know if Sanders winced because Tessa spilt crumbs on his floor or because she insulted him about the coasters. Either way, Sanders was clearly becoming more and more irritated with Tessa.

'Phoebe?' Joe said.

'As I said, I met her when I bought the penthouse. Pretty thing. Though a little too short for my one eighty-five centimetres. I always insisted she wore her high heels when we were in public together. Quite smart for somebody working at an estate agent. She had a lively sense of humour. She was young and had a lot to learn about the finer things, but as I said, she was smart and a quick learner. You could do with a few lessons about the finer things, Miss um …' he nodded towards Tessa.

'Detective Mariani,' Tessa said. 'Do I need to spell it for you?'

'Did Phoebe stay here often, overnight?' Joe asked.

'Once or twice.'

'Was Phoebe gay?' Tessa asked.

Sanders opened his mouth and closed it. He crossed his arms over his chest. 'That's absurd.' He shook his head vigorously. 'No. No. I wouldn't have had anything to do with her if she was.'

Joe rolled his shoulders, trying to get comfortable in a lounge that was more form than function. 'How long were you in a relationship with Phoebe?'

'I don't know precisely. I imagine just under three months. From the twenty-fifth of October to the eighteenth of January.'

Joe raised his eyebrows. 'What did you say?'

'Really, do I have to keep repeating myself? I said about three months.'

'From the twenty-fifth of October to the eighteenth of January,' Joe said. 'That's very precise for somebody who doesn't know precisely.'

'I have an excellent memory for dates and I'm marvellous with numbers. I'm a stockbroker.'

'Stockbroker, right. Trustworthy. Good with numbers.' Joe smirked. 'Why did Phoebe end the relationship?'

'Ungrateful little lesbian bitch.'

'But you said you didn't know she was gay,' Joe said.

'Well … you just told me.'

'And,' Tessa said, 'you just confirmed it for us.'

Sanders reached for his cigarettes. 'I imagine you're waiting for an explanation.'

Joe raised his eyebrows and nodded.

Sanders' hand trembled as he took a cigarette out of the packet and placed it in the ashtray. 'I gave her gifts, clothes, a new laptop, took her to restaurants,' Sanders said. 'I didn't like the cheap little Japanese car she drove, so I ordered a BMW Coupe for her. Red. My TT is red. I like red cars.'

'Of course you do,' Joe said. 'Continue.'

'I even put up with that sister of hers who always glared at me with disapproval in her eyes. And that brother-in-law who wouldn't shut up but had nothing interesting to say.'

'We asked why Phoebe ended the relationship,' Tessa said.

'Did she find out you're married?' Joe said. 'That you have a wife living in Melbourne?'

16

'It's no secret I have a wife,' Sanders said. 'It's a convenient business arrangement for both of us.'

'Your marriage is a business arrangement?' Tessa said.

'We married way too young, in our early twenties. We came to realise the only thing we had in common was our combined wealth. So, for tax reasons and the smooth operation of our businesses, we agreed to remain married, but ... um ... well, you know, not keep our vows.'

'Did Phoebe find out you're married?' Tessa said. 'Is that why she ended the relationship?'

'Must I always repeat myself? I said it's not a secret.'

'So Phoebe knew?' Tessa probed.

'Yes.'

'If you just answer our questions without your bullshit beating around the bush, we can get this over and done with,' Joe said. 'Is that why she ended the relationship?'

Sanders hesitated, bit his bottom lip, lit the cigarette he'd left in the ashtray. 'There's no need to get testy.'

'Answer the question,' Joe said.

Sanders turned his head and blew out a large puff of smoke.

At least he didn't blow smoke in our direction this time, Joe thought.

Joe took a deep breath, puffed his cheeks as he exhaled. 'I would like to leave here, get in my car and drive home in the not-too-distant future. But I can guarantee we are not leaving until we get what we came here for. So work with us. Your relationship with Phoebe. Why did it end?'

'Okay, okay.' He stood and paced. 'She said I was too old for her. I would have given her the world.'

'So, you had feelings for her?' Joe said.

'Of course I did.' Sanders took a long, hard drag of his cigarette. Then removed his glasses and rubbed his eyes as he walked to the balcony door. 'I was just what she needed. I can't understand why she didn't appreciate me more than she did. As I said, I gave her gifts, tolerated her annoying family. She couldn't possibly find anybody better for her than I am.' He shrugged as he sat again. 'I was astonished that I was so generous. I mean … I mean that I cared …'

'Astonished you cared about anybody else but yourself?' Tessa said. 'I'm astonished too, a guy like you …'

Sanders raised both hands in a clenched fist, closed his eyes, took a deep breath, and then slowly lowered his hands. Red faced, he glared at Tessa. Clenched teeth replaced his clenched fists. 'What do you think you know about, as you say, a guy like me?' Sanders lit another cigarette, and this time blew the smoke in Tessa's direction. 'Not everyone is as they appear.'

Joe noticed Tessa frown, just for a split second, and then sit straight in the chair as if composing herself. He wondered why Sander's words bothered her, and then almost immediately realised why.

'Okay, so you cared,' she said. 'Is that why you harassed

her with phone calls every day and sent roses every other day? Which florist did you send the roses from?'

'I didn't harass her. I was just showing her I care, the only way I could.'

'Buying her affection,' Tessa said.

'However you want to interpret it, I cared for her. Has anybody ever said that about you Detective what's your name?'

Tessa slammed her card on the table in front of Sanders. 'Just look at this when you need to remember my name. You can read, can't you? Which florist?'

'The one just around the corner, if you must know. Not sure why that's significant.'

'Every detail is significant in a murder investigation,' Joe said. 'Did you know she was bisexual?'

'No, I …'

'What's your mother's date of birth?' Joe asked.

'Why, what does that have …'

'When was your mother born?' Joe repeated.

'Um, it's um December one, nineteen hundred and um …'

'When did you find out Phoebe was bisexual?' Joe repeated Tessa's question.

'I didn't know …'

'You're lying,' Joe interrupted. 'Your eyes move left when you're lying. I tested you when I asked about your mother's date of birth. They move to the right when you're telling the truth.'

'Okay, okay. I knew from the start. But it's not like she was totally gay. I always thought her desire for me and what I could give her would be strong enough to overcome any desires she had for women.'

'Did she leave you for a woman?' Tessa asked.

'No, no, of course not. I repeat. It was the age difference.'

Joe looked at the card where Sanders had written his friend's contact details and then looked directly at Sanders. 'If we find out you fabricated an alibi, we can arrest you and your friend, Andre. Sleep on it.'

'Thank you for your time, Mr Sanders,' Joe said as they walked to the front door. 'We'll be in touch but contact us immediately if you think of anything that will help in our investigations.'

'By the way, Sanders, what do you do for a job?' Tessa said with a sly grin as she stepped into her boots.

'I don't have a job, I'm a stock …' He stopped, red faced and clenched fist again. 'You think you're smart, don't you, Miss what's your name?'

The deafening bang of Sanders' door reverberated through the hallway as Joe and Tessa walked to the elevator.

***

Tessa pressed the elevator button for the ground floor. '*Not everyone is as they appear*. Did you see the way Sanders looked at me when he said that?'

'I noticed your reaction to what he said.'

'Was he taunting us about the note? *Trust not too much to appearances.*'

'I don't know. Probably a coincidence. He's obnoxious, but he doesn't come across as a …' Joe trailed off when he saw two people waiting to get in the elevator when the doors opened on the ground floor.

'So, you were saying that Sanders doesn't come across as a vicious killer,' Tessa said when they left the building.

'No, he doesn't. But Ted Bundy didn't either. Bundy was intelligent and charismatic. According to some reports, he even appeared to be kind and empathetic when he worked on the suicide hotline.'

'I guess Sanders is intelligent. He must be. He's a stockbroker.' Tessa snickered. 'But he doesn't have a charismatic bone in his body.'

'He might give the impression of charisma if the situation calls for it. Phoebe's sister said he had a superficial charm.'

'Did you notice him rubbing his eyes? Was he hiding tears when he said he had feelings for Phoebe?' Tessa said. 'Or did he just get smoke in his eyes?'

'He was smoking at the time. Most of the time, in fact.'

'You're right, it was smoke. I'm not convinced he had any feelings for Phoebe,' Tessa said. 'Just about every sentence he muttered began with "I." Talk about an inflated sense of his own importance. The world revolves around Sanders.'

'Agree. He might try to convince himself, and us, that he had feelings for Phoebe. But I doubt he did. All Sanders cares about is his own need for admiration. He thinks he can get it by boasting about how much money he has and his trips to Europe. Buying Phoebe gifts, sending her roses. I think it was just his way of trying to control her, under the pretence of caring. Just a big charade.'

'Trust not too much to appearances,' Tessa said. 'Who can trust anybody? I guess we all have a hidden side.'

'I trust you one hundred percent,' Joe said. 'You're an open book. Well, not open. More um … closed with a bookmark in it ready to be opened.'

'You're talking about my parents and Alex, aren't you?'

'If you can't be honest and open with your family, well …'

'It's not just Mamma and Papa—there's my brother, and what would my nonnas say? They adored Damien.'

'So you won't invite them to your wedding if you and Alex get married?'

Tessa froze mid-stride. 'Married? Married—I never thought

that far ahead. Married … imagine me a bride, and Alex …'

Joe nudged her elbow. 'C'mon. Enough daydreaming. Keep walking, I want to get back to the station before Christmas.'

'I'm feeling peckish, let's grab a …'

'I want to beat the peak hour traffic.'

'We've got time for take-away.' Tessa pointed to the Golden Arches. 'There's a Maccas down there.'

'Okay, but you have to eat on the way to the car, not in the car. You dropped fries on the floor last time.'

17

Joe and Tessa spent most of the next morning sifting through interview after interview from the task force. Joe ran tired fingers through his hair and then rubbed his eyes so hard stars pulsated behind his eyelids. Nothing. A wave of nausea and helplessness drained through his body. He felt in his pocket for his father's button and read the sticker on his laptop, '*Failure is not an option.*' It's not an option, but what if it's out of their control? Ten to twelve percent of murders go unsolved. 'Don't let Amber, Issy, and Phoebe end up in the unsolved statistics,' he murmured.

'What?' Tessa looked up from her laptop.

Joe stood. 'Coffee?'

'Tea. Peppermint. No—water. No—coffee.'

Joe said nothing, just looked at her, head tilted, raised eyebrows, then eyebrows raised even higher.

'Coffee,' Tessa said. 'Yes, definitely coffee. Thanks.'

Joe turned and found himself almost nose to nose with Des. 'Jesus Des, how can a behemoth your size creep up as quietly as you do?'

'I'm a delicate behemoth. My night job is a ballerina.'

'I heard him. He didn't creep.' Tessa said. 'Ninety-nine percent of the time you're oblivious to what's happening around you.'

'It's not oblivion. It's focus,' Joe said.

'Whatever,' Des said. 'I'm here and I've got something for you.' He handed Amber's iPad to Joe. Username, 'Des.' Password 'Imagenious.' He winked. 'Remind Olivia for me about the seats in the Members' Stand for the first international cricket match of the season.'

***

'We're getting closer, Tess.' Joe sipped the third coffee he'd made since they started to explore Amber's iPad. In addition to being a frequent visitor to a similar dating site as Phoebe Duncan, Amber kept a journal.

'Journal or dating site first?' Tessa had asked when they connected Amber's iPad to a monitor.

'Journal. Hopefully, we'll get some more insight about who Amber really was.'

Amber wrote in the journal almost every day. Some days just a half dozen words like *Went shopping with Mum* or *No time for you today dear diary, exams tomorrow.* Other days she poured her soul out, revealing her thoughts and feelings about her friends, relatives, and colleagues.

Dear diary,
Jayden is the best flatmate. He even offered to take down his posters when I moved in. I'm so busy. I barely notice them. And he's been so understanding while I've been studying for exams and finishing my last assignment for the semester. I plan to help

Jayden with the housework this weekend. I need to be tidier around the unit. I promise to make more of an effort.

'This correlates with what Jayden said about Amber not being the tidiest person around the unit,' Tessa said.

'The apartment.'

'What?'

'Jayden said she wasn't the tidiest person around the apartment.'

Tessa rolled her eyes.

Joe shrugged, 'Well, I remember because ...'

'Because you have a photographic memory.'

'I told you, the existence of photographic memories is open for debate. Anyway, I just remember important things—details about the case, my mother's birthday. That reminds me. My mother's birthday—I should book now.' Joe scrolled through the contacts on his mobile, selected 'Mum's restaurant,' called, and booked a table on the balcony.

Dear diary,

I can't wait to move on to another project—away from Ed Kowalski. He's been a pig to me since I refused to meet him for drinks. Why would I be interested in him? He's married. And he's a ... well he's a 'he.' Walks around like he's king shit. Talks over me at meetings. Does nothing, gets into the office late, sucks up to management, and then gets promoted. I HATE, HATE him. When I walked past his desk the other day, he and his slimy mates were watching porn on his laptop. Sackable offence. Married cockroach vomit.

'So he did ask her out,' Joe said. 'I'm sure Mrs Kowalski would be interested in that diary entry.'

'Yep,' Tessa agreed. 'I wonder if Mrs Kowalski knows she's married to cockroach vomit. Cock being the operative word.'

Dear diary,
I met somebody on the dating site. She sounds intelligent, like somebody you could have a meaningful conversation with. So many of them on that site just want to 'party and have fun'. She doesn't sound like the partying type. She's got a computer science degree, loves art and classical music and visiting museums and galleries when she holidays in Europe.

I can't wait to get back to Europe. Maybe we could go to Europe together. No, I'm daydreaming. Getting ahead of myself. But it would be wonderful to meet a soul mate one day. Especially one as pretty as Zoe. Well, she looks beautiful in her photo. She has long, long thick, wavy dark brown hair. And her eyes. OMG, those sexy, come to bed eyes.

Joe read out loud. '*But it would be wonderful to meet a soul mate one day. Especially one as pretty as Zoe.* Zoe. This has to be the same person Phoebe connected with. Same name. Same description. Beautiful, with long, dark hair. Zoe is our guy. Has to be. There'll be a photo on the dating site,' he said as he keyed in the web address.

'Yes.' Joe pushed his chair back from the desk. Stood. Kissed Tessa on the top of her head. 'It's the same Zoe. The same person Phoebe connected with.'

Joe sat, sighed heavily, and slumped in his chair. Reality replaced elation. 'Now all we have to do is find Zoe.'

They opened Amber's journal again and spent the next three hours collating the relevant diary entries.

Dear diary,
If a relationship develops between Zoe and me, I'll tell Mum and Dad. They'll be shocked at first, but I'm sure they'll come to accept Zoe. If I love her, they'll love her too. They've always said all they want is for me to be happy. Such a cliché. I bet all parents say that to their kids.

Dear diary,
I just re-read what I wrote yesterday. 'If I love Zoe!' Really! I'm jumping ahead of myself. I haven't even met her. I believed what she wrote in her profile because I want to believe it. She sounds perfect. Maybe too perfect.

Dear diary,
Tonight's the big night. I finally get to meet Zoe. I let myself have an extra sleep in this morning, so I'll be extra fresh and look my best for her.

This has been the very, VERY, best week for me. I got my assignment back yesterday, an A plus. Finally, I'm almost finished—on the homestretch, one more semester. And I'll finish with a distinction in every subject this year.

I can't wait to tell Mum and Dad. No, I'll wait. I'll gift wrap my results and give them to Mum and Dad for Christmas. I can see the look on their faces. OMG, they'll be so proud.

At last, I'll be living the study-free life.
The future is looking amazing. I wonder if Zoe's in my future.

18

Touched by its poignancy, Joe re-read, '*At last, I'll be living the study-free life.*'

He banged his fist on the desk. Coffee splashed, just missing a stack of documents. 'We have to catch this monster, Tess. Before he ...' Joe paused mid-sentence. 'What are you looking at?'

'Your coffee. You're so OCD, you even spill your coffee neatly.' Tessa laughed. 'I'm sorry, I've got the tired giggles.'

'Do you want to call it a night?'

'No, no. I'll pump some caffeine into my system, and I'll be good for another hour or two. You're right, we so have to catch this monster, demon—there's no word bad enough to describe him.'

Joe opened the file that contained the transcript from the dating site. 'Another hour and we'll call it a night. We won't be able to catch a tortoise if we're dead on our feet.'

***

ReadyForASoulMate8

I'm in my final year of university, at last. Looking forward to travel, Sunday drives in the country, dumping the textbooks for a while and reading for pleasure. Not that I didn't enjoy my studies. I love learning and I'm so proud of what I've achieved. But I'm ready now, so, so ready to meet a soul mate who I can grow with and enjoy all the wonderful things life offers.

TravelGirl08

Hello ReadyForASoulMate.

Let me introduce myself.

I'm what you might call the academic type.

Somewhat serious, but I do enjoy lively conversation with friends.

And I love museums, art galleries and picnics.

I enjoy most types of music, but mostly classical.

It sounds like we might have a lot in common.

I majored in computer science.

Some might say that's boring, but I loved it.

What are you studying?

ReadyForASoulMate8

Hi Travel Girl. I agree, we do have a lot in common. I'm studying law. I love it and I'll specialise in criminal law one day. I think computer science sounds fascinating, not boring. You're obviously very clever.

TravelGirl08

Law has always fascinated me, especially criminal law.

You must be very clever too.

And beautiful, judging by your photo.

ReadyForASoulMate8

Thank you. And you look beautiful too. I just love your long, thick brown hair. Do you think we could meet, maybe get to know each other?

TravelGirl08

I would like that.

But let's take it slow.

Are you free for coffee on Sunday afternoon?

ReadyForASoulMate8

Taking it slow is good. Coffee sounds perfect. But if we're meeting for coffee, we should know each other's name. My name is Amber. What's your name?

TravelGirl08

Amber, a pretty name for a pretty girl.

Coffee it is then.

We could meet outside the QVB, near the Queen Victoria statue, say around three.

ReadyForASoulMate8

Three is good. But I still don't know your name.

TravelGirl08

Perfect.

See you then.

And BTW my name is Zoe.

TravelGirl08

Something has come up.

Can't make coffee.

Can I buy you dinner tonight to make up for it?

Say 7:30 at the new restaurant near the beach.

The Sandpiper.

It's had excellent reviews.

We should swap mobile numbers.

I'll text you the address.

And we can text when we get there.

ReadyForASoulMate8

It's Sunday, will the restaurant be open?

TravelGirl08
Definitely.
I've booked.
Looking forward to my evening with you.
Ciao.

***

Tessa sat back in her chair. 'He's done the hard return again, after each sentence.'

Joe nodded. 'And he says, "Looking forward to my evening with you". It's all about him. Most people would say "Looking forward to meeting you."'

'You're right. It is all about him. He's looking forward to *his* evening and what he's got planned for his vile entertainment.'

Joe emailed Des. We're looking for TravelGirl as well as PartyGirl.

Des replied. *Step ahead of you. Already on it.*

Joe emailed Des. *Why weren't the dating site charges on her bank statements on her laptop?*

Des replied. *Different account. Different bank. On her iPad. Not on her laptop.*

'So we have a connection between Amber and Phoebe,' Joe said. 'And Zoe is definitely our guy. All we have to do now is find the connection with Issy. And find Zoe.'

'Not necessarily in that order,' Tessa said.

'Yep, the sooner we find Zoe, the better. But finding a connection with Issy, might help.'

'Issy led such a private life, no Facebook, just a few friends,' Tessa said. 'Her studies were her focus. And she was a virgin.'

'At last, I'll be living the study-free life,' Joe murmured to himself.

'What?'

'Amber was looking forward to a study-free life. Phoebe was looking forward to having her own real estate business one day. I wonder what sort of life Issy was looking forward to. What future did Zoe steal from her?'

19

The weekend didn't distract Joe from the case. He spent Saturday morning catching up on domestic chores and talking to his chooks while tending his herb garden. After lunch, he settled in his study with Bonnie, coffee, his laptop, and the case files. Banjo found a sunny spot to curl up in, on the top shelf of the bookcase next to Joe's copy of *To Kill a Mockingbird*. The same book that sat on Phoebe's bedside table. Joe had been reviewing the files for about an hour when his mobile played Jimmy Barnes' 'Working Class Man'. 'Hi Dean.' Dean and his wife Lorna were family friends since before Joe was born. 'Sounds good. Around five, okay?' Joe hadn't seen Dean for a couple of weeks and looked forward to catching up.

'Come on, Bonnie. We're going to visit Dean and Lorna,' Joe said as he opened the car door three hours after Dean's call. Bonnie hesitated, looked up at Joe. He patted her blanket on the back seat. 'C'mon girl. You'll soon look forward to riding in the car. Sammy will be there. You love playing with him. He might even share his favourite doggy nibbles with you.'

Joe's mind drifted back to his youth as he drove the familiar route to Dean's house. He thought of the happy times years ago spent with his parents visiting Dean and his wife, Lorna. He smiled when he remembered himself as a young boy sitting in Dean's lounge room pretending to watch TV but listening to adult conversation between his parents and Dean and Lorna. Dean and Joe's father shared stories about when they studied together at the Goulburn training academy. They talked about the different cases they were working on, and then the conversation always gave way to less serious topics, peppered with jokes and sudden outbursts of laughter. He remembered his parents still laughing as they drove home.

Joe stopped at a red light, looked at Bonnie in the rear-view mirror. She sat on the same spot on the back seat he sat on as a boy. He realised it didn't bother him in those days that his mother always had to drive home, because his father had one or two, probably more, drinks too many. But they were carefree days at Dean's place. Remembering those happy, untroubled days was emotional therapy for Joe. He looked at Bonnie in the rear vision mirror. He hoped spending time and playing with Sammy would be emotional therapy for her, too.

The sun was casting a five o'clock shadow when Joe pulled up outside what used to be a red brick, and now a more charming grey clad and rendered house. He walked up the path bordered by tall, gold and red silky oak trees that were just a metre high when he was a boy. When Dean opened the front door, Bonnie didn't wait for an invitation. She squeezed past Dean, ran through the house and out the pet door into the backyard to find Sammy, her black and tan German Shepherd friend. Despite, or because of, being a retired police dog, Sammy had a gentle and devoted nature. Although retired, Sammy still had his police dog instincts. Dean often talked about a time when Sammy uncharacteristically growled at a tradesman who Dean found out three months later had been charged with abusing his wife.

'You'll stay for dinner,' Dean said. 'Lorna's gone to the movies and dinner with her book club. I could do with some company for a couple of hours.'

They sat down to stuffed zucchini, salad, and homemade bread rolls. *Not bad for a Saturday casual meal,* Joe thought. 'Your culinary skills have improved since you retired, Dean. A level or two up from vegemite sandwiches. Have you been watching MasterChef?' Joe teased.

They ate in silence for a while, then Joe looked up to see Dean watching him.

'You're toying with your salad.' Dean nodded towards Joe's plate. 'What's the matter. You don't like the salad dressing?'

'The dressing is perfect.'

'What's on your mind, Joe?'

'Nothing. All good. The entire meal is delicious. Thank you.'

'What's happening on the job? Not that I miss it, but I haven't walked away from it completely. I don't think you ever do. I like to keep up to date with what's going on.'

Dean drank from his beer bottle. Joe drank from his bottle of mineral water. Then Joe outlined the key details of the three murders, a description of the three victims, the white roses, and the notes.

Dean stroked a beard that had more grey than his thinning salt and pepper hair and nodded. 'He's smart and methodical. The way he left the victims, no regrets, no feeling for the victims, cold, calculating. Do you have any suspects yet?'

'The usual. Jealous colleague, I've seen people murder for less. A married colleague whose advances were rejected. A dumped boyfriend.'

'Those motives sound more like one-off personal motives.

None of them sound like reasons for multiple murders. Could be a religious nut.'

'Yeah, it's an angle. Unless he's, we're pretty sure it's a *he*, unless he's killing everybody who reminds him of the person who pissed him off,' Joe said. 'But if there's a religious angle, he could be using religion to justify his hate of gays and bisexuals. Whatever the motive, we have to get him before he kills again—and make no mistake, he will kill again.'

Sammy wagged his tail as he made his way to the dining table, followed closely by Bonnie. Joe noticed Sammy favoured one of his back legs. 'Why is Sammy limping?'

'It's the arthritis. Seems to bother him more at night. We're seeing the vet tomorrow morning.' Dean rubbed Sammy's head. 'Well, well, well, Sammy, me ol' mate. I'm surprised you didn't come in earlier. You're after a treat, aren't you?'

Dean turned to Joe. 'Is Bonnie allowed to have a treat?'

'Of course.' Joe laughed. 'She's expecting a treat.'

'And I've got special cat treats too, you can take home for Banjo,' Dean said as he walked to the back door with two bowls, followed by two tail-wagging dogs.

When Dean returned to the dining table, he had another mouthful of beer, sat back in his chair, and folded his arms over a belly that had seen slimmer days. 'This is a tough case, Joe, and you're probably losing sleep over it. But there's something else, something more personal. Tell me to mind my own business if you want to. But I've known you too long and your family, your father long before he ... sorry. Anyway, you're almost a son to me, you know that. I care. I know when something is wrong.'

'Have you been talking to my mother?'

'Lorna and I talk to your mother all the time.'

'Have you been talking to my mother about me?'

'I don't need your mother to tell me when something's

bothering you.'

They were both silent for a minute or two. Joe stood, walked to the window, and looked at the dogs curled up together, contented in each other's company, innocent and unaware of the evil they were sharing with the world. The evil that was happening right at that moment, always happening right at that moment, no matter when the moment was. Joe wondered what was going on in their minds. He wondered if Sammy and Bonnie remembered unhappy times. Did what happened in the past make them the dogs they are today? Especially Bonnie. He wondered if they dwelled on those times. Or was it just certain events that reminded them? Like the wife-bashing tradesman, who reminded Sammy of all the criminals he helped capture. What reminded Bonnie of her unhappy past events? How long will it take her to mend? Will she mend? Bonnie looked up at that moment, put her head to the side, looking at Joe, and gave her tail a slow, gentle wag. Joe smiled. *That's my girl; you are mending aren't you.*

Joe returned to the dining table, sat forward, and folded his arms on the table. He looked into Dean's eyes, pressed his lips together and slowly shook his head. 'How did you do it, Dean? Stay on the job for over thirty years? Sleep at night? I hate going to bed at night. And the sorrow of the families, I feel it. I don't show it, I can't show it on the job. Tessa calls me Mr Iceman. But I feel it. It stays with me. The cesspool we face day after day. I sit up half the night watching re-runs of *Frasier* to get the images out of my head. Is this what my father went through? Is this why he ...'

'Are you afraid you're going to suicide?'

Joe looked down, didn't answer.

'You're a different person from your father. He turned to alcohol to forget. But the alcohol only made it worse for him. We lost a dedicated, talented officer when we lost him. Your father was one of the best officers I knew. He didn't know how good he was.' Dean paused, buttered two bread rolls, and placed one on Joe's plate. 'But you're better. You're as smart, if not smarter, than he was. You've got the confidence he didn't have. Don't lose it, Joe. Don't lose your confidence. You have to keep believing in yourself.'

'I know he was good. But the job beat him, Dean.'

'Don't let it beat you. Your father cared about the victims and the families, exactly the way you do. But he tried to run from his demons. He turned his back on them and turned to the bottle instead. That's why the job beat him. You can't outrun the demons. They'll always catch you, overtake you, so you have to face them. Face the demons, Joe and you'll win.'

'What's the point. You put one away, and there's two, three, more to take his place. It's like—well, you're a gardener, you know what it's like—you pull out one noxious weed, but more come to take its place. Somehow the evil just spreads its roots and multiplies uncontrollably.'

'Everyone you put away, means one less out there. You know that.' Dean stood, picked up the empty dinner plates, rinsed, and stacked them in the dishwasher. 'Coffee?'

Joe nodded. 'Thanks.'

'You'll be impressed. I made muffins with overripe bananas.'

'I am impressed. One of my mother's recipes?'

'You guessed it.'

Dean returned to the dining table with coffee and the muffins. 'Who knows how many lives you've saved, how many families you've saved from heartache? That's what I had to keep reminding myself. And then I'd come home to Lorna. Sometimes I cried. Not sometimes, I cried often.' Joe noticed Dean's eyes water. 'I cried, and she held me. She'd say, *you can't save 'em all, but think of the ones you have saved, will save.'* He paused, sipped his coffee. 'Did you see the movie, *Schindler's List?'*

Joe nodded. 'Sure, Thomas Keneally wrote the book. One of Mum's favourites.'

Dean toyed with a muffin, broke it in half. 'Towards the end of the movie, do you remember? The Jews gave Schindler a ring engraved with a quote from the book of Jewish law. The engraving read, *Whoever saves one life saves the world entire.'*

'Very inspirational. But it's just a quote. Just because somebody wrote it, and it was a line in a Hollywood movie, doesn't make it true.' Joe slouched in his chair and shook his head. 'My first week on the job, still wet behind the ears, we got called to a domestic violence. I held a dying woman, told her the ambulance was on the way and she'll be fine. I told her that her dead baby was safe. The husband broke free from my partner, grabbed a gun, and shot himself. We lost an entire family that night.' Joe sipped his mineral water. 'I've never spoken about it before. Don't know why I'm burdening you with it now. You've been through it. We all go through it. Too many dead bodies. And we get shot at, stabbed, abused, and spat on for our efforts. All I want to do ... what we all want to do—is put the bad guy away. For years I've prayed I don't get killed doing it. Now I pray I don't ...' Joe shook his head. 'Never mind.'

Dean studied his coffee cup, then looked at Joe. 'Now you pray you don't kill yourself. Right?'

'I get angry—hurt—sad,' Joe said. 'Sometimes I feel the job rips the soul out of me. The images I have of what I want to do to the bad guys scares me. Keeping Tess under control helps keep me under control. Tess and I usually want to punch the same guy at the same time. And well ... stopping her makes me stop myself. When she loses her cool, I can see myself, and I can see that it won't achieve anything. Just makes matters worse. But

I don't sleep, Dean.'

'Ask yourself the question. Do you want to not sleep at night because of the job? Or do you want to not sleep at night because you're not helping those who need you most?'

'I'm qualified. I'm thinking I could teach. I'd still be in the force. I could work with the programs that support PTSD sufferers.'

'Those programs do amazing work. I know at least two retired officers who are still with us thanks to the support and nurturing from those great people. But catching the bad guy is in your DNA.'

'I don't know, Dean. I don't know what I want to do. I know the feeling when you put one away—the relief, the satisfaction. The exhilaration even. But the exhilaration is short lived. And quickly replaced by the dread you get in the pit of your stomach when you get called to the next crime scene. And there's always a next one.'

'Then quit now, Joe.' Dean shouted. He stood and shoved his chair under the table. 'If you're gonna quit, do it now. If doubting yourself is stopping you from doing your job, then quit.'

'Quit now?' Joe stood, shook his head. 'I can't, not now, not with this maniac on the loose.'

'So, you just answered your own question.'

'I don't know, Dean. I don't know.'

'Yes, you do.' Dean placed his hand on Joe's shoulders and squeezed encouragingly as he whispered, 'Talking about it is a good thing. And you know what you have to do. It's in your blood.'

20

Sunday afternoon, on the fourth floor of a ten-storey nineteen-seventy-something block of units, Yolanda looked up from the year nine assignments she was marking and checked the ticking clock on the lounge room wall. Five o'clock. That gave her another hour before she needed to get ready for her date. She wrote 'congratulations' and stamped a gold star on the last maths assignment and smiled. She hoped Jason's excellent grade would help the bright but disruptive boy overcome his feelings of inferiority and lack of confidence. Watching students like him improve under her care was what she loved most about teaching.

She put the assignments in her laptop bag and turned her attention to the fast-approaching blind date, her first proper date in six months. Her stomach fluttered. Maybe another cup of camomile tea would settle her nerves. She stood, put the kettle on to boil, grabbed a tea bag and an apple scone to tide her over until dinner.

What will they talk about? Yolanda's bookcase overflowed with maths and science books, journals, and magazines. Would her date want to talk about chaos theory or game theory, or even the golden ratio? Doubtful. Few people did. Being pretty was enough for the initial attraction, but not enough to sustain a meaningful relationship. And Yolanda yearned for a meaningful relationship. If she had a hobby outside school, she'd be better at small talk. *I'll investigate that at the end of school term*, she decided.

Yolanda's iPhone stopped playing the latest Pink album just as she took her first soothing sip of tea and played the melody to 'By the seaside' instead.

'Hi Mum.' Yolanda put the phone on speaker, taking the opportunity to apply pink polish to her toenails.

'Hi sweetie, just ringing to see how your hand is after that nasty burn.'

'It's fine. It blistered, but the pain's gone.'

'You need to be more careful with the oven. You need new oven mitts. I'm going to the shop tomorrow. I'm making a note for myself now to buy oven mitts for you. I've got some news about ...' While her mother shared neighbourhood chatter about cows, brown snakes, and the Marshall's blue heeler, Yolanda finished painting her nails.

'Well, say hello to Mrs Marshall for me.' Yolanda examined her toenails and smiled, pleased with the finished product. 'How's Dad? Is he looking forward to next weekend?'

'Oh, he's so excited. He's on his ride-on lawn mower now, getting the place in apple-pie order.'

'Speaking of apple pie,' Yolanda said, 'are we getting him a special cake for his sixtieth?'

'I've got it ordered, caramel mud, his favourite.'

'Great. I'm so looking forward to coming home for a couple of days.' Yolanda walked into her bedroom to choose an outfit for her date. With the mobile in one hand, she shuffled coat hangers with the other, looking for her black cocktail dress. 'I'm leaving school as soon as the three fifteen bell rings and I should be there between seven thirty and eight. I'd say closer to eight.'

'We miss you, sweetie. But you know we support your move to the city. We love you and just want you to be happy. I know all parents say that. But it's true, we mean it.'

'I know that, Mum, and I love you both. See you next Friday night.'

Yolanda found her dress and went back to the kitchen.

She sat at her dining table, which also served as a desk, opened the dating app on her laptop and re-read her correspondence with tonight's date.

***

Yolanda3

New to the area. Moved from the country about 9 months ago and love living near the beach now. Shy, but looking for new friends and maybe a special relationship. I'm 26, 5'4", slim with long, thick, dark blonde hair. I enjoy intimate dinner parties, picnics, and entertaining conversation. I'm a good listener. I'm passionate about the environment, animal welfare and social justice.

LookingForAFriend103

Hi Yolanda.

Such a pretty name for a pretty girl.

You sound like a person I'd enjoy spending time with.

Let me introduce myself.

I share your passion for the environment and social justice.

And animals are my best friends.

I'm not a party goer but I enjoy stimulating conversation, watching old movies and fine dining restaurants.

Yolanda3

Hi LookingForAFriend. We don't have fine dining restaurants

where I grew up in the country. It sounds like a new experience I might enjoy.

LookingForAFriend103

I would love the opportunity to get to know you.

Can we meet sometime?

Are you free for coffee on Sunday afternoon?

We could meet outside the QVB, near the Queen Victoria statue, say around three.

Yolanda3

Coffee. Yes, sure. Coffee is good.

LookingForAFriend103

Perfect.

See you then.

Ciao.

Yolanda3

I can't keep calling you LookingForAFriend. I don't want to be forward, but do you mind telling me your name?

LookingForAFriend103

Something has come up.

I can't make coffee.

Can I buy you dinner tonight to make up for it?

Say 7pm at the new restaurant near the beach.

The Sandpiper.

It's had excellent reviews.

It's a splendid opportunity for you to experience fine dining.

We should swap mobile numbers.

We can text when we get there.

And BTW my name is Zoe.

Ciao.

Yolanda3

A fine-dining restaurant. Sounds wonderful. What should I wear?

LookingForAFriend103
Something pretty and feminine.
Just like you.
Looking forward to my evening with you.
Ciao.

***

Yolanda wondered if it was a lie when she said she enjoys entertaining conversation. And decided that maybe it was just a little white lie. *I am a good listener,* she thought. *Mainly because I'm not a good talker in social situations.* She looked over at her laptop bag and thought of school. *If only I could always have the confidence I have when I'm in a classroom.*

At six Yolanda showered. Applied mascara. No lipstick. She didn't need lipstick. Her lips were naturally full and pink. She dressed in her short black cocktail dress. High heel, open-toed silver shoes. She checked her toenails, assuring herself that the pink polish matched her shoes perfectly. She tied her hair in a ponytail. Took her hair out of the ponytail. Fluffed her hair. Brushed her hair. Changed her mind. Tied her hair in a ponytail again. She was ready just after six thirty.

***

He reversed his car into a park opposite Yolanda's and four cars down. He checked his watch. Plenty of time before she comes down the lifts to her car, he thought. The car park was poorly lit with few vehicles in it. Perfect. Everything was working as he planned. It always did. He was meticulous in his preparations.

Ten minutes elapsed. There she is. All dressed up for her lesbian night out, or so she thinks. He watched her walk to the car. Petite, pretty, high heels. He loves high heels, the higher the better. Too high for running away. This one is easy, too easy, no challenge. He reached for the door handle as he watched her fumble and drop her keys. They fell under the car.

***

'Damn,' she muttered as she got down on her knees to reach for her keys.

A voice behind her, 'Let me help you.'

'I'm fine, thank you.' She stood to face the man.

At the sound of screeching tyres, they both turned to see a dark coloured car speeding out of the car park.

'Wow, he's in a hurry. Do you live in this building? I haven't seen you before. My name's Andrew, Andy. My wife and I are on the seventh floor.'

'I've been here a while. I'm on the fourth floor.' Yolanda thought Andy was okay looking if you like that kind. If you like men, that is. And she did like men, but she accepted now that she's more at ease with women. 'I'm running late, so I have to get going. But it was nice to meet you, Andy. Thanks for the offer to help.'

She wasn't late. That was another white lie, but Yolanda rationalised her lie by telling herself she would have been late if she got into a conversation with Andy. Then chastised herself about her obsession with lies. Nobody is one hundred percent truthful. She remembered reading that the average person lies one point six five times a day. *Has she reached her daily quota yet?* she wondered. She took a deep breath, held it for six seconds and reminded herself to relax and enjoy the evening.

Yolanda climbed into her old model MG convertible. Pleased she'd decided to put her hair in a ponytail, she drove with the top down. She listened to the latest music her students were listening to. She could tell they liked that she knew the names of their favourite bands and trivia about the band members.

Yolanda tapped on her restored wooden steering wheel to the beat of the music. Five minutes into her journey she heard a text come through. It must be Zoe. Jesus, she thought, what would her parents think if they knew she was going on a blind date? A date with another woman! She could hear her mother saying, 'Bradley is just right for you. And he's a doctor.' It was always Bradley, never Brad, as far as her mother was concerned. She dated Bradley, but they hadn't progressed past the first kiss. He was awkward and she wasn't interested.

Yolanda arrived just before seven and parked about ten metres from the restaurant. She read the text. 'Beautiful evening. Meet me near the surf club—we'll go for a walk before dinner.' She replied, 'On my way' and attached a smiley face symbol.

Yolanda agreed. It *was* a beautiful evening for a walk. Zoe was right. The ocean breeze provided a cooling relief after a warm, humid day. But the clouds in the distance looked threatening, and the sky was quickly getting darker. She thought there could be a storm coming and made a mental note to put the top up on her car on the way back to the restaurant.

A park led to the surf club. It wasn't easy walking on grass with high heels. She took her shoes off, not wanting to risk a twisted ankle. She kept walking, enjoying the feel of the soft grass under her bare feet. The closer she got to the surf club, the more her tummy fluttered with nervous anticipation.

***

The dark and deserted garage was the perfect place to coax her into his car. Perfect, that is, until that idiot turned up unexpectedly out of the shadows when Yolanda dropped her keys under the car. Where did he come from? Probably from the lift, just a few cars up from Yolanda's pathetic little MG.

He regretted screeching his tyres and hoped they didn't notice. He chastised himself for his uncharacteristic loss of control. But things didn't go as planned. He hated when things didn't go his way. That happens to those with less attention to detail, not him. She'll pay for it. He had a plan B.

He watched her short, unsteady steps on the grass. This is going to be too easy.

Then she took off her shoes. She was more sure-footed now and took longer strides. She might present a challenge after all.

***

Yolanda looked for Zoe but couldn't see her. She walked closer to the surf club but still couldn't see her. She frowned, confused. *Where's Zoe?* she wondered. Yolanda thought Zoe might have noticed the storm coming and headed back to the restaurant. *But surely she would have sent a text. Maybe she's late. Why didn't she text?* Yolanda kept walking.

Yolanda thought she must be the only one who didn't check the weather forecast. There was nobody else around except a man in a black car near the surf club. He must be waiting for the storm to pass. The car looked like the one that screeched out of her garage. But she was no car expert. Most of them looked the same to her, especially black ones.

She reached the surf club. Still no Zoe. Yolanda felt a sprinkle of rain on her face. She turned to head back in the direction of the restaurant and her car. *I'll text Zoe when I get back to the restaurant.* The sprinkle turned into fat droplets of rain. *Or just get in my car and go home. I'm kidding myself. Zoe probably won't turn up anyway.* The black car's door opened. A tall man somewhere between thirty and forty got out. 'Hi, you look a little lost. Where are you going? I'll give you a lift, it's going to rain cats and dogs shortly.'

'Oh, you're too kind … thank you …' *What are you thinking, you silly girl?* Her mother's voice invaded her thoughts, again. 'I mean … um …no thank you. I'm going to the restaurant, it's not far, I'm fine. But thanks for the offer.'

'Are you going to the restaurant on your own?'

'Oh, no. I'm meeting a friend.'

'I can drive you there. I'm meeting a friend too, but she's late. I could buy you a drink while we're waiting.'

Yolanda laughed. 'And if neither of our friends turn up, we could have dinner together.'

He smiled. 'Perfect. I'd like that.'

Oh that smile, Yolanda thought, *that smile would charm anyone, male or female.* She walked towards his car. *What are you doing?* Her mother again. Common sense took over. She put her arm out to feel the rain on her hand. 'Thanks anyway, but the weather and it's Sunday. I think I'll call it a night.' Yolanda turned to walk towards the restaurant.

'Hey, Yolanda, where are you going?'

Yolanda stopped. 'Who, who are you?' She stuttered. 'How did you know my name?'.

More droplets of rain fell on her face, heavier now.

'Not who you were expecting? Wrong gender? You look lovely, Yolanda—all dressed up for a special date.'

'Who are you?'

'Not Zoe. Zoe couldn't make it.'

'But Zoe sent a text. She's … who are you?'

'The last face you'll ever see.'

Yolanda dropped her shoes as she turned to run. He grabbed

her arm and put his hand over her mouth. The stench of tobacco fingers made Yolanda want to gag. Her heart pounded. She struggled to get air into her lungs. Metal bruised her back as he pushed her against the car. She kneed him in the groin. Not hard enough. He didn't double over, but he let go of her for an instant. Long enough for her to escape. She slipped on the wet grass. Regained her balance.

'A fighter,' he said, as he grabbed her again. 'I enjoy a challenge.'

She kicked him again. His grip loosened. Loosened long enough for her to pick up one of her shoes. Yolanda aimed the sharp end of the heel to his face. Blood spurted from his forehead.

'You bitch,' he hissed through clenched teeth. 'You dirty, little lesbian bitch,' he said as he punched her in the face.

She tasted rain and blood on her lips. 'Help, help.' She didn't know if she whispered or screamed the words. Her stomach contracted. 'Why are you doing this?' Her words choked on bile and chunks of undigested apple scone that clogged her throat. The world spun as she fell to the rain-soaked ground. She felt herself choking on her vomit, felt his knees dig in as he straddled her. She noticed his eyes for the first time, cold and dark. She saw only his eyes. She looked into those dark, soulless eyes. Penetrating, vile eyes oozing more hate than she ever knew was possible. Her own eyes pleaded back at him as his fist rose, then plunged toward her face. *'The last face I'll ever see.'* Her thoughts echoed his words as he punched her again and again. *Mum and Dad, I'll never see them again. Dad's birth...* The world stopped spinning and faded into blackness. And then ... nothing.

21

The warm, humid spring day ended in a blustery spring thunderstorm. The table that Joe sat at opposite his mother in the restaurant had a starched white tablecloth and silver cutlery that sparkled reflections from the white candle in a small crystal candelabra. From their table on the enclosed second-floor balcony, protected from the rain, they watched lightning in the distance and the trees below lashed by fierce winds. The wildness of the weather outside heightened the warm, cosy atmosphere inside.

Joe studied the menu, enjoying the ambience of the restaurant, the aroma of garlic and herbs, sounds of clinking glasses and Bublé crooning 'Quando, Quando, Quando' in the background.

Joe's mum sighed. Joe lowered his menu.

'Problem, Mum? This is your favourite restaurant.'

'There's absolutely nothing wrong, darling. Everything is perfect. It's just that ... well ... this song ... well, it reminds me of when your father and I were young together. It's an old song, you know. This is a remake. Bublé has done quite a pleasant job of it, though.'

The restaurant owner came over and kissed Joe's mother on her cheek. 'It's good to see you again, Billie.' He handed her a red rose. 'And I've got a special red wine tonight to match the rose, for a special lady on her special day.'

Billie laughed. 'I bet it's a special price too.'

'Don't worry about the price, Mum. It's your night.'

The owner filled their water glasses. 'I'll get it now for you.'

Billie drank from her glass, put it down and refilled it. 'Your father would have enjoyed this restaurant. The intimacy. And the gourmet food and fine wine.'

He enjoyed wine, fine or otherwise, too much and too often, Joe thought.

Billie sighed again. 'I still miss him. It doesn't get easier. Time doesn't heal. When I look at the empty chair across from me at the table, I ...well ... eating alone every night ...' She trailed off, a hint of a tear in her eyes. 'Anyway ...'

Joe placed the menu on the table, folded his arms, and leaned toward his mother. 'It's been fifteen years, Mum. Fifteen bloody years.' He reached out and took his mother's hands. 'Sorry. I shouldn't have said that. But there's no need for you to eat alone every night. How many times have I asked you to come back to our family home?'

'How many times have I told you—too many memories?' Billie released her hands from Joe's grip and frowned. With a barely noticeable shake of her head, she said, 'You didn't cry. You didn't cry when he died.'

He didn't die. He killed himself, Joe thought, but didn't say.

She toyed with her water glass. 'When are you going to let go of your anger?'

'When are you going to let go of your guilt? Baseless guilt. When are you going to stop asking yourself if you could have done more for him?'

Billie dipped her bread in oil. 'Have you thought any more about applying for a promotion?'

Joe sat back in his chair, sipped his water, and made no comment about, but appreciated, the sudden change in the topic. 'I know you've been talking to Dean.'

'Of course I have. Dean and Lorna are my friends. We talk all the time.'

'You know what I mean. You've been talking to Dean about me.'

'You're so sullen lately. I think it might be good for you to have a role that will get you off the field.'

'Dean would disagree with that. Anyway, I failed the exam, remember?'

'You didn't even turn up for the exam, Joseph ... remember?'

Joe shrugged. 'I can handle the field. I won't break down ... Not like Dad,' he added, almost as an afterthought, as if trying to convince himself, and then regretted he had. 'Sorry, Mum.'

'It's not that. It's just that, well, spending less time in the field would give you more personal time. Maybe find someone special. You need ...'

'Why is everybody so focused on my love life, or lack of? I'm doing fine in that department.'

'You can't spend the rest of your life in short-term relationships. Not even short-term. When did you last date somebody for more than one night?'

Joe tapped his chin with his index finger, pretending to consider the question. 'Um, let me think. Yes, I dated somebody for two nights in a row just last month.'

'Funny. The point is, I never meet any of your girlfriends.'

'You wouldn't approve of my girlfriends.'

'Why? What sort of girls do you date?'

'I meant that you wouldn't approve because nobody would be good enough for your son. Anyway, I'm happy with the status quo.'

'That's what you like to believe. Your problem is your mood swings. Well, not so much mood swings, but not letting go. Not talking about how you feel, what's on your mind. Nobody wants to spend the rest of their life with somebody who they don't know. It's comforting to know who you're waking up next to each morning.'

Joe put up his hand in a stop now gesture.

He handed his mother the menu. 'We've been here twenty minutes, we should order.'

Looking at his mother over the top of the menu, Joe admired her healthy glowing skin, the sparkle in her blue eyes, her lean, toned body. The three or four days at the gym each week kept her in shape and looking ten or fifteen years younger than her age. And despite her short, no-nonsense grey hair, his mother exuded more than enough femininity to feature in a L'Oréal commercial or women's health magazine.

Billie ordered salmon. Joe the garlic, mushroom risotto.

Relaxed again, Joe winked. 'Will the red wine go with your salmon?'

Billie chuckled. 'Sweetie, I've never had a good red that doesn't go with everything.'

Joe raised his glass. 'Happy birthday, Mum. I love you.'

They ate in silence, enjoying the meal, the music, Billie the wine, relaxed in each other's company. A relaxation that comes with familiarity and mutual love.

Halfway into their main course, Billie broke the silence. 'Tell me about the case you're working on.'

'Haven't you followed it in the news?'

'You know me—I only believe half of what I read or hear

141

on the news. I want to hear it first hand from a reliable source.'

Joe put his fork down, wiped his mouth with his serviette, sipped his mineral water, and summarised the case, careful not to include any details kept from the public.

Billie sipped her wine, contemplated. 'This person is smart, driven, analytical. He thinks ahead.'

Joe finished his risotto and put his plate to the side. 'And that's the considered opinion of an English and History teacher.'

'I've seen *Silence of the Lambs*,' Billie grinned. 'Seriously though, teachers have to know a lot about human nature, understand motivation, recognise unique personality types. Your father never wanted to talk about his cases ...' Billie paused, looked down and said almost inaudibly, 'Things might have turned out differently if he had.'

'We don't have any solid clues yet,' Joe said, wanting to steer the conversation topic away from his father. 'Dean agrees he's cold and calculating. And possibly a religious nut. I'm leaning to jealousy or revenge as a possible motive.'

'Maybe,' Billie continued. 'Maybe all the above.'

'All the above. Sounds like the answer to a multiple-choice question you might set your students.'

'I never set multiple-choice questions ... too easy. In any case, he—maybe she—is probably overconfident to the point of arrogance, which will probably lead to his downfall. The violence of the act makes me agree it's a "he."'

'That's true,' Joe said. 'Most women have different, less violent methods. But the outcome is the same. The victim is dead. So I hope you're right. About him being overconfident, I mean. Time is running out. Dean agrees with me ... he will kill again ... soon.' Joe sat straight in his chair. 'Anyway, we shouldn't be talking about this on your birthday. Finish your meal so we can salivate over the dessert menu. My mouth is watering for a

Tiramisu. And I want to hear about your holiday plans.'

Joe's mobile rang just as they were ordering dessert. 'Where?' He gave the waiter a 'Just one minute,' signal. 'I'll ring Tess. We'll be there in about an hour.'

'What is it, sweetie?' Billie asked.

'Sorry Mum. We'll have to order a take-away dessert for you. I'll explain in the car.'

Fifteen minutes later, they arrived at Billie's house. 'I'm sorry …' he said as she opened the car door. 'I'm sorry to have to do this to you on your birthday. I'll make it up, I promise.'

'It's okay Joseph, I'm a cop's wife, I understand.'

You were a cop's wife, Joe thought. *Were, past tense. When are you ever going to let go?*

22

Joe caught a faint scent of lemon myrtle when Tessa got into the car. 'You've shampooed your hair. I guess you'd settled in for the night.'

'Kinda. You should get a job as a sniffer dog.'

Joe made a U-turn. 'A sniffer dog? Right, the shampoo thing.'

'Anyway, Alex is in Melbourne for a few days researching an article. So I was filling in time, switching between Netflix and looking at the dating sites Phoebe and Amber had been visiting. Just to get a feel for who visits, you know—what they write, their profiles, how they arrange a date.'

'You haven't been on a dating site before?'

'No, have you?'

Joe shook his head. 'No way. I think I'd feel—I don't know, I'd feel …'

'Embarrassed? Shy?'

'I guess. Anyway,' Joe smirked. 'Contrary to popular opinion, I'm doing fine in the dating department.'

Tessa rolled her eyes. 'No comment. Back to business. What did the hospital say about the woman who was attacked? What's her condition?' Tessa asked.

'She'll be okay. Physically, anyway.'

'Is it connected to our case? Do you know any details about the attack?'

'Not much. There was a witness. Two witnesses. A young couple. We'll talk to them tomorrow. Could be connected to Amber, Issy and Phoebe.'

'It's the same guy, isn't it? Zoe?' Tessa said.

'Sunday night. Near the same restaurant. It's a stretch, I know. And it's too soon. Only a few weeks since Phoebe. I don't know. Probably no connection. But we'll have a better idea after we speak to her.'

'It's him, Joe. Like Paul said, he's growing in confidence, escalating. He won't stop. He'll keep adding to the garland of roses, his string of rosary beads, until we catch him and put him away. Or kill him.'

Joe glanced at Tessa. 'You're right,' he said as he sped up past the speed limit. AC/DC's 'Highway to Hell' thundered from his speakers as he uncharacteristically weaved in and out of the traffic and swore at the red lights. He parked in the hospital car park fifty minutes after he got the call.

Joe and Tessa raced from reception, up a flight of stairs and past the nurses' station. Joe didn't notice patients in wheelchairs, orderlies pushing trolleys, buzzers alerting nurses that patients need attention, or doctors being paged over the intercom. But he couldn't ignore the unmistakable, sickly smell of hospital disinfectant and bleach. A smell that Joe had experienced too many times since joining the force. The hospital odour always evoked bad memories for Joe. Never good memories. But he managed to disregard his growing nausea as he raced to Yolanda's room.

Despite her long legs, Tessa's run-walk just kept pace with

Joe. But she almost ran into him when he froze in the doorway to Yolanda's room. Joe turned and walked out.

Tessa grabbed his arm. 'What are you doing?'

'Did you see the mess she's in? I was so pumped, so ready to go in there and drill her for information. But look at her, she needs … I don't know what she needs. But she doesn't need us probing her for answers right now.'

'I know she's in a bad way, but we still have to talk to her tonight. Get some information from her while it's still fresh in her memory.'

'She'll never forget what happened to her tonight. But you're right—again. We need to talk to her now.'

***

Joe and Tessa crept into the room. Yolanda's closed eyes half opened as Joe and Tessa approached.

'Hello, Yolanda. I'm detective Joseph Paterson and this is Detective Tessa Mariani. We're so sorry this has happened to you.'

A tear fell from a bloodied, swollen eye and rolled down Yolanda's red and purple bruised face.

'If you're up to it,' Joe said, 'we'd like to ask you some questions. We're going to catch the man who did this to you.'

'I'm a bit drowsy. They gave me something for the pain,' Yolanda slurred. 'It worked, but I'm a bit …' Yolanda closed her eyes, took a deep breath, and opened her eyes again. 'I'll do my best. He terrified me.' Yolanda paused. She shook her head. 'I don't want to think about it. I thought he was going to kill me. Everything went black … I thought I was dying. My parents … I thought I'd never see them again.'

'But he didn't kill you.' Tessa sat in the chair next to the bed.

'You fought back. And you will see your parents again.'

'They're on their way, driving from the country. They'll be here soon. Oh God, I hate to think of them seeing me like this. How bad do I look?'

Joe sat in the chair next to Tessa. 'You look like a strong woman who fought off a vicious attacker and survived.'

'We need you to tell us everything you remember about him and what happened,' Tessa said. 'You survived his attack, but his next target, and that's what you were, a target—his next target might not survive. And we're sure he will do this again.'

Joe saw the alarm in Yolanda's eyes. 'You're safe now. But we need to stop him before he does it again, to another young woman.'

Yolanda swallowed. 'My throat, it's dry—I'm so thirsty.'

Tessa poured water for her. Yolanda winced when the straw touched her split lip. She sipped the water and handed the glass to Tessa. 'Thank you.'

Tessa placed the glass on the side-table. 'Okay, Yolanda, we need you to tell us, from the beginning, what happened, everything you can remember.'

Yolanda told Joe and Tessa about meeting her blind date online to the time of the attack.

'We arranged to meet at the restaurant. Then I agreed to meet at the surf club, but my date ...' Yolanda lowered her head. 'The person who I thought I was meeting,' she said softly. 'My date ... was late.'

Tessa moved her chair closer to Yolanda. 'What name did your date give on the dating site?'

'It doesn't matter.' Yolanda shook her head. 'I never met my date. I never will now. My date doesn't exist. Never did. The man attacked me before I could get back to my car. I knew ...' Yolanda reached for a tissue. 'I knew when I decided to go back to my car that my date wasn't going to show.'

'Okay, tell us about the attack,' Joe said. 'And the man who attacked you.'

'He seemed sweet. Offered me a lift because it was raining. I said ...' Another tear trickled down her cheek, moistening her split lip. 'I said yes at first, then thought better of it. I turned to leave, but he grabbed me. He knew my name.' More tears. 'How did he know my name? I tried to get away. I kicked him, but he kept grabbing me. I hit him in the face with my shoe. I was carrying my shoes because it was hard to walk on the grass in high heels. I remember dropping them when he grabbed me. But I must have managed to pick one up. He punched me to the ground. I ...' Yolanda looked away as her voice faltered. 'I can't remember. I ...'

Tessa took her hand. 'You can. Just a few more details about the man. Relax. Take your time.'

Yolanda closed her eyes and inhaled deeply. After a few moments, she opened her eyes. 'Yes. Tobacco. I remember tobacco.'

'What about it?' Tessa said.

'He stunk of tobacco. I can't stand the smell. It turns my stomach. And he had his hands over my mouth at first. My nostrils were full of tobacco stench. I gagged.' Yolanda started to cry again. 'I thought I'd vomit,' she said through her tears. 'Choke on my vomit.'

'You're doing great,' Joe said. 'We know now that he's a smoker. What did he look like? How old was he? It's important. The more detail, the better chance we have of stopping him before he does this again.'

'How old was he?' Yolanda took another deep breath, composed herself. 'I don't know. Not old. Well, older than me. Not as old as my father. Somewhere in between.' She looked in Joe's direction. 'Maybe about the same age as you.'

'Would you say mid-thirties to forties?' Joe said.

Yolanda nodded.

'What about height and hair colour? Did he have a beard?' Tessa asked.

'He's tall, much taller than me. Hair, not dark, not blonde. No beard.'

'This is very good, Yolanda,' Joe said. 'Just a few more details and then you can rest. What sort of build does he have?'

'Build? Normal, I guess, not fat, not skinny. Much like you Detective ... Detective ..., sorry I've forgotten your name.'

'That's okay. It's Detective Joe.'

Yolanda studied Joe. 'I could almost be describing you, Detective Joe ... except for the eyes. You've got gentle blue eyes. His were ...' Yolanda closed her eyes. Shook her head and started to cry again.

Tessa looked at Joe and then back at Yolanda. 'His eyes, Yolanda. What about his eyes?'

'Dark, piercing.'

'You're doing great.' Tessa passed the water to Yolanda. 'Just a few more questions. What was he wearing?'

'I don't know. I wasn't really interested. I think trousers, not jeans. And ...' Yolanda hesitated. 'No, I'm wrong. He was wearing jeans. I remember now. He was wearing jeans because I remember thinking how well his shirt matched his jeans. And I thought I'd look for the same shirt for my father's birthday. The fabric was soft and silky, a pale blue, I think.' Yolanda paused and licked her lips. 'The shirt had long sleeves, pushed up at the elbows. Kind of casual, but elegant.'

'Is there anything else you can remember?' Joe said. 'Was he wearing glasses?'

'Glasses. Yes. He had glasses on when he first grabbed me. But when he was on top of me on the ground, he didn't. That's when I noticed his eyes.' Yolanda shook her head. 'The glasses, no, I remember now. He wasn't wearing them. They were on top of his head. But I don't remember when he was on top of me. They might have fallen off when I hit him with my shoe.'

'Did you notice what sort of car he was driving?' Tessa said.

'Not really. Only that it was a dark colour, maybe dark blue or black. I think it was black, and it looked fancy.' Yolanda shrugged. 'I don't know much about cars. On the farm, I grew up with mainly Ford pickup trucks.' Yolanda sat straight in bed. 'My car. I almost forgot. What happened to my car?'

'Your car is safe.' Tessa plumped Yolanda's pillow. 'Sit back. The officers found your keys and your car is in a safe place. Back to the attacker's car. You said the colour was dark, and it looked fancy. What else do you remember? Maybe the number plate?'

'No. I didn't see the number plate, but the car looked like the one in the car park.'

'What car park?' Joe asked.

Yolanda told him about dropping her keys and meeting one of the other residents. 'And then this car screeched out of the garage. I only saw the back of it. They were in a hurry, whoever it was.'

'Did you see who got into the car before it left the car park?'

'No, they must have got in it when I was searching for my keys under my car. The only person I saw was … was, I'm sorry, I can't remember his name.'

'What's the name of the dating site?' Joe noticed a pink blush on the parts of Yolanda's face that weren't bruised.

'Is that important?'

'Very important,' Tessa said.

'My parents will be here soon.' Yolanda turned her head away, in the direction of a window that overlooked the hospital car park. 'I don't want to talk about this in front of them. I don't want to upset them any more than they already are.'

'We just need a few more details and then we'll leave you to rest,' Joe said. 'Now, the name of the dating site.'

Yolanda looked in Joe and Tessa's direction again, with weary eyes that Joe knew were barely focussed. 'I'm tired.'

Tessa looked at Joe. He shook his head.

Tessa patted Yolanda's hand. 'Okay, that's enough for tonight. We'll come back tomorrow when you've rested. We'll bring photos. You might recognise him.'

'You know who it is?'

'No, we're not sure. We're following some leads.'

'Because he's done this before, hasn't he? Oh my God, oh my God—he was going to rape me—wasn't he?' Yolanda's face grimaced in pain as she sat straight in bed again. 'If those people hadn't come along, he was going to rape me.'

'Don't think about what might have happened,' Joe said. 'You were brave, and you survived. Just rest tonight and we'll visit you tomorrow morning.'

Joe and Tessa were just outside the door when Yolanda called after them.

They walked back towards her bed. 'Did you remember something else?' Joe asked.

'No. Nothing. But my car.' Tears filled Yolanda's eyes again. 'It was raining, and the top was down.'

'Don't you worry about your car, my poor baby girl,' a man's voice said from behind them.

23

The following morning Joe and Tessa interviewed the young couple who witnessed the attack when they were returning from a walk along the beach. They were running. They were trying to beat the heavy rain they knew was coming and nearly missed what was happening. The wife thought she saw something, but thought it was probably just a couple making out. 'It happens a lot around here,' she told Joe and Tessa. So she kept running. But something didn't look right to her about the scene. Was the guy being aggressive? The couple ran back about fifty metres and saw a man and woman wrestling on the grass. They heard a stifled cry. The man was punching her, over and over. And then the woman stopped struggling. They called out to him, 'Stop. We've called the police.' The man jumped up and sped away in a dark-coloured car. It was raining, and the car was going too fast to make out what it was, but they both agreed that it looked upmarket. They didn't see the man clearly enough to give a description. They ran over to the woman after ringing triple O. Her face was streaked with blood. And she was so still they didn't know if she was dead or alive. They didn't move or touch her and waited for the police and ambulance to arrive.

After interviewing the two witnesses, Joe and Tessa returned to the hospital. Tessa scanned the evidence report while Joe circled the hospital car park. On his second time around, Tessa pointed to a park between a Jeep and a Toyota Hilux. 'Over there.'

'It's too narrow.'

'I could fit a semi in there.'

'You could and you would. I could, but I wouldn't.'

Joe eventually parked at the back of the car park at the end of a row, metres away from the nearest car. 'What does the report say?'

'There was a lot of rain last night, so not much. They found her shoes and a pair of broken glasses.'

'Sunglasses or clear lens?'

'Clear. The arms were bent, but they made out the brand, Cartier. If the evidence gods are on our side, we might get a partial fingerprint from them.'

'Designer brand. And an expensive-looking car, according to the witnesses. And Yolanda said it looked fancy. Our guy is well off.'

They made their way unnoticed past the busy nurses' station to Yolanda's room. Yolanda's parents, who Joe recognised from the previous night, sat either side of Yolanda. Another lady, who appeared to be in her fifties, sat next to Yolanda's mother.

Yolanda's father, a burly man with a woodchopper's build, stood and loomed towards the door. 'What are you doing here?' Red faced, he waved a muscle-bound arm and pointed to the window. 'Why aren't you out there catching the son of a bitch who did this to our baby girl?'

His wife hurried over and put an arm around his shoulder. 'Sit down, Jim. They're here to talk to Yolanda. They're doing their job.'

Jim put his arms around his wife and sobbed. 'I'm sorry. It kills me to see her like this.'

It wasn't the first time in his career that Joe saw a big, strong man sobbing. And he knew it wouldn't be the last.

Yolanda reached out her arms. 'Come here, Daddy. I'll be fine. I am fine. I'll be out of here, home, in a day or two.'

Jim composed himself and sat again next to his daughter's bed.

'We didn't formally meet last night,' Joe said to Yolanda's parents. 'I'm Detective Joseph Paterson and this is Detective Tessa Mariani.'

Yolanda's mother introduced Mrs Robinson, Yolanda's school principal.

Joe looked at Yolanda. She sat up in bed, still bruised, her lip still split and swollen, but her eyes were alert now. 'We've got more question for you, so ...'

Yolanda shook her head. 'No, I told you everything last night. I've got nothing more.'

'We've got some photos to show you,' Tessa said. 'And we need to know more about the dating site.'

'What dating site?' her mother asked. 'What's a dating site got to do with this? You were meeting a friend. She was late. What's her name? We should ring her. She'll be wondering why you weren't there.'

Joe saw the anxious look in Yolanda's eyes. 'There's been a misunderstanding. But I think we can clear this up if we talk to Yolanda alone.'

Jim stood again. 'No, we need to be here with her. Make sure there's no more, as you say, misunderstandings. We ...'

Mrs Robinson stood, took Jim by the arm. 'C'mon, I'll buy you two a coffee. We could all do with some refreshment. And I can ring school and give them an update. They'll be concerned.'

'We can talk freely now,' Tessa said as she closed the door

when Yolanda's parents and Mrs Robinson left. 'This is important if we're going to find the man who attacked you. What is the name of the dating site?'

'I don't want my parents to find out.'

'Find out what?' Joe asked.

'I …' Yolanda wiped a tear from her cheek. 'I went to a bar one Friday night after school when I first moved to the city, you know, to meet people. But I didn't like it. I'm not good at socialising.'

'So you tried the dating site,' Tessa coaxed. 'What's the name of the dating site?'

Yolanda told them about the site, meeting Zoe online, and gave them her login details.

'We need you to look at these photos.' Joe handed Yolanda his iPad. 'Do you recognise any of these men?'

Yolanda dismissed Harvey Cosgrove, Amber's jealous colleague, without hesitation. He was the wrong build. Aaron Thompson, Ed Kowalski and Sebastian Sanders were all the right colouring and build. She wasn't sure about Aaron. He looked too young in the photo. Yolanda pointed to the photos of Kowalski and Sanders. 'I might have seen them before. Do they have children? Could be one of the fathers who pick up their kids from school.'

Tessa pointed to Kowalski. 'He has a child. But not at your school.'

'I'm not sure. It was dark and raining. I didn't take any notice of his face until I saw those eyes. Except …' She hesitated.

'Except?' Tessa coaxed.

'I just remembered. I've been so focussed on his eyes. But I thought at first he had a charming smile. Nice teeth.'

She went back to Kowalski's photo. 'I might have seen him at the bar. I noticed a man there with a blonde woman and another woman with long, brown hair.' She pointed to Sanders. 'Or it could have been him, I don't know. To be honest,' she lowered her eyes. 'I, um, I was looking more at the women. I guess that's why I didn't really look at the man before he attacked me. I just wasn't interested.'

'All I wanted last night was to meet Zoe.' Yolanda looked from Tessa to Joe and back to Tessa. Her face flushed between the red and purple bruising. 'Please, please don't tell my parents.'

'I'm sorry, Yolanda,' Joe said. 'We can't make any promises. We don't know …'

'We understand,' Tessa interrupted. 'But we don't know where this investigation will take us.'

'Just one more question. You said you saw a man with a blonde woman.' Joe showed her a photo of Amber. 'Is this the woman?'

'It was so long ago, months.' After a moment Yolanda's eyes widened in recognition. 'That's the woman in the news. The one who was murdered. I remember. It was not long after I moved here. The man who attacked me. It's him, isn't it?' Yolanda whispered. 'It's the man who killed that woman. He killed her, and he was going to kill me, wasn't he?'

24

Later that day, back at their desks, Tessa closed a file, stretched, and looked at Joe. She tilted her head to one side, contemplated.

Joe looked up. 'What? Did you find something?'

'No. I was just looking at your scar. I like it. It adds character to your features, somehow brings out the Mcdreamy blue in your eyes, and …'

'The interview notes?' Joe interrupted. Tessa and Joe spent most of the afternoon reading interview notes from the other detectives on the task force. The team had been working overtime gathering information, interviewing friends, relatives, and colleagues of the victims. The interviews with the other staff and patrons from the Sandpiper beach restaurant produced no leads for them to follow up. The man who left his glasses case behind emailed a reply to say thank you for keeping it, but he has other cases and won't be needing it. His contact phone number on the email had an area code that was either Perth or Adelaide. When Tessa called him, he confirmed he lived in Perth and had been in Sydney for three days on a business trip.

He dined at the restaurant on the Thursday night and caught a flight home the next day.

'I think it's a chick magnet.'

'The interview notes?' Joe repeated.

'No, your scar. And no, I've found nothing so far from the interviews. You?'

'Nobody we need to revisit,' Joe said. 'Not yet. Unless the interviews with Yolanda's friends, family and the other teachers at her school uncover more suspects, Kowalski and Sanders are still at the top of our list. Not that two is a list. Their alibis are far from rock solid, but ...' Joe's moblie played the theme from *Law and Order*. 'Detective Paterson ... Yes I remember you ... We interviewed you weeks ago. Why have you decided to tell the truth now...We made it clear when we spoke to you that this is a murder investigation ... I hope you do understand now ... We'll make a time with you to get a full statement.'

Joe rocked back in his chair, stretched his legs, folded his arms, and nodded. 'He lied.'

'Who was that? Who lied?'

'The arrogant, egotistical shit lied.'

It was Tessa's turn to nod. 'Sanders.'

'That was his friend, Andre. He was at his girlfriend's place that night, and he had made no arrangements to meet Sanders. Apparently, he's been fretting about this for a couple of weeks. And his girlfriend finally convinced him to tell us the truth.'

Tessa picked up her mobile. 'I'll make a time with Sanders now for another interview. And Kowalski, too.'

'No don't. If I pick you up in the morning, are you okay to make an early start?'

Tessa nodded. 'Sure. How early?'

'Instead of calling Sanders and Kowalski, I'd like to make a surprise visit,' Joe said. 'If we leave early enough, we can catch

Sanders before he leaves for work, and then catch Kowalski before lunch.'

'Sounds like a plan. We should …' Her mobile buzzed. After a few moments she said, 'Hang on a sec. No, wait. I'll call you back shortly.'

Joe looked up from the interview notes. 'What is it?'

'It's Paul. He just had a call from a woman who said she'd been raped.'

'When, who is she? It can't be connected to our case. Not rape. There's no evidence of rape.'

'No. It's not connected to our case. But it could be connected to Paul's case. Apparently, it happened a while back, but she didn't report it. She, Julie, I think Paul said her name is, read the news report about two rape victims. The description of what happened to them was the same as what happened to her.'

Joe blew out a breath. 'So she could be another one of Johnson's victims?'

'That's the one. The scumbag Damien is defending for rape. Anyway, I guess finding out about the other victims changed Julie's mind about reporting her rape. And she said the rapist shoved a twenty-cent piece in her hand when he finished. That's a detail about the previous rapes we held back from the media.'

'The trial's this week, isn't it?'

'I know, it's last minute but Paul's meeting with her this afternoon and wants me to go with him.'

'I thought he was working with Jeff on the rape cases.'

'Jeff's interstate overnight chasing up on another case. Should only take a couple of hours.'

'I hope Jeff is giving Paul the support he needs,' Joe said. 'Jeff's competent, but he's young. I'm not sure he's the right partner for Paul.'

'Paul will be fine. He's so much more confident now. And

Trudi is the best for him.'

'You're right. Do you want me to come along?'

'No. It might be too much if three of us turned up. We may be stretching it with me going. I don't know. But Julie might feel better if there's a female there. Who knows?'

'Okay, I'll be here when you get back. I've still got a stack of interviews to go over.'

Tessa pressed favourites on her mobile and called Paul. 'On my way.'

***

Ten minutes later Tessa and Paul turned out of the station car park and headed west. 'Thanks for coming along, Tess. I think Julie will feel more comfortable with you there.'

'What's her surname?'

'Porter, Julie Porter.'

'Yeah, I wasn't sure if it was a good or bad thing, me being there with you.'

'To be honest, I'm just guessing it's a good thing,' Paul said. 'I haven't met Julie yet. I've just spoken to her over the phone.'

'What did she tell you about the rape?'

'Not much.' Paul put on his indicator to change lanes. 'Only what I told you. It took me some effort to get her to agree to meeting with me.'

'Thanks again, Tess, for coming with me. I really appreciate the support.'

'No need for thanks. You've come back fighting Paul, I'm so proud of you.'

'I couldn't have done it without Trudi. And Joe, of course. He was there for me the entire time.'

John Paul Young sang 'Love is in the air' on the radio.

Paul turned the radio down. 'Did Joe tell you?'

'That he was there for you? I knew …'

'No, I mean, did Joe tell you about Trudi and me?'

'What? You're not splitting up, are you?'

'So Joe didn't tell you. It's so like Joe not to discuss personal stuff—his own or anybody else's.'

'Tell me. Tell me about you and Trudi.'

Paul grinned. 'Maybe I should let Joe tell you.'

Tessa shook her head as she massaged her temples. 'Jesus Paul. Don't do this to me. If I could reach it, I'd slam the brake on. Tell me. I have to know.'

'Okay, okay. I'm going to ask Trudi to marry me.'

'Oh, my God. Oh, my God. That's wonderful.' Tessa almost squealed as she clapped her hands. 'When? Where? How many guests? How many bridesmaids? I'm one of them, of course. Obviously, Joe will be best man.' She reached for her mobile.

'Who are you calling?'

'I'm calling Trudi. We need to shop for a wedding dress and bridesmaid's dresses and…'

'Tessa, put your mobile away. I said I'm going to ask her. I haven't asked her yet.'

Tessa laughed. 'You're right, it's probably better you ask her before I talk to her about wedding plans. When are you going to get down on bended knees and give her an engagement ring? Oh my God—have you got an engagement ring? I can help you shop for one.'

'My grandmother left me her diamond ring. It's old fashioned, but beautiful. I think Trudi will love it. What do you think?'

'That is so romantic. I know she'll love it.' Tessa dabbed her eyes with a tissue.

'Are you crying, Tess? I didn't mean to upset you. I thought you'd be happy.'

'I am happy, so happy for you. I'm just, well, you know, feeling emotional. It's the Italian in me. So, when are you going to ask her?'

'That's what I was going to ask you. Would your parents mind if I asked her at your Dad's birthday bash? Would that be appropriate? I don't want to steal his thunder.'

'Mamma and Papa would be ecstatic … Oh my God. They'd be thrilled … honoured. They would burst with joy.'

Paul grinned again. 'So they won't mind?'

Tessa sang 'Love is in the Air', harmonising perfectly with John Paul Young.

25

Joe and Tessa pulled into the car park in Bondi at seven the next morning and walked just over a kilometre to Sanders' apartment building. It took Joe four attempts before Sanders answered the security buzzer.

'It's seven-fifteen in the morning. You didn't ring to say you were visiting.'

The annoyed tone in Sanders' voice told Joe they had made the right call by catching Sanders off guard with an early morning surprise visit. 'This isn't a social call, Mr Sanders,' Joe said. 'Buzz us into the building immediately.'

'I was in the shower,' Sanders said as he opened the door in a white robe and still wet. 'I'm leaving to meet a client in a few minutes.'

Tessa didn't wait for an invitation. She marched straight to the white lounge.

'Your boots. Remove your boots.'

'My boots will be up your arse, Sanders, if you don't start telling us the truth.'

'You will address me as *Mr* Sanders.'

'You lied to us.' Joe sat on the lounge next to Tessa and pointed to the lounge opposite. 'You might as well sit, Mr Sanders. We might be here for a while. You lied about where you were the night Phoebe was murdered. You didn't make any arrangements with your so-called friend, Andre.'

Tessa stretched her long legs, leaned back in the lounge, and folded her arms. 'I'm ready to sit here as long as it takes to get the truth out of you. I'm not in a hurry to get back to the station.'

When Sanders sat, he lit a cigarette, took one puff, and wrinkled his nose as he stubbed it out. 'Too early for this. I haven't had breakfast yet.' He stood. 'Can I offer you a coffee?'

'You can offer us the truth,' Joe said. 'Sit.'

'I did have an arrangement with Andre.' Sanders sat. 'We had arranged to meet for a drink. But he changed his mind and stayed the night with his girlfriend. That's why he rang to say he couldn't make it.'

Tessa unfolded her arms, sat forward, and glared at Sanders through narrowed eyes. 'Do you bullshit your clients, the way you're bullshitting us? Where were you the night Phoebe was murdered? Like I said. I'll stay as long as it takes to get the truth out of your lying arse.'

'The truth, Mr Sanders,' Joe said. 'Now. This instant. I'm not as patient as Detective Mariani. I'll repeat the question. Where were you the night Phoebe was murdered?'

Sanders' hands trembled as he lit another cigarette. 'I was … I was … well, it's embarrassing.'

'It might be embarrassing for you, but it won't be for us. We've heard it all before,' Tessa said. 'And our empathy for your feelings? Well, we have none. So out with it.'

'I, um … I ah …was with a lady who provides favours. Um … for a price.'

'A prostitute.' Joe shook his head as he let out a slow

breath. 'Name?'

'I don't know. I didn't need to know her name.'

'Credit card receipt?' Tessa asked.

'Oh, of course,' Sanders snickered. 'Ladies of the night hang around on corners with their credit card machines.'

'So you still can't prove where you were, the night Phoebe was murdered,' Tessa said.

'But I can. You can ask the escort provider. She hangs around the same place all the time.'

'Seriously,' Tessa laughed. 'Ladies of the night? Escort provider? The word is prostitute. Do I need to spell it for you?'

'You said she hangs around the same place,' Joe said. 'So, you're a regular client?'

'Not regular, but sometimes. I like certain things, and well … she's good at what I like.'

Tessa shook her head. 'And you don't even know her name.'

'Brandy,' Sanders blurted.

'It's seven-thirty in the morning,' Joe said through clenched teeth. 'No coffee, no brandy. Just the truth about where you were when Phoebe was murdered.'

'No, not the drink. Her name. The escort's name is Brandy. She's got a website.'

Sebastian stood. 'I need a coffee.'

'It's odd,' Joe whispered, 'that he doesn't use the word prostitute. Does this fit with the possibility of a religious connection?'

'Certainly worth exploring. Maybe …' Tessa paused when Sanders returned with his coffee. She focussed her attention on Sanders again. 'Why did you make up a bullshit story about going to a bar?'

'When I heard about Phoebe, I knew the police would ask me questions.'

'This is a murder investigation, Sanders,' Tessa said. 'But you would rather lie and waste our time, than feel a little embarrassed about what you were doing when Phoebe was murdered.'

'I didn't want to talk about my private life.' Sanders glared at Tessa. 'Everybody has their little secrets. As I'm sure you would understand.'

Joe noticed Tessa frown. The same split-second frown he noticed the last time they interviewed Sanders when he said, 'Not everything is as it appears.'

'Were you with Brandy last Sunday evening?' Joe asked.

'No.'

'Where were you?' Joe asked.

'This is becoming quite tedious. You're wasting my time. My time is money and I have important clients who depend on me.'

Tessa held out an open palm. 'Give me the names of your important clients.'

'My clients are none of your business.'

'Give me their contact details,' Tessa said. 'So I can ring them and let them know you'll be late because you're refusing to co-operate in a murder investigation.' Tessa returned Sander's narrow eyes glare. 'Where were you Sunday evening?'

'Here. In my penthouse. Alone, if you must know.'

'So you don't have an alibi for when Phoebe was murdered,' Joe said. 'Or for last Sunday.'

'So, I'm a suspect, am I?'

'Oh, you're so quick off the mark,' Tessa said. 'No wonder you're a bank teller.'

Sanders' face flushed. 'Stockbroker.'

'Where did you go to school?' Joe asked.

'Relevance?' Sanders snapped.

'The relevance is,' Tessa said, 'Detective Paterson asked you a question. And you have to answer his question. Truthfully.

You should check the word truth in the dictionary. You may be surprised at what you learn. Where did you go to school?'

'St Joseph's. Hunters Hill.'

'Do you attend Mass regularly?' Joe asked.

'I haven't seen the inside of a church since I finished high school.'

***

'He did it again,' Tessa said after Sanders slammed the door behind them.

'Are you talking about when he said everybody has their little secrets?'

'Yes, how did you …? My body language. I gave it away, didn't I?' Tessa thumped her right fist into her left palm. 'I need to control my involuntary emotional expressions.'

Joe raised his eyebrows and shook his head. 'Really, Tess. Think about what you just said. Control … involuntary.' He pressed the down arrow. The door opened to an empty lift. 'Anyway, Sanders wasn't even directing the comment at you. He's too self-absorbed. We just caught him out as being a liar who hangs around with prostitutes. And he's trying to minimise the damage,' Joe continued as he pressed the button for the ground floor. 'And, if you weren't keeping a secret, a particularly important secret, from your family, you wouldn't have had an involuntary emotional expression.'

'Doesn't appear to be a religious connection if it's true he doesn't attend Mass.'

'If there is a connection, probably not a traditional organised religion.'

'Brandy,' Tessa said. 'She's a bit like Vivian Ward. Hooker meets obscenely rich businessman.'

'Julia Roberts, *Pretty Woman*. Right?' Joe said. 'I bet her relationship with Sanders doesn't have the same Hollywood fairy tale ending. Anyway, you're changing the subject, again, about telling your parents,' Joe said, as they got out of the lift.

'He didn't ask why we asked him about Sunday night.'

'Good sidestep, Tess. But you're right, he didn't ask. And no way are we going to rely on his Brandy alibi. Not sure anyway, that we could count on her remembering back as far as the night Phoebe was murdered.'

'And even if she says she remembers,' Tessa said. 'He could have paid her to say she does.'

Joe nodded. 'Agreed.'

'So Sanders doesn't have an alibi for Phoebe or Yolanda. No point in asking him where he was when Amber and Issy were murdered. But we know he was in the country and in the state,' Tessa said. 'Let's see if Ed Kowalski can produce a credible alibi for Sunday.'

'Edward,' Joe reminded her with mock disdain.

Joe turned left out of the Bondi Beach car park exit. When he was sure he was heading in the right direction he said, 'Siri, play "Pretty Woman" by Roy Orbison.'

26

Joe spent the better part of five minutes driving around the double helix car park at the Opera House before he found a vacant spot that provided ample separation between his Monaro and the next car.

When Joe and Tessa exited the lift from the car park and made their way past the Opera Bar and up the steps that led to the walkway, Joe stopped. He looked at the Harbour through the eyes of somebody who had been there many times before and took all it offered for granted. Then, as he always did, he consciously looked through the eyes of a tourist who was visiting for the first time and, as always, felt in awe of its beauty.

'Circular Quay is one of Mum's favourite places to visit,' Joe said as he led Tessa along the Sydney Writers Walk between the Opera House and the Overseas Terminal. 'There's Banjo Paterson's plaque.' Joe pointed to one of the sixty writers' plaques embedded in the walk.

Tessa laughed. 'Detective Paterson. You named your cat after an author?'

Joe grinned and shrugged. 'Anyway, Mum and Dad used to

go to a show at the Opera House at least three or four times a year. Dad would buy her … never mind. Too many years ago.'

'It's okay to reminisce about the good times, Joe.'

Joe shrugged. 'I don't know. Do you remember what Amber's mother said about happy memories making the loss worse? Anyway, let's drop it. I don't know why I even mentioned it.'

***

They arrived at Kowalski's office ten minutes after parking the car.

'According to his calendar, Mr Kowalski is in a meeting for another fifteen minutes,' the receptionist, on the ground floor foyer of the multi-storey office building, told Joe and Tessa. 'I can leave a message for him. Do you have an appointment?'

'No.' Joe said. 'But we will—once I call his mobile.'

They waited in the coffee shop on the far end of the ground floor.

'I think you should take the lead on this one, Tess.' Joe winked. 'You get on so well with Kowalski.'

'My pleasure. I don't think the gay bar Yolanda told us about will take us anywhere with him. But I'll give it a go.'

'Agree. It's unlikely Amber would've gone anywhere with him, let alone a bar.'

Twenty-five minutes later Kowalski got out of a lift and approached their table. 'What is it this time? I'm busy and I have nothing else to tell you.'

'We just have a few more questions for you,' Joe said. 'Can we go somewhere private?' Joe nodded towards the parade of people coming and going through the foyer revolving doors. 'And somewhere quieter.'

'We're investigating another murder. Where were you last

Sunday night?' Tessa asked after they settled in a small meeting room behind the reception area.

'Is this really necessary, Detective, um …?'

'Detective Mariani. Do I have to keep reminding you, Ed, this is a murder investigation? So, yes, this is really necessary.'

'Do I have to keep reminding you, my name is Edward?'

'Where were you Sunday night, Kowalski?'

Kowalski glared at Tessa across the table and said through clenched teeth, 'I stayed in, watched TV, like I do most Sunday evenings.'

As agreed, Joe made notes and remained silent while Tessa interviewed Kowalski.

'We'll confirm with your wife.'

'She wasn't there.'

Silence. Tessa's turn to glare.

Kowalski shifted in his chair. 'She, my wife, and our son were in Canberra visiting her parents.'

'How often does she go? Your wife had been in Canberra last time we interviewed you.'

'Interrogated.'

'We're just having a friendly chat here.' Tessa leaned forward and spoke in a quiet, calm voice. 'But if you don't want to co-operate, Mr Edward Kowalski, you can come to the station with us, and you'll find out what an interrogation really is.' Tessa sat back and smiled her best fake smile. 'Now, Ed, how often does your wife visit her parents?'

Kowalski responded in a monotone voice. 'About once a month. Am I a suspect?' His mobile rang. 'I'll be there in five minutes … yes, we'll go over the project plan with them.'

'Five minutes. I doubt it,' Tessa said.

'I told you where I was on Sunday.' Kowalski stood. 'I'm not a suspect, so we're done here.'

'The less you cooperate, the more we suspect you might be involved. So sit.'

Kowalski turned his attention to Joe. 'You're a reasonable person. Can we get this over and done with so I can get back to work? My project team is waiting for me. The meeting can't go ahead without me. I need to make important decisions for them.'

Joe looked at Tessa, then back at Kowalski, shrugged, and continued making notes.

'We're going to interview your wife,' Tessa continued. 'So we need to know exactly what your relationship was with Amber Thompson.'

'We've been over this. I didn't have a relationship with Amber. We were colleagues, that's all.'

'We have a positive ID from a witness that you were at a bar with Amber Thompson and another woman, with long brown hair, just days before Amber was murdered.'

'That person is mistaken.'

'We have the witness, and we have the video from the bar.'

'It was probably a work social. We often get together. Team bonding.'

'You told us you didn't socialise with Amber.'

'I don't. Amber wouldn't have been there. She doesn't go to work functions. I've never socialised with her—I would not want to. She was nothing but a...' Kowalski paused, closed his eyes, and breathed deeply. 'What I mean is, well, it's sad what happened to her.'

'You were saying. She was nothing but a ... but a, what?' Tessa said.

'What I meant to say was, that Amber Thompson was nothing but a colleague. She was not somebody I would socialise with.'

'Was not somebody ...?' Tessa tilted her head and crossed her arms. 'You know, liars tend not to use contractions. You didn't say wasn't somebody. You said was not somebody. Just like Clinton when he said, "I did not have sexual relations with that woman."'

'I did not …' Kowalski paused and took a deep breath. 'I didn't want to socialise with Amber Thompson.'

Joe looked up from his notes. 'What about the brunette? From what we saw on the video, you did more than socialise with her.'

Kowalski looked down, twisting his wedding ring the way he did in the first interview. 'It was probably just a harmless flirt. After a few drinks … well, you know what it's like. It was probably just an in the moment thing. Nothing serious.'

'So, you went to a work social at a gay bar?' Joe joined the interview. 'And flirted with another colleague.'

'A gay … what are you talking about? I wouldn't go to a gay bar.'

'What was the name of the bar?' Tessa asked.

'It was …' Kowalski stopped, frowned. His complexion turned bright pink. He stood, pushing the chair back with so much force it toppled to the floor. He strode towards the door. 'You're full of shit. You haven't seen any video from any bar.'

'Correct,' Joe said. 'But you've just confirmed you spent time at a bar with a woman other than your wife. So we haven't finished with you yet.'

Tessa pointed to the chair on the floor. 'Please, take a seat, Ed. Now, what's her name? The woman at the bar.'

'It's not important. Like I said, it was just a simple flirt, not meant to be serious.'

'Is your simple flirt where you spend your Sunday evenings?' Tessa said.

'No, no, no.'

Joe handed him a business card. 'Write her name and contact

details and we're done, for now.'

Kowalski snapped the card from Joe and scrawled the woman's mobile number on it.

Joe placed the card in his wallet. 'One more thing.'

'You said we were done. I'm leaving.'

'I did, but then I said, "One more thing," so you're not leaving just yet. I'll repeat. One more thing—Sunday evening, three weeks ago, where were you?'

Kowalski twisted his wedding ring. 'I don't remember.'

'Think,' Tessa said. 'You won't be going to your meeting until you remember.'

Kowalski glared at Tessa. 'I was probably finishing a report that was due the following morning.'

***

'I can't believe he fell for the video footage line,' Joe said when Kowalski left the meeting room. 'I thought he was smarter than that.'

'Of course he fell for it. He's smart enough, but he thinks with his cock. He had the hots for Amber and now this brunette. But it looks like it was a different bar from the one Yolanda was at. Was it a coincidence that she saw somebody who resembled Kowalski with a brunette at her bar?'

'There's a lot of bars in the city. On any Friday night at any of these bars there's going to be men flirting with a brunette. And Friday night drinks at a bar is a tradition for Kowalski and his mates.'

Joe looked at the card where Kowalski had written the contact details. 'Kowalski didn't have to check his contacts for her number. He knew it. He's guilty. Even if he's not guilty of murder, he's guilty of something. It was more than a simple flirt.'

'What was he really going to say when he said Amber was nothing but a…?' Tessa said. 'He has an angry streak. Amber said in her journal that he treated her badly after she refused to go to Friday night drinks with him. Did he kill Amber because she rejected him?'

'It wouldn't be the first time that rejection was the motive … not by a long shot.'

'He has no alibi for any of the murders or the attack on Yolanda,' Tessa said. 'If Kowalski is Zoe, why would he kill Phoebe, and Issy too. And Yolanda. Why not just Amber? And why wouldn't he make sure he has an alibi?'

'If he's our killer, I guess he figures having no alibi, is better than us disproving a false alibi.'

'Like we did with Sanders and his Andre mate,' Tessa said.

'Kowalski has no alibi. Sanders has a weak alibi at best.' Joe said. 'Sanders is a liar. Kowalski is a liar. So, which one is our main man?'

27

Joe and Tessa spent the rest of the day back at the station after meeting with Sanders and Kowalski, poring over files and interview notes. The next morning, they pored over more files and interview notes, met with the team and prepared reports before leaving for a midday appointment with Damien to discuss the Johnson rape case. When they left, the sky was thick with heavy dark grey clouds. Ten minutes into the trip, lightning struck, thunder rolled, and the grey clouds turned into rain. The rain turned into a torrential downfall and then came the hail. Along with the harsh weather came the inevitable front bumper bar of one car introducing itself to the rear bumper of the car in front, slowing traffic to a crawl.

Joe frowned and bit his bottom lip.

'Your car will be okay,' Tessa shouted over the noise of the hail. 'They're only pea size stones.'

'Am I that easy to read?'

'Too easy. Your shoulders are almost hugging your ears and your knuckles are as white as Sanders' teeth. I don't know why you didn't use the station car.'

'Hopefully, the hail won't last long. But let's park anyway. Just till it eases.'

'We'll be late for the appointment with Damien.'

'Better late than hail damage.'

'But …'

'There's a Maccas.' Joe pointed to the golden arches. 'Over there. We can grab a coffee and wait in the car park till the weather eases.'

'Get out in this rain?'

'We'll go to the drive-thru. I'll park under that tree. It might offer some protection.' Joe frowned again. 'As long as a branch doesn't fall on it.'

'I can have Maccas? In your car? I thought you banned me from eating in your car.'

'Coffee only–as long as you don't spill it.'

Five minutes later, as they sipped their coffees and watched the rain and the hail, the tension eased in Joe's neck and shoulders. 'It's been a while, but we haven't talked about what happened when you split with Damien. You're a first, you know. He's always the one to end a relationship. How did he take it?'

Tessa shrugged. 'Oh, I don't know. I've never been able to read how he feels about anything. And I should be able to, it's my job to read people.'

'You were too close. Sometimes the people we're closest to are the hardest to read. And often we don't even try to read them, because we think we know them, so there's no need,' Joe said. 'Anyway, how did he react?'

'You know Damien. He never says much. Unless he's in court or being Prince McCharming at a social gathering. But what I do know is, Damien wants to be in control, and he hates to lose. When he lost a case defending a drug dealer last year, back at his apartment, he sat for twenty minutes on the outdoor terrace, not talking, just staring into space. And then, with no warning hurled his drink against the concrete wall. Why would he care what happens to a drug dealer?'

'He doesn't,' Joe said. 'It's all about winning and not losing for him. As you said, he hates to lose.'

'You're right. Even when he's playing computer games, he hates to lose. He'll play for hours until he wins. Until he beats a stupid bloody machine. I guess that drive to always win is why he's such a successful lawyer.'

'Yeah, you're right. He loves to win. When Damien and I were in high school together,' Joe recalled, 'he always got top grades, straight As. Refused to fail at anything. He wasn't allowed to fail. His father wouldn't permit it. Even sport. I was good at sport, but he was excellent. I was good academically. Actually, I was exceptional. But he always outdid me there too. Just by one or two marks most times. Except one time. He only got a B plus grade for a maths exam once. I always got an A plus for maths.' Joe sipped his coffee. 'Anyway, it was in the middle of the rugby season. His mum was okay about it. She always doted on him. Well, before her breakdown.'

'The word is schizophrenia?'

'Whatever. Anyway, when he didn't score an A for his maths exam, Damien's dad wasn't okay about it. Damien didn't play rugby for the rest of the season. Wasn't allowed to play rugby. So, I guess he made sure he never got a poor grade again. And I beat him at chess once. He avoided me for a month. Even now, twenty years later, he always has to prove he's smarter, stronger, more successful ... he's so ... so driven to win—every time at everything. I remember a time when ...' Joe stopped mid-sentence. 'Wow, talking about Damien got my verbal juices flowing. So, what did he say when you told him about Alex?'

'Do you really think he's more successful than you?'

'It's obvious, for a start, compare the cars we drive. And…'

'Depends how you measure success, doesn't it?' Tessa interrupted. 'If keeping criminals out of prison is your measure, then yeah, he's successful. And yes, your verbal juices, whatever that means, flowed.' Tessa smiled in Joe's direction. 'You're good company when you let your hair down. When are you going to ask Olivia out?'

'What did he say when you told him about Alex and that you and he were finished?' Joe asked again, changing the Olivia subject.

'I didn't tell him about Alex. He thinks we're sort of, well, work colleagues.'

'Work colleagues? Alex is a journalist.'

'Doesn't matter what he thinks. I don't care.' Tessa sipped her coffee. 'I just told him I'd had enough of him trying to dictate everything I do. I remember as if it was yesterday. He just stood shaking his head. "Yeah, right," he snickered. "Do what you do second best, darlin' and get me a drink." I turned and walked out. He shouted after me, "You'll be back, you need me." I kept walking. Arrogant jerk. Sorry, I know you two are friends. Anyway, I should have walked away long ago. I guess he was an insurance policy for me.'

'We were pretty good friends in high school, not so much at uni. Even less now, I guess. Anyway, how do you feel about going to see Damien today? Are you okay?'

'It's my job. I can't avoid him forever.'

'This is not your job,' Joe said. 'And you're not the one avoiding Damien. I'm not sure this is the right thing to do. But if anybody is going to do it, it should be Paul. It's his case. And he's the one who convinced Julie Porter to testify against Johnson.'

'Paul's not ready yet to face Damien yet. It's too soon for him.'

'Paul has to accept Damien for who Damien is. And what he

does. He has to accept that it's a defence lawyer's job to defend the guys we catch.'

Tessa stared out the window as she sipped her coffee.

'The sooner Paul accepts it, Tess, the better it will be for him. It's part of his recovery.'

Tessa continued to stare out the window as she spoke. 'You, me, Paul—we all know it's a defence lawyer's job—Damien's job, to defend the bad guys. We accept that. But ...' She stopped and looked directly at Joe. 'You know as well as I do—when the drug dealing rapist that Damien got off, did it again, raped that boy, and the kid committed suicide. Well ... that was the final straw. That's what broke Paul.'

The wild weather eased, but the tension returned to Joe's neck and shoulders. 'It's the system, Tess. That's all we've got. We have to work with the system.'

28

The hail stopped, but the rain didn't. It took them another thirty minutes to drive to Damien's office. Joe knew at this time of the day, in this weather, he wouldn't find a safe park close to the office. He found one three streets away.

'I'm not wearing my new boots in this weather,' Tessa said, as she reached over the back for gumboots. 'We're already late. And you had to park almost in the next suburb.'

'So you think red Wellingtons are a better alternative?' Joe said, shaking his head. 'We have an interview with a lawyer—did you forget?'

'I lived with the lawyer guy for three years—and dumped him. I'm not out to impress him with my gumboots—or anything else.'

'And how did your Wellingtons end up in my car?'

'Gumboots, not wellies. And I checked the weather forecast.' She held up three fingers with her thumb, holding down her pinkie. 'Prepared.'

'But how did they ... never mind.'

They walked the three blocks dodging puddles and the

pointy ends of umbrellas and arrived at Damien's office twenty minutes late. Damien shared the second floor of a modern two-storey glass, concrete, and steel building with financial planners, a firm of accountants and another lawyer. The streamlined reception had pale grey walls and low-level black and chrome lounges. The back wall, a deep charcoal, displayed abstract paintings and prints selected to match the office décor. A selection of Picasso and Ken Done prints on the other walls added colour and the pretence of a welcoming warmth to the reception area.

A man in his late forties with greying ginger hair sat in a chair against the charcoal wall. He didn't look up from his magazine when Joe and Tessa walked in. The thirty-something receptionist, with very bleached platinum blonde hair in a bun and black-rimmed glasses, tapping long red fingernails on her computer keyboard, didn't look up either.

Joe looked at Tessa. Tessa raised her eyebrows and leaned over the receptionist's desk. 'I really hate to disturb you, but …'

'One moment.' The receptionist continued tapping. Tessa tapped her red gumboots, which were almost the same red as the receptionist's fingernails, on the grey-tiled floor.

Joe wondered with amusement which one would win the tap, tap battle when the receptionist stopped tapping and looked up with a smile that didn't quite reach her eyes. 'Can I help you?'

Tessa stopped tapping too. 'Detective Joseph Paterson and Detective Tessa Mariani to see Damien. We have a midday appointment with him. Apologies, we're a few minutes late—the weather…'

'Mr Beresford will be back in about fifteen minutes. Take a seat. There are magazines on the table.' The receptionist turned back to her computer.

'You're new, aren't you? Your name is?' Tessa said.

'Sarah.'

'Well, thank you for your hospitality, Sarah. Yes, we would love a coffee while we're waiting.'

Joe half grinned at Tessa, amused at her 'don't give a shit what anybody thinks,' attitude. Sarah asked how they took their coffee and strode to the kitchen, pursed lips, in three-inch red stilettos.

'Her shoes are the same colour as your Wellingtons,' Joe teased.

'Gumboots.'

'And I don't want to rub it in. But. Aren't you glad we weren't on time?'

Joe and Tessa sat in a lounge diagonally across from the ginger-haired man. 'Don't touch the magazines,' Joe said as he pulled Tessa's hand back from the glass coffee table and nodded at the man across the room. 'You don't know who's been touching them with God knows what on their fingers.'

Tessa watched the ginger-haired man pick his nose, then lick his finger to turn a page. She grimaced. 'Ugh—point taken, you're right,' and flicked through her iPhone instead.

Damien arrived twenty-five minutes later. His charcoal grey suit sat well on a tall, athletic frame. Dark brown eyes contrasted with sandy-coloured hair and a fair complexion.

'Joe, Tessa,' Damien said, nodding in their direction. 'I'll be five minutes. Black coffee, Sarah. And hold all calls.'

'Yes, of course, Damien.' This time the smile reached Sarah's eyes.

Tessa rolled her eyes. 'Yes sir, yes sir, three bags full ...' she whispered. Joe nudged her with his elbow.

Ten minutes later, Sarah announced that Mr Beresford would see them now.

It wasn't the first time Joe and Tessa had been in his

office. The mahogany desk imported from England, matching bookcase, and plush pile grey carpet were in stark contrast to the ultra-modern reception area.

Damien had positioned his desk so he sat facing the door with his back to a large curtainless window overlooking a park, a meandering river, and more office buildings on the other side of the river. He sat behind his desk, polishing his glasses as they entered. The rain had stopped, making way for a bright afternoon sun. The sun shone through the window, backlighting Damien's hair and face, giving him an almost boyish appearance.

Joe studied the glasses and noticed how similar they were to Sarah's. His and hers black-rimmed glasses. *Now I'm catching Tessa's sarcastic sense of humour,* Joe thought, but managed to keep a straight face.

As if reading Joe's mind, Tessa said, 'New frames? I don't remember seeing them before.'

'They're my spares. I'm waiting for a new prescription. But it's no concern of yours, so, let's do away with the pleasantries and get on with it.'

'Your new receptionist, did you find her at the bottom of your cereal box?' Tessa said.

The corners of Joe's mouth twitched in an effort to control his amusement.

'It's after one. I've got a busy afternoon,' Damien said, not amused. 'And I have a paying client, unlike you, waiting for me in reception.'

'And here I was, thinking you'd set aside the entire afternoon for us,' Tessa said. 'I forgot about your drug-dealing clients like ginger megs out there.'

Damien's eyes narrowed. 'Tessa, darling, you really do need to work on your wit. Now, as I said, I'm busy.'

Tessa tilted her head, examined Damien, and stuck out her

bottom lip in a sympathetic gesture. 'Ooh, that's a nasty scratch on your forehead. Aren't you too old to be still playing rugby, Damien? I would have thought ...'

'Damien,' Joe interrupted. 'We've got an update on the Johnson case. We've come across more evidence that Johnson probably wasn't the only one involved in the rape. Another victim has come forward, willing to give evidence.'

'I thought Paul took charge of that case. Anyway, there's nothing to discuss.' Damien stood and walked towards the door. 'And even if Paul was here, there's still nothing to discuss.'

'Sit down, Damien,' Joe said. 'You know Paul's been on stress leave. We're helping him out while he finds his feet again. Just a few minutes of your time. That's all we need.'

Damien sat and started polishing his glasses again. 'Why are you speaking to me about this, Joe? It's not like you to take advantage of our friendship.' He swivelled his chair to face Tessa. 'But I'm not surprised *you* would try to take advantage of whatever there was between us.' Damien glared at Tessa with a tilt of his head and half-lidded eyes. 'What exactly was between us, Tessa?'

'Mm. Let me think.' Tessa rested her chin on her hand and closed her eyes. 'We had … um.' She opened her eyes, pursed her lips, and shook her head. 'Oh, That's right. We had … nothing.'

Damien shook his head and then turned his attention back to Joe. 'Anyway, this is not a conversation we can have. Try speaking to the prosecutor. Not that it'll do you any good. I've got witnesses who place Johnson elsewhere when the rape happened.'

'Druggies. How much is Johnson paying them to lie for him?' Tessa said.

'When you speak to Johnson, tell him there might be a deal to be made if he's willing to name the other person involved,'

Joe said.

'Do I have to repeat myself?' Damien said. 'Speak to the prosecutor.'

'We did,' Tessa said. 'We spoke to him this morning.'

'My darling Tessa, I've known you too long,' Damien said. 'I know when you rub that little notch between your collarbones, you're lying.'

'And I know when your lips move, you're lying,' Tessa said.

Damien stood. 'Obviously, there is nothing to discuss. You're wasting your time. And more importantly, you're wasting my time. As I said, I've got a busy afternoon ahead of me, a paying client waiting for me, and I'm already running late. So …'

'I know it's your job to …' Tessa interrupted.

'I didn't know I had finished speaking,' Damien said.

'I didn't know I was interested in what you were saying,' Tessa retorted. 'As I was saying, I know it's your job to defend this guy. I don't understand how you can, but I know you have to.'

Damien started to interrupt again. Tessa put her hand up in a stop signal. Joe raised his eyebrows and nodded at Damien in a, *You might as well listen,* gesture. Damien sat, leaned back in his chair, and folded his arms.

'I know you have to defend him,' Tessa continued. 'But do you really want to see him get away with this?' Tessa took the photos of the victim out of her bag. 'It's been nearly a year, and Tracy's still under the care of a psychiatrist—unable to return to work.'

The attacker had grabbed Tracy and pulled her into the back of a van when she was walking home from the train station after work. He blindfolded, bashed, and repeatedly raped her. Unfortunately for Johnson, she remembered the letters and the first digit of the van's number plate. A simple process of elimination led the police to Johnson.

'Do you want to see a vicious rapist walk free to do it again to another innocent victim? Win your case at what cost to society?' Tessa said.

'Do you want to convict an innocent man just to close the case? Win the case at what cost to justice?' Damien looked at the photos with cold, unemotional eyes. 'Anyway, she's mistaken about the number plate. The prosecutor won't be able to convince anyone she's a reliable witness. Just like Paul isn't a reliable police officer,' Damien added with a smirk.

'She's not mistaken about the number plate,' Joe said. 'And her name is Tracy. Not a hard name to remember.'

'We'll get him for this one and for Kaitlin Whitaker,' Joe said.

'Kaitlin who?' Damien asked, picking invisible lint from his jacket.

'Kaitlin with a "K", Whitaker,' Joe said. 'Remind Johnson about Kaitlin. She's still in a coma.'

'An even less reliable witness,' Damien said with a half-smile.

'What about some empathy for the victims?' Tessa said.

'Empathy doesn't win cases.'

'Johnson and his cockroach mate are serial rapists.' Tessa pointed at the photos. 'They're low-life cowards who should be in prison getting done to them what they've done to at least three victims.'

'An eye for an eye. How Old Testament of you, Tessa.' Damien stood and marched to the door. 'I repeat. Stop trying to use our relationship to influence the outcome of this case. And because I'm a gentleman, I'll open the door so you can leave, now.'

'C'mon, Tess.' Joe tugged at her elbow. 'Damien is right. We should be talking to the prosecutor.'

Damien examined his fingernails. 'You know I'm always right. Well, once I was wrong when I considered for a split second that I might be wrong sometimes. I dismissed that thought immediately.'

Tessa stood. 'Once again, it's been a pleasure,' she said, giving Damien the middle finger.

'Ever the professional, my darling, Tessa.' Damien returned to his desk. 'Joe, you need to teach your partner better manners.'

'We'll talk to the prosecutor,' Joe said. 'But pass on the message to Johnson. Thank you for your time.'

'Hey, Tessa,' Damien's stern, professional face transformed almost instantaneously into his smiling Prince Charming face. 'I'm looking forward to catching up with your Dad for his birthday. And your Mum. Oh, and Alex, of course. I'm so looking forward to meeting your ... what is Alex exactly?' Damien tilted his head and frowned. '... Your new bed partner? What did your Mamma and Papa say when you told them about Alex? Oh, and your nonnas?'

'Alex and I are just friends. Besides, Alex is none of your business.' Tessa walked to Damien's desk, leaned over the desk so her face was inches from his. 'Everything about me is none of your business.'

Damien stood, forcing Tessa to straighten. 'Can I bring a date?'

'How did you even know about Papa's birthday?'

'Social media, of course, my darling Tessa.' Damien jutted his chin and smirked. 'So, I can bring a date?'

'If I looked up the word "smug" in the dictionary, I'd find a photo of your face next to it.' Tessa turned from the desk towards the door. 'Sure, whatever. Bring a date. It'll be fun to see how the bleached blonde bombshell excuse for a receptionist scrubs up for a barbeque.'

'My date won't be Sarah. And my date won't be wearing red gumboots,' Damien said.

Tessa turned back to face Damien. 'I remember when you used to insist on me wearing my gumboots when we …'

Joe didn't want to hear what was coming next, afraid it might be an image he couldn't unsee. He grabbed Tessa's elbow. 'Come on, we need to get back to the station.'

'Odds on she'll wear pink stilettos,' Tessa mumbled as they walked past Sarah's desk.

Just as they opened the door to leave the office, Damien called out. 'Hey Joe, I just remembered. I'll be down your way next Monday night. Do you want to catch up? It's been a while since I spent some quality time with my old school buddy—just you and me. Away from work. I've got a new boat. It's a nine metre Whittley, but I can tell you all about it when we catch up. And, of course, you can fill me in on what you've been doing. You're going to love seeing the photos of my boat. Give me a call.'

Joe looked at the calendar on his mobile. 'Um … yeah, sure, that should be fine. Around eight. We can grab a bite at the club.'

'My shout. We'll go somewhere a little, no, a lot more upmarket than the club.'

29

It was after one thirty when they left Damien's office. Tessa strode ahead on the footpath still damp from the rain.

Joe wondered how she could walk so quickly in her gum boots. 'Wait up, Tess. What's the hurry? I thought we might stop for coffee, maybe a sandwich. We haven't had lunch yet.'

'Not hungry.'

'Rubbish. You're always hungry. What's wrong?'

Tessa stopped. 'Seriously, Joe? You were pretending to look at your calendar. Your social calendar is empty. Your dates are always spur of the moment. Who are you trying to impress?'

Joe stifled a laugh. 'Are you jealous of me catching up with your old boyfriend?'

'No, that's bullshit. It's just … I don't know, it's just … well, I know you and Damien have been friends for a long time. But the only time he contacts you is when he's got a new car or boat to show off. He's not unlike Sanders. The way he brags about all the stuff he's got. Paid for by drug money.'

'Not drug money. Legal fees. And I know Damien has his faults. But, like you said, I've known him for such a long time. Since we were kids in school together. We've got a history. And I guess I can just ignore the bad bits. No, not bad bits. Irritating bits.'

'Forget it. I just thought you might have better taste in friends by now.'

'Why? Because you broke up with him? Does that mean I have to as well? Anyway, what about your taste? You lived with him for how long?'

'Three years.'

'Right, three years. So, there must have been something about him you thought was okay. Besides, just because he's a talented lawyer, doesn't make him a bad person.'

'Yeah, I guess he has some redeeming qualities. He's not bad looking, if you like that type. He's rich. And most people like that type. Well, not necessarily like. But at least attracted by that type. Perfect teeth—paid for by drug money. I'm sorry, how I feel about him has nothing to do with your friendship. And yes, you're right.'

'I'm right?' Joe said, eyebrows raised.

'Yes, you're right. It's lunchtime and we haven't eaten. And yes, you're right, I'm hungry. There's an okay café around the corner.'

The lunch time rush hour had finished by the time they arrived. They sat at a table near the window and ordered coffee, a hamburger and chips, and a roasted pumpkin salad. Less than ten minutes passed when the waiter brought the meals over. They waited till he left, not wanting to embarrass him, before they swapped their meals with each other, the hamburger for Tessa and the pumpkin salad for Joe.

'What do you think Damien will do about Johnson?' Tessa asked as she pushed her chips towards Joe. 'Have some. I thought I was hungry. I lose my appetite when I think of Damien defending Johnson, and Kaitlin in a coma and God knows how many other rape victims.'

Joe polished his knife and fork with his serviette. 'Damien will do what a good defence lawyer does and defend Johnson to the best of his ability.'

'Without his family,' Tessa said, 'and the wealth they've accumulated from their chain of restaurants, Johnson wouldn't be able to afford Damien.' She poured a glass of water for each of them. 'I hope Julie Porter comes through in court, for Paul's sake and for all the victims, however many that might be.'

They ate in silence for a few minutes. Then Joe put his fork down, folded his arms on the table and looked at Tessa till he got her attention.

'What? Have I got sauce on my nose?'

'You can't keep denying your relationship with Alex. How do you think it would make Alex feel if …?'

'Just like you can't keep denying your relationship with Olivia?'

'It's different. Olivia and I don't have a relationship.'

'That's right, Joe, you just keep denying it.'

'Damien will be at your dad's birthday. What do you think he's going to say to Alex? And to your parents about Alex?'

Tessa pushed her plate away and stared out the window. 'I'll tell him not to come.'

'Yeah, right, that'll work.'

'I'll tell him I'm bringing a pet snake. He hates snakes. The reptile ones, not the slimy ones he defends.'

'You have to tell your family. Don't let them find out from anybody else, especially Damien.' Joe leaned across the table. 'Look at me Tess. You know I'm right.'

'I'm done.' Tessa scrunched her serviette, slammed it on the table, stood, and walked out.

Joe finished his pumpkin salad, folded his serviette neatly so all hemmed edges were hidden, and paid the bill.

***

When Joe turned the last corner, he saw Tessa leaning against the passenger door of his car devouring a chocolate coated ice cream. She looked at him, looked at the ice cream and shrugged. 'Good for the mood.'

On the way back to the station, Joe agreed not to say the Alex word, if Tessa agreed not to say the Olivia word.

Joe took his eyes off the road briefly to look at Tessa when she adjusted her seat to sit straighter. She'd been silent for longer than was normal for Tessa. 'Problem?'

Tessa frowned and shook her head slowly. 'I was just thinking about what I said back at the café. You know, about hoping Julie Porter comes through in court. I just hope she doesn't let Paul down.'

'And the other rape victims,' Joe added.

'I'm just not sure about her.'

'You don't believe her story?'

Tessa nodded. 'I believe her, okay. Remember the first day she contacted Paul, she told him about the twenty-cent piece the rapist shoved in her hand. We hadn't released that information to the media.'

'Sick bastard. Trying to make out his victims are prostitutes.'

'Anyway, the day Paul and I interviewed her—I'm sure she wasn't telling us everything. She told us the truth, but not the whole truth.'

'Why do you think she's holding back?'

'Don't know. She was nervous, understandably upset. But she was reluctant to answer specific questions about Johnson.

We eventually managed to persuade her to provide the details we needed. But it took a lot of coaxing from both of us.'

Joe turned into the station car park. 'From what Paul has told us, Julie's testimony is the icing on the cake for the case. Without it, who knows?'

30

'Y̶ou were right.'

Joe looked up from the interview notes over the partition that separated his desk from Tessa's. 'What about?'

'We shouldn't have gone to see Damien yesterday. Waste of time. Achieved nothing.'

'We got to meet his charming new secretary.'

'Jesus, Joe.' Tessa gaped wide-eyed at Joe. 'Are you kidding? You wouldn't date her. Surely not.'

'Can I have a split second to think about it?' Joe grinned and winked at Tessa, amused at her horror at the thought of him dating Damien's not so charming secretary. 'No, no, no. I wouldn't date her.'

Fifteen minutes after Joe and Tessa resumed digging for clues and possible leads to follow up, Tessa suddenly stood and sang in her best female imitation of Rex Harrison. 'By George, I think I've got it.'

'Really, Tess. Professor Henry Higgins? *My Fair Lady* is even older than the movies I watch.'

'No, Joe, really, I've got it. Issy's link with Amber, Phoebe and Yolanda. Come here, look.' Tessa pointed to her monitor. 'She bookmarked a gay dating site and accessed it a couple of times a month.'

'By George, you have got it.' Joe shook his head. 'You're a genius.'

'I know. I'm good. I had to do a bit of digging to find it. But I did have a few hints and tips from Des and his IT team.' Tessa stood, tilted her head from side to side and stretched. 'By the way, *My Fair Lady* is my favourite musical. I grew up watching it with Mamma. Rainy Sunday afternoons, hot chocolate, homemade amaretti biscuits and *My Fair Lady*.' Tessa rubbed her eyes and stretched again. 'I need coffee before we go any further with this. My turn to make.' She turned to go to the kitchen.

'No wait. Not more kitchen coffee. My shout for a cappuccino.'

'And baklavas?' Tessa said. 'Nik's are the best.'

***

When Joe and Tessa returned with their coffees, they studied the contents of Isabel Reinhard's laptop. Just as Amber had kept her personal activities on her iPad, Issy kept hers on a personal laptop, which she left at her father's house when she visited with him twice a month. It was only after they re-interviewed Issy's father that he remembered she kept her laptop locked in his filing cabinet.

'I hate doing this,' Tessa said. 'Reading their personal correspondence.'

'Agree. It feels intrusive. But ...' Joe shrugged. 'We have to, for Issy. And Amber and Phoebe.'

Tessa sliced off a portion of her baklava. 'And now Yolanda.'

Joe sat back and folded his arms over his chest. 'So, Zoe is

PoodleMum this time.'

'The same Zoe with beautiful long dark hair.'

***

VetChick4

This is my first time here. I'm a little shy and not used to social media. My veterinary science studies take up most of my time. I'm not a vet yet, but I will be in a couple of years. I would love to meet somebody who shares my love of animals. And maybe over time develop a deep relationship. When I have time, I enjoy movies, music and reading, mainly historical novels.

PoodleMum104

Hi VetChick.

You sound like a special person.

Let me introduce myself.

Animals are my best friends.

I have a poodle, a labradoodle, and a cat, and I volunteer at the local animal shelter.

I'm also looking for somebody who shares my love of animals. I'm happy to take things slow if that means developing a deep and lasting relationship.

It sounds like we have a lot in common.

You're going to be a vet, and I have just finished my medical degree.

I spend a lot of hours at the hospital.

So I don't get much spare time either.

But I would love to meet you, maybe over coffee.

VetChick4

You have a medical degree. That's impressive. I'd love to meet you over coffee. Weekends are best. My name is Isabel.

What's your name?

PoodleMum104

Isabel, a pretty name for a pretty girl.

Are you free for coffee on Sunday afternoon?

We could meet outside the QVB, near the Queen Victoria statue, say around three.

VetChick4

Three works for me. What's your name?

PoodleMum104

Perfect.

See you then.

And BTW my name is Zoe.

Ciao.

PoodleMum104

Something has come up—can't make coffee.

Can I buy you dinner tonight to make up for it?

Say 7:30 at the new restaurant near the beach.

The Sandpiper.

It's had excellent reviews.

We should swap mobile numbers.

We can text when we get there.

Ciao.

VetChick4

I don't normally go out Sunday nights. But I'm in between semesters, so maybe I can break the rule just this once.

PoodleMum104

Looking forward to my evening with you.

Ciao.

***

'If only they visited the same dating site,' Joe said when they finished reading the messages. 'We might have a better chance of tracking down Zoe. Before he does it again.'

'If only Zoe hadn't visited any of the sites, maybe we wouldn't have to be tracking him down.' Tessa said. 'Of course we would.' She contradicted herself. 'There will always be victims—until we catch him. Just not Phoebe, Amber and Issy.'

Tessa sipped her coffee and wrinkled her nose. 'This is cold. I'll make fresh coffees then start with Issy's emails.'

'I'll make.' Joe stood. 'I need to stretch.'

'Look at this,' Tessa said, less than ten minutes after she opened Isabel's Inbox. 'An email exchange between Issy and her father. Issy forwarded the emails to her personal laptop at her father's house from her everyday laptop. She must have deleted it—it wasn't on her everyday laptop.'

Dad. *Why is there a charge on my credit card for a dating site?*

Isabel. *Sorry, I lost my credit card. I'll pay you back. You know I'm good for it. Love you. xoxo.*

Dad. *Love you too, baby. But just be careful. I know you will. You're a sensible girl.*

'Explains why there were no charges on her bank statement,' Joe said.

'Just like Amber, Issy kept her very private life totally separate from her daily life.'

Joe sat forward and re-read the email exchange. He slowly shook his head. 'If only she'd taken notice of her father's advice about being careful.'

31

'You guys look pleased with yourselves,' Paul said as he walked towards Joe and Tessa's desks. 'Have you cracked the case?'

'We're on the right track,' Joe said. He felt a renewed energy since Tessa confirmed the link between Issy and the other three victims.

'What've you got that's new?' Paul sat on the spare chair next to their desks.

'We've got our three victims and an attempt on a fourth. And three suspects,' Joe said. 'You know about Aaron Thompson and Ed Kowalski. We've added Phoebe's ex to the list, Sebastian Sanders. But I think we can rule out Aaron Thompson and reduce the number of suspects to two.'

'Agree to a point,' Tessa said. 'But let's go over what we know about Aaron before we cross him off the list.'

'I've been pre-occupied with Julie Porter and the rape case. Can we start from the beginning, so I can catch up?' Paul slid his chair in closer. 'This will be good to get my mind off Johnson and the trial tomorrow.'

'Good idea,' Joe said. 'We need fresh eyes anyway, and it'll be useful for us to recap.'

'The victims. What do we know?' Paul said.

'Female, between the ages of twenty-two and twenty-six, petite, blonde, and either gay or bisexual.' Tessa walked to the board. 'And they subscribed to similar online gay or bisexual dating sites, where the killer lured them to a meeting. That's where the similarities end. There's no work, university, or social connections. Amber was a compliance analyst studying law part time. Issy studied veterinary science—at a different university from Amber. Phoebe worked as a receptionist for a real estate agent, and Yolanda was the last victim. She survived the attack. Yolanda's a high school science and maths teacher. She moved from the country to the city about nine months ago.'

'Let's go back over the timeline,' Paul said. 'When did it start?'

Joe opened his notes but didn't refer to them. He didn't need to. Joe had lived and breathed the case since April. 'The first victim, that we know of was Amber, in April. But I think we can start before that. Sanders, one of our two primary suspects, was in a relationship with Phoebe Duncan until she ended their relationship. That was in January.'

'Agree, the chain of events could have started before the first murder in April.' Paul said. 'If Sanders is the killer and Phoebe broke up with him, the breakup might have been the stressor that triggered him.'

'So, if it's Sanders, he didn't act straight away.' Tessa returned to her desk. 'He controlled his rage for three months, long enough to plan the attacks. But why Amber and Isabel? And Yolanda. Why not just Phoebe? And Phoebe would have recognised Sanders. It would have set off alarm bells for her. She'd arranged to meet a woman, but Sanders turned up instead. Surely, she would have left as soon as she saw him. So did he overpower her before she could run?' Tessa rubbed the back of her neck. 'Too many questions and too many loose ends.'

'Yep, there are still a lot of loose ends,' Joe said. 'But we're getting closer. We've found the link and we've narrowed it down to two suspects, and a possible third.' He went to the board. 'Back to the timeline. Isabel was murdered in July, three months after Amber, and Phoebe was murdered in September, two months after Isabel.'

'Less than a month after Phoebe,' Tessa said, 'he attempted to murder Yolanda.'

'We knew he would escalate,' Paul said. 'And based on what you said the other day about most of the stab wounds being on the left side of the victims, we agreed he's probably right-handed. What else do we know about him?'

'We've got most of what we know about him from Yolanda,' Joe said.

'The one who survived.' Paul frowned. 'What a frightful experience for her. How is she?'

'People are saying she's lucky to be alive. Such a throw away statement,' Joe said. 'She's not lucky. She's a brave young woman who fought hard for her life. And she's smart. Despite the trauma she went through, she remembered several important details about him.'

'Our killer is tall, dark eyes, fair not blonde hair, maybe light brown,' Tessa said. 'And he smokes.'

'Did they find cigarette butts at the murder scenes?' Paul asked. 'You mentioned nothing about cigarettes before.'

'The only evidence they've found so far is a pair of broken glasses with clear lenses,' Tessa said. 'They found them where he attacked Yolanda. And the roses and notes, of course.'

'No cigarette butts.' Paul said. 'So how do you know he smokes?'

'Yolanda smelt tobacco on him when he attacked her,' Tessa

said. 'From what she said, he reeked.'

'So, you've got three suspects,' Paul said. 'With a question mark against Aaron Thompson narrowing the list down to two.'

'We should at least keep Aaron at the bottom of the list but remove him from our focus,' Tessa said. 'He matches the general physical description, and he's a slime and a liar.'

'We know he's a slime,' Joe agreed. 'He made that bet about getting Issy into bed. And he was going to film it as proof. But being a slime doesn't make him a killer. I don't think Aaron is our Zoe. But you're right, we won't cross him off just yet.'

'Zoe,' Paul said. 'Who's Zoe?'

'Zoe is the name the killer used online with all four victims, pretending to be female.' Joe handed Paul printed transcripts between Zoe and the victims. 'Zoe's clever. He changes his persona to reflect the image of the woman he's communicating with online.'

'For example,' Tessa pointed to Phoebe's transcript. 'Phoebe described herself as bubbly, outgoing, and loves to party. Zoe called herself PartyGirl. Amber, on the other hand, was more serious than Phoebe. She was studious, loved learning, but was looking forward to travelling and swapping her textbooks for some lighter reading at the end of the semester. This time Zoe called herself … himself, TravelGirl. Zoe was academic, and of course, enjoyed all the same things Amber enjoyed.'

'And he did the same for Issy and Yolanda,' Joe added. 'He's able to recognise what they need, who they're looking for, and he becomes that person. But he's always Zoe. Beautiful Zoe with long, dark hair.'

'Not only did Zoe enjoy the same things, he also used a similar number in his online name,' Tessa said. 'Amber was 8, TravelGirl was 08. Phoebe was 11 and PartyGirl was 011 and so on.'

'Do you think he meant this to be a sort of subliminal message,' Paul said. 'So they would unconsciously start to feel a familiarity with her—him—and a level of comfort?'

'It's a theory,' Joe agreed.

'Zoe always arranges to meet the dates for an afternoon coffee,' Tessa said. 'Innocent, safe. Who wouldn't agree to a coffee in the middle of Sydney? But something always comes up, so the killer lures them into an evening meeting. *Can I buy you dinner tonight to make up for it? Say 7:30 at the new restaurant near the beach. The Sandpiper.*'

'The Sandpiper,' Paul said. 'So he's a local?'

'Not necessarily,' Joe said. 'But he selected victims from the general area.'

'They're already feeling comfortable with Zoe,' Tessa said. 'So they agree to a Sunday night dinner. Yolanda said she was excited about going to the Sandpiper. Imagine, the anticipation, being from the country and never having been to a fancy restaurant.'

'Yes, you're right,' Paul said. 'Zoe knows how to get his targets interested at the initial contact. Look at Yolanda's transcript. She's passionate about the environment, animal welfare and social justice. Zoe shares Yolanda's passion for the environment and social justice. And animals are Zoe's best friends.'

'Animals are PoodleMum's best friends too, when he's messaging Issy,' Joe said.

Paul skimmed the other transcripts. 'We agreed Aaron is smart and probably creative. But, making a bet with his mates about getting Issy into bed is juvenile behaviour for a man his age. So I doubt he would have the maturity to adapt his persona the way Zoe has. But we can't be sure.' Paul shrugged. 'On the other hand, how smart do you have to be to echo another person's likes and emotions? I'm passionate about animal welfare. Animals are my best friends. What else have we got that puts

Aaron in doubt?'

'He knew Amber and Issy, of course,' Tessa said. 'But there's no evidence that he knew Phoebe or Yolanda.'

'Didn't he say he didn't know Amber?' Paul said.

'Yep, but he lied,' Joe said. 'Amber was a compliance analyst at his company. And when we questioned Aaron's colleagues, it turns out Amber gave compliance feedback on one of his marketing campaigns.'

'So that's why you said he was a slime, *and* a liar. How did he slither his way out of his lie?' Paul asked.

'He said Amber was so insignificant, he forgot,' Tessa said. 'We couldn't prove otherwise. Anyway, Zoe smokes. Aaron's not a smoker. He said he's never smoked and there wasn't a hint of tobacco odour on him or in his unit.'

'When Yolanda looked at the photos,' Tessa added, 'she said he looked younger than the man who attacked her. He's left-handed, and he's the only one of the suspects who doesn't wear glasses.'

'I agree,' Paul said. 'I think you can put Aaron aside. He's a smart, slimy liar. But besides being left-handed, and a non-smoker, he lacks the maturity.'

'We haven't come up with anyone associated with Yolanda yet, who we consider as a possible suspect,' Tessa said. 'And out of all of Issy's family, friends and colleagues, Aaron was the only one that came up as a possibility.'

'It might be somebody that none of them knew,' Paul said. 'Somebody out there who resents whatever it is the victims represent for him.'

'Yeah, we haven't dismissed the possibility,' Tessa said. 'We've got so little to work with. We've got the team following up with online dating companies, to see if we can track down who Zoe is. But he's smart, so odds are he concealed his identity and location by using a virtual private network. We may be able to track him eventually, if he hasn't given the VPN provider a fake identity for billing. So that leaves us with Ed Kowalski and Sebastian Sanders, unless we get a better lead.'

'Pray we don't have to wait for another attack for a better lead.' Joe walked to the window overlooking the car park. The renewed energy and confidence he felt less than thirty minutes ago was beginning to wane. He felt in his pocket for his father's button. 'Which one, Kowalski or Sanders?' he murmured to himself. 'Which one?'

32

'We've all but eliminated Aaron Thompson,' Paul said. 'Can we eliminate either Kowalski or Sanders, or both?'

Joe continued looking out the window. 'We're running out of time, Tess.'

'Can we eliminate either Kowalski or Sanders?' Paul repeated.

Joe ran his hands through his hair. 'All we're doing is theorising. We don't have any evidence. We know how the victims are linked. But we don't know how the killer is linked to them or what his motive is. We know nothing.'

'We do.' Tessa stood, walked over, and placed herself between Joe and the window. 'We've got a description of the killer, we know he smokes, he's right-handed. He has dark, menacing eyes. Although admittedly, victims often remember their attacker as looking more menacing than reality.'

'We have no DNA, no fibre,' Joe said. 'All we have is a possible partial fingerprint on a pair of broken glasses.'

'You know as well as anyone, Joe, that what the killer doesn't leave behind is often a clue.' Paul joined Joe and Tessa at the window. 'Because he doesn't leave anything, we know the killer plans ahead. He's meticulous. He plans every last detail and leaves nothing to chance. He has to maintain control. It's a compulsion. What do we know about Kowalski and Sanders? How do they compare? Can we eliminate one or both?'

Tessa walked to the murder board. 'We have to keep moving on this, Joe.'

'You're right. I'm wasting time we don't have.' Joe took a deep breath and followed Tessa to the murder board. 'Kowalski and Sanders share similar physical profiles. They're around the same age, height, build, hair and eye colouring.' Joe pointed to the facial composite based on Yolanda's limited recall. 'Both vaguely resemble the composite. But look at it, so do I.'

'Only if you dyed your hair and wore coloured contact lenses.' Tessa smirked. 'I think we can cross you off the list.'

'They're both right-handed, and they both smoke,' Joe continued. 'Sanders practically chain-smoked when we were interviewing him. Both are married, but Sanders is separated. They are both well off and drive a dark coloured German car. Although, Sanders is off the scale wealthy.'

'Both are intelligent, self-centred and arrogant,' Tessa said. 'Phoebe's sister, Sally, described Sanders as having superficial charm. Pretend charisma if that's possible. Sanders did display superficial charm when we were at his unit the first time we interviewed him.'

'Penthouse, Tess.' Joe grinned. 'Sanders corrected you several times about that.'

Tessa rolled her eyes. 'As I was saying, he offered us drinks, prepared a plate of cheese, crackers, and strawberries. But the charm slowly slipped away. When we delved more deeply than he expected into his relationship with Phoebe, his demeanour changed. His true, arrogant self, surfaced.'

'What about Kowalski?' Paul said.

Joe shook his head emphatically. 'Not even pretend charm when we interviewed him.'

'According to what Amber wrote in her journal, he was a pig to her,' Tessa said. 'And she caught Kowalski and his mates watching porn at work.'

Joe frowned. 'I don't know why people use pig to describe unpleasant people. Pigs are highly intelligent and can make a nice pet. Sorry, I digress. Kowalski's team had positive comments about him as a manager. They like him.' He shrugged. 'So maybe Kowalski can be charming when it counts.' Joe made a finger quote sign when he said 'charming.'

'And of course, they denied the porn thing,' Tessa said. 'Do you remember Harvey Cosgrove, the jealous colleague, didn't want to speak ill of the dead, but said Amber sucked up to the bosses. Well, Kowalski's team had nothing positive to say about her either. Amber didn't win any popularity contests at work. But her friends and family loved her.'

'How many on Kowalski's team?' Paul asked.

'Five men,' Tessa said.

'How many women?' Paul asked.

'Five men,' Tessa repeated.

Paul nodded. 'Boys' club. So, both men are smart, arrogant, can be pleasant when it suits them, and not so pleasant when they're not getting their way. Anything else?'

'There were times when we interviewed them that each of them displayed signs of anger. But they both managed to keep their cool,' Joe said.

'Interesting,' Paul said. 'Obviously, neither has an airtight alibi.' He walked to the murder board and studied the photos of the victims. Joe could see the pain in his eyes, but Paul didn't look away this time. 'Who *are* you, Zoe?'

33

Tessa loved her family, her mamma and papa and her brother. Her very Catholic family. Tessa loved Alex too—loved her so, so much. She kept thinking about what Joe said, that she should tell her family about Alex. Her mamma and papa were so fond of Damien. They had hopes of Tessa marrying Damien, giving them grandchildren. Oh God, grandchildren! She and Alex could have children. She knew two other gay couples who have children. Would her parents accept that? Would her brother accept that? Shit. Holy shit, what would her nonnas say?

Marriage. Joe was the first to mention the marriage word as they walked back to the car after they interviewed Sebastian Sanders. What if she and Alex do want to get married one day? Joe is right. She can't keep her relationship with Alex a secret forever. What if her family found out before she told them? That would hurt them. But how to tell them? When to tell them? They know Alex. They like Alex. And they think she's a nice friend, a good influence, the way she dresses, the way she talks, sort of refined, not unlike Damien in a way. But not like Damien. Damien was self-centred, controlling, and domineering. Alex cared for other people. She was kind. Damien would complain that Tessa spent too much time playing her guitar. Alex promised they would have a dedicated music room one day where Tessa could play her guitar and write music. Damien and Alex were so similar in some ways, but polar opposites where it counted. Just like Joe and Damien. The same, but different. They were both intelligent, attractive, successful, although Joe would deny his own success. But unlike Damien, Joe cared for the victim. Fought for the victim. Damien fought for the accused. Even if the accused was guilty. But that was his job. Wasn't it?

Damien will be at the barbeque. And Alex. Joe was right. Tessa couldn't trust Damien not to blurt out what he thinks her relationship is with Alex.

There was only one person in Tessa's family who she felt comfortable with, who she could tell and get advice from and rely on that advice. Her mother's sister. Sister Rose.

Tessa sat in her car, parked across the road from the convent school, leaned back in the seat and thought about the phone call that changed her life. She remembered the day clearly, even the weather. The rain drizzled all day with no end in sight. A grey day that didn't foreshadow the happiness that she would soon experience. Just over a year ago her life was heading in one direction, and then as the saying goes, life turned on a dime for Tessa, with just one phone call. She remembered that call as though it happened that morning.

'Detective Tessa Mariani.'

'Hello, detective Mariani. My name is Alexandra Jackson. I'm a journalist.'

Tessa poked her tongue out at the phone. 'I have nothing to report.'

'Just give me ninety seconds to explain.'

'Clock's ticking.'

'I'm a freelance journalist and I'm researching an article about women in the police force. How they're treated by other officers, how they advance their careers, the impact on their family life, why they joined in the first place. I'm researching the history and progression of female police officers in Australia.'

'And you want some first-hand insights from me, blah, blah, blah. Right?'

'Well, yes, I'd really appreciate your time. My shout for coffee, lunch, a glass of wine—whatever. Your choice, my wallet.'

Tessa warmed to the sound of Miss Jackson's mellow voice. Or is it Mrs Jackson? And to a free glass of wine. She wouldn't choose a very expensive one, but it would be a nice one.

'Mm ... okay. I'll meet you at the local tonight. Say six-thirty. How will I recognise you? What are you wearing?' Tessa said.

'Don't worry,' Alexandra Jackson said. 'I'll recognise you.'

Tessa could hear the warm smile in Alexandra's voice when she said, 'How many times has your photo been in the media? Tall, with long hair that has the colour and gloss of tempered dark chocolate, alert but soulful brown eyes. Right?'

Tessa smiled at the memory of the tingling sensation she felt at the sound of Alex's voice and her seductive way with words.

When she finished the call with Alex, Tessa called Damien to let him know she'd be about forty to forty-five minutes late and could he grab some take away for dinner.

When she walked into the pub that evening, a pretty woman at a table near the middle of the room stood and waved to her. She looked a little younger than Tessa, maybe twenty-eight. She had blonde hair cut in a shoulder-length bob and wore glasses with dark green frames.

They ordered a bottle of sparkling mineral water, a glass each of a Western Australian chardonnay that Tessa selected, and potato chips.

'Thank you so much for meeting with me. And my friends call me Alex.'

Tessa raised her eyebrows. 'Oh, so we're friends now, after five minutes and one sip of wine?'

Alex blushed. 'Sorry, I didn't mean …'

'No, I'm sorry,' Tessa said. 'I can be sarcastic sometimes, no, not sarcastic, call me rude. Let's start again—Alex.'

'Okay, thanks. Let me tell you where I'm up to so far with my research.' Her eyes, the colour of jade, sparkled as Alex moved her chair closer to the table. 'Lillian May Armfield, who was born on the third December eighteen eighty-four, was one of the first female police detectives in Sydney. She joined the New South Wales police force in nineteen-fifteen.'

For the next ten minutes Alex described her research about the struggle by female police for equality, integration, and acceptance by their male counterparts. Tessa was impressed by her intelligence and her eloquence. But what really impressed Tessa was Alex's passion for the subject.

'I don't want my name associated with your article.'

'No, absolutely not, I promise.'

They met again a few nights later. And Alex published her article the following week. Tessa called Alex the next day. 'Congratulations. Great article.'

'Thanks. Can I buy you a thank you drink?'

'Um … ah,' Tessa hesitated. Her tummy was fluttering. *What's happening here?* 'Thanks, but I've got to get home. Maybe we can catch up for coffee one day. My shout this time.'

They met the following week, and then the following day, and then the following night.

***

The clanging of the three-fifteen school bell, and the squeals of the students free at last, took Tessa even further back in time to when she was a student at that same school. The old brass school bell, the same bell that signalled the start or the end of the day when Tessa was a student at St Joseph's, reminded her of a time … *No, enough reminiscing,* she thought. Tessa sat up straight, tightened the band around her ponytail and got out of her car. She took a deep breath, held it for a count of six, and then walked across the road to the path that led to the convent. She hesitated at the door, took another deep breath, and then pressed the doorbell.

After about fifteen seconds, Tessa changed her mind and turned to leave just as an elderly nun opened the door. 'Hi Tessa, how are you? Is Sister Rose expecting you?'

'How are you, Sister Therese? Yes, she is. I called her earlier.'

'I'll let her know you're here.' Sister Therese opened the door wider and beckoned Tessa in. She gestured towards a room at the end of a long, dark hallway. 'You can wait in the library. Would you like tea?'

'Coffee. No, sorry, not coffee. Water would be great. Thanks.'

The library where Tessa had visited her aunt many times over the years was used more often as a meeting room than a library. When she entered through the double doors, her eyes were drawn to the floor-to-ceiling stained-glass window at the end of the room. The light from the afternoon sun reflected a rainbow of colours through the stained glass, giving a soft warm glow to an otherwise dark, cold room. An old lounge with cracked brown leather sat in front of the window. The permanent deep indents in the cushions were testament to the many who had sat there over the years. Six ornate chairs encircled an oval timber table, polished to a mirrorlike gloss, at the end of the room opposite the window. Tessa wasn't an expert on period furniture, but she thought the table looked to be from the late nineteenth or early twentieth century. Reminiscent of the furniture in *My Fair Lady. Would that make it Victorian,* she wondered? A large, ornate grandfather clock dominated the corner near the window. The library's walls were a pale yellowy cream, not a colour Tessa would choose. The middle of one wall had a crucifix surrounded by four large, brass-framed photos of nuns from a time long past, wearing habits rarely seen these days. The only concession to the twenty-first century was a laptop which sat on an antique desk under the crucifix.

Tessa wandered over to the bookcase that occupied the entire wall opposite the crucifix. The bookcase housed mostly primary school textbooks, Bibles, history books and various reference books, mainly religious studies. The scent of the highly polished timber floor reminded Tessa of her primary school days when she went to the convent twice a week for piano lessons. And of the horrified look on Sister Mary Angelica's face when Tessa told her she wanted to stop piano lessons and learn guitar instead. Tessa smiled at the memory. The smile faded when Tessa heard the door open and remembered why she was there.

***

Just as the grandfather clock chimed three-thirty, Tessa sat next to her aunt on the lounge. Despite, or because of its age, the lounge was comfortable, even comforting.

Tessa studied her aunt. Sister Rose was three years younger than Tessa's mother but looked older. *It's the grey hair and no makeup,* Tessa thought. Tessa's mother coloured her hair every four weeks and didn't leave the house without foundation and mascara.

'It's so lovely to see you my sweet girl. What've you been up to? How's Damien? I'm looking forward to catching up with him at your papa's birthday. He will be there of course, won't he? Such a lovely young man. And I understand he used to visit his poor dear Mamma in the nursing home every Sunday. How long has it been now? From memory she died just after Christmas.'

It was a family trait to ask a question and then another without waiting for an answer to the first and then continue their dialogue as if they hadn't asked a question in the first place. It didn't bother Tessa. She'd inherited the same trait. She sipped her water and waited for Rose to pause for air.

'I need to talk to you about something.' Tessa fought back tears. *No, not now,* she thought. She didn't want to lose control in front of her aunt.

'Oh, my poor sweet thing. You're upset. What is it? Is it Damien? How can I help? Tell me what's happened.'

'In a way it's about Damien, and it's not about Damien.' Tessa swallowed. 'It's about somebody else. And I don't know how to tell Mamma and Papa. I love you Aunt Rose. I love Mamma and Papa too, of course, but you're the only one I can talk openly to.' Tessa wiped a tear from her cheek. 'I don't know how to start, where to start.'

Rose took Tessa's hand. 'Just start at the beginning, my sweet.'

So she did. Tessa told her story. Rose held Tessa's hand and listened for a full ten minutes without interrupting. Tessa let out a breath and sank deeper into the lounge. 'That's it. Thank you for listening.'

Rose remained silent. She let go of Tessa's hand, stood, and walked to the desk under the crucifix. She looked up at the body on the crucifix and made the sign of the cross.

Oh God, she's shocked, Tessa thought. *What was I thinking?*

'I'm sorry Aunt Rose. I shouldn't have burdened you with this.'

'Yes, you most definitely should have.' Rose returned to the lounge. 'And you're not burdening me, my dear.'

'But ...' Tessa frowned and shook her head. 'But you're not saying anything. I've never heard you not say anything before. You always have something to say. I'm sorry, I've upset you.'

'If I'm upset, my sweet girl, it's because I feel the pain you feel ... thinking you can't be open and honest with your parents. Joe is correct. You must tell your parents. Listen to Joe. He's a good friend. He's a good and honest person.'

'If it wasn't for the Catholic thing,' Tessa said. 'You know, what the Church says about homosexuality.'

'And what do you think the Church says?'

'I've done some research. I've got notes ... from a Catholic website. For example, and I guess this passage applies to women too.' Tessa read from her notes. 'You shall not lie with a male as with a woman; it is an abomination ... If a man lies with a male as with a woman, both of them have committed an abomination; they shall be put to death, their blood is upon them.'

Tessa handed Rose her notes. 'Really, put to death? Obviously, that won't happen. But the Church is serious about this.'

'That passage is Old Testament. How much research have you done?'

'Not too much. Joe and I are caught up in a case.'

Sister Rose stood and walked to the desk. She opened the laptop. 'It might surprise you, but I'm not a stranger to this topic. We often counsel young gay men and women. There's a website I want you to see. It provides support for gay Catholics and their families.' Rose emailed the link to Tessa and returned to the lounge. 'Look at the site when you go home. It will give you comfort and assurance that God still loves you.' Rose winked. 'And the Church isn't going to put you to death.'

'That's all good. But what about Mamma and Papa? And my brother? What am I going to tell them?'

217

'Give them the credit they deserve for who they are. They love you and they are so proud of you, my sweet. Tell them exactly the same way you told me. Be honest with them.'

'I have to wait for the right time.'

'Now is the right time. It's my turn to quote now. It's my favourite quote, and it's from the New Testament.' Rose held Tessa's hand again. 'Faith, hope and love. The greatest being love. Have faith in your parents, hope in yourself, and love for your family. It might be a cliché. There are so many songs about it these days, but love *is* the greatest gift.'

Tessa's eyes watered again. 'You're right. Thank you.'

Sister Rose frowned. 'Why haven't I heard before now that you broke with Damien?'

'You've been busy, I've been busy, you know how it is.' Tessa patted her aunt's hand. 'Mamma and Papa were in Italy visiting all our relatives for over three months earlier in the year. Time slips by. I'll let you know how I get on. And you'll meet Alexandra at Papa's birthday. You did say you were coming, didn't you? Nonna Bella and Nonna Bernadetta and …'

'Yes, yes my dear, I'll be there.'

Tessa grinned. 'You know, this might be a good article for Alex. "The Catholic Church and homosexuals." I guarantee she'd research the shit out of… Sorry I mean, she'd do more in-depth research than I did.'

Rose laughed and hugged Tessa. 'Feeling better now are you my sweet thing.' Then with both hands still on Tessa's shoulders, Rose looked directly into Tessa's eyes. 'You will tell them … won't you?'

When Tessa reached her car, she turned to wave to her aunt. Sister Rose waved and smiled a half smile that quickly faded and was replaced by a frown. *She knows,* Tessa thought. *She knows I still have doubts about telling Mamma and Papa.*

34

The marquee, decorated with party balloons and streamers, occupied the end of Tessa's parents' half acre backyard closest to the kitchen. Joe sat at the large teak timber table between Sister Rose and Dean. Dean's wife, Lorna, sat opposite, next to Joe's mother.

Despite the loud conversation and laughter of friends and family enjoying each other's company, celebrating Tessa's father's birthday, the sounds were a muffled background noise to Joe's thoughts. Abba sang 'Dancing Queen'. Wind chimes glistened in the sun and played their own tune in the gentle breeze that carried the mouth-watering aroma of garlic bread and barbequed onions. Saturday. It should be a time to relax and not think about work. But Joe couldn't relax. Tessa's guitar leaned against the wall next to her brother's, ready for a jam session. Maybe he should have brought his guitar—might have helped him strum the tension from his shoulders. His mind drifted back to the case. *Edward Kowalski, Sebastian Sanders—which one? What are we missing?*

The track changed to 'Take a chance on me', tugging Joe's

mind back to the barbeque. He watched the cheerful faces. Tessa's father pouring drinks, his mother and Lorna laughing at something Dean said, Damien passing cheese and crackers to the nonnas, Damien's date—*whatever her name is, and who cares*, Joe thought, *we'll probably never meet her again*—was talking to Sister Rose. *What the hell did they have in common?* Joe wondered. He sniggered to himself. *Sorry, Sister, I meant what on earth* … He wondered what time Paul and Trudi would turn up and guessed they were caught up with wedding plans. *Has Paul proposed to Trudi yet?* Joe wondered.

Then his eyes drifted to where Olivia was placing Bonnie and Sammy's water bowls under the shade of an Acacia tree. Sammy had growled at Damien when he arrived. Joe chuckled when he thought about what Dean said to Sammy. 'It's okay, we know he's a lawyer, but somebody's gotta do it.' He watched Sammy limp to the bowl. The limp was more pronounced than it was the other night when he had dinner at Dean's house. Joe thought about going over to Olivia. Maybe share Dean's lawyer joke with her. 'Take a chance on me' played over in his mind. She looked up from the water bowls, looked at him, her lips parted and full for an instant, and then they were a thin line as she looked down again. What was in her eyes? He couldn't tell. Was it hurt, confusion, even anger? He didn't know.

Joe turned his attention to Tessa and Alex. They were talking to Tessa's parents and her brother. Tessa's mother smiled, put an affectionate arm around Alex. Her father refreshed their drinks. Tessa tapped her chest and blew a kiss to her aunt, Sister Rose. Tessa's brother left the group, hands in his pocket and head bowed. Joe noticed Tessa frown as she watched her brother until he disappeared inside the house and then turned her attention back to her parents and Alex.

Joe smiled. *You did the right thing at last, Tess. You told them.*

Not sure this was the right time, but … Joe had noticed Tessa call her parents to one side when Damien arrived. He guessed Tessa hoped Damien wouldn't show. But when he did, Tessa probably had no choice but to tell her parents. Tell them before Damien made one of his smug comments about her relationship with Alex.

Joe's eyes wandered over the gathering again. *Such good people,* he thought. *Why can't everybody be good people? Be happy?*

Joe hadn't noticed that Dean had left his chair until he sat next to Joe again and placed a bottle of sparkling mineral water in front of him. 'Looks like you're having your own party. Can I join? You've been quieter than usual. The case?'

'No. Just enjoying being here with all my friends.' Joe pointed to the dogs. 'Looks like Bonnie and Sammy enjoy barbeques. Bonnie is handling the noise and the people better than I thought she would.'

'I'd say they're enjoying Olivia's attention. I'd say you'd enjoy Olivia's attention too.'

'Jesus, Dean. Don't *you* start too. Olivia and I are colleagues—that's all.'

'Do you look at all your colleagues with those puppy dog eyes?'

Joe stood. Dean tugged Joe's arm. 'Okay, I'll stop. Sit down. Keep me company. Tell me about the case. What's new? You can deny it. But I can tell, it's been on your mind all afternoon.'

Joe felt his eyes sting—the sting you get when you hold back tears. He thought about what his mother said. *You didn't cry when your father died.* He opened his mouth to say something—couldn't—swallowed.

Dean handed him the mineral water. 'Here, drink. Get rid of the lump I know is in your throat. And talk to me.'

Joe drank from the bottle, wiped his mouth, and took a

deep breath, fighting off the anxiety attack that was threatening. 'I know it's a cliché, but I can't think of another way to describe it. I can't unsee the victims. I'm here with these beautiful, wonderful friends. They mean the world to me. *You* mean the world to me. But I can't let go of the images long enough to be a part of the festivities, to enjoy myself.'

Dean squeezed Joe's arm. 'You're starting to let your emotions show, not hold back. That's the beginning. That's how you'll get through this. I told you, I lost count of how many times Lorna held me while I sobbed. I let go. You have to let go.'

Joe looked up and saw Olivia watching them. This time, he knew what was in her eyes. It was understanding. It was the same gentleness he saw in Paul's eyes, saw in his father's eyes. He knew she saw his pain. He looked away, unsure how he felt about being so transparent.

***

The gathering ate, sang 'Happy Birthday', and indulged in the Italian rum birthday cake. Then they demanded live entertainment. Tessa's brother, Tony, had a spare guitar. With some not so gentle persuasion from Tessa, Joe joined the brother and sister in a medley of eighties' rock songs.

'It's my birthday,' Tessa's father said. 'How about a nice ballad for your papa?'

They sang George Harrison's 'Something'. Joe focussed on not letting his eyes meet Olivia's as he sang. Then he looked at her for a split second. She was smiling. Was there something, somewhere in that wonderful smile that crinkled her nose?

Joe had that special butterflies-in-the-tummy feeling that Tessa talked about. But not just his tummy, his entire body. *Don't get carried away*, he thought. *It's just a song … the most beautiful love song ever, but just a song.* He looked up again. Olivia held his gaze for just a moment before he looked down at his guitar again.

The trio declined the encores and Joe finally relaxed, joined in a game of backyard cricket with the lucky ones who weren't clearing the tables or in the kitchen loading the dishwasher. The game finished when Damien, true to form, forgot it was a friendly game and not a competition and hit the ball over the fence. 'Sorry,' he said. 'Maybe one of the hounds can fetch it.'

'Maybe you can go woof, woof, and jump over the fence and fetch it yourself,' Tessa said.

'I've missed your charm, my darling Tessa.' Damien smiled, but dark sunglasses masked whatever feelings his eyes might reveal.

'Anyway, we have other arrangements this evening,' Damien continued. 'So, we must be on our way now.' He walked over to Joe, put his empty glass on the table, and extended his arm to shake hands. 'Don't forget Monday night. Call me.' He kissed Tessa's mother and each of the nonnas on the cheek, shook Tessa's father's hand and said, 'Happy birthday, sir. Thanks for the invite, Tessa. It's been fun. Ciao everyone.'

Joe's eyes narrowed as he watched Damien leave. He remembered a twenty-year-old Damien tackling an opponent in a touch football game when his team was behind in points. The tackle, in what was supposed to be a friendly touch, not tackle, football game on the beach at the end of the semester, put a young man, fifteen kilos lighter than Damien, in hospital. *You hate to lose, don't you, Damien? So, is this what it's come to?*

Joe turned his attention to Tessa, tall, long dark hair, and Alex, petite and blonde. He watched them watching Damien leave. Alex smiled a shy, almost embarrassed smile as Tessa gave Damien not one, but two, birdy fingers behind his back.

The gentle breeze that cooled the day turned into a blustery howl that threatened the weaker branches on the tall Eucalyptus trees. Joe didn't notice the wind. He sat with his elbows resting on the table, fingers interlocked under his chin. *Alex, petite and blonde. How did we miss it? It's been there in front of us the whole time.* He didn't know how much time had passed when he felt a tug on his arm.

'Joe,' Tessa said. 'Mission control to Joe. Where are you?'

'Sorry, just thinking about something.'

'The case. Right? You were off the planet when you first got here, then back on earth, and now you're gone again.' Tessa looked around. 'And where's Paul? Did he tell you he's going to propose to Trudi today? He's giving her his grandmother's diamond ring. When he told me in the car the other day, 'Love Is in the Air' was playing on the radio. It was so perfect—it could have been staged. So, so romantic.'

Olivia carried a plate of cupcakes over and sat next to Joe. 'I thought you might need some refreshment after your performance. I didn't realise you were so talented. The three of you. I thought maybe ...'

Joe kissed Tessa on the cheek. 'I'm sorry, Tess. It's been a great afternoon. And it's wonderful you told your parents about Alex. But ... um ...'

'I know, you have to go.'

Joe nodded, turned to say goodbye to Olivia, and realised he was talking to an empty chair.

35

The words to 'Run For Your Life', kept replaying, over and over, in Joe's head as he drove to the station. He wondered how many men would really rather see their wives or girlfriends dead than with somebody else. He was thinking about how John Lennon regretted composing this song when he missed his turn.

Joe's head was spinning, alternating between Lennon's song and something else that nagged him in the back of his mind. *It's there,* he said to himself, *it's in the files.*

When he drove into the car park, he saw Paul's car. *What the … why is Paul here?*

Paul wasn't at his desk when Joe walked into the station. Joe checked the kitchen. Not there. He shrugged and went to his desk. He took out the case files and opened his laptop, but now something else nagged at him. This time, it wasn't the case distracting him. It was something distracting him from the case. *Where are you, Paul?*

Joe rang Paul's mobile. Paul's mobile played the standard iPhone ringtone. It was on Paul's desk. Joe rang Trudi. 'Do you know where Paul is? His car and his mobile are here, but I can't find him… Don't worry, he was probably meeting somebody about one of his cases … forgot to take his mobile … I know, he's too conscientious… Yes, I promise I will. And you let me know if you hear from him.'

Joe searched the station. No Paul. He went back to Paul's desk. He froze. Why hadn't he noticed it before? The note.

It won't leave me. I'm desperate. I can't face it anymore. I know it'll still be here when I'm gone. But I can't. I just can't face it. Understand me, Joe. I love you. Forgive me, Trudi. I love you so much.

The note, written with a trembling hand and smudged with tears, was barely legible.

Joe tried to get into Paul's head. Where would he go? He wasn't in the station. Joe searched every office, meeting room, even the toilets. He can't be far. His car is here. Could he be at the park? No. Paul is too kind. He wouldn't do what Joe knew he was going to do. Or has done. Not where a child or civilian would find him. Paul has to be here. Of course he's here. Joe ran outside, behind the station.

Paul was slumped on the concrete ground against the recycled brown brick wall at the back of the police station, unaware of Joe's approach. His Glock rested loosely in his hands between his knees. He stared off into the distance. Joe recognised the look on Paul's face, the thousand-yard stare. The unfocused gaze of someone who has seen too much horror, too much trauma. Had Joe seen the same empty stare in his father's eyes fifteen years ago, he wondered.

Joe walked to Paul with measured, quiet steps, and sat against the wall next to him. He put a protective arm around Paul's shoulder.

'Why aren't you at the barbeque?' Paul said without looking at Joe.

'Why aren't you? Trudi is waiting for you to call her.' Joe looked at Paul, saw tears run down his cheeks and mix with tears already shed.

'Everything has gone to shit. Johnson … not guilty. Damien got him off … they found the bastard not guilty. Julie Porter didn't turn up to court. I rang. She didn't … wouldn't answer her phone.' Paul wiped the tears from his face. 'Tracy is still seeing the psychiatrist. She testified. But Damien, true to form, rattled her. Had her convinced she didn't remember Johnson's number plate. And…'

'And what?'

'And Kaitlin is dead. She never came out of the coma. They took her off life support.' Paul's voice was monotone, emotionless and empty, like his gaze. 'What's it all for, Joe? What we do is meaningless.'

'Don't do this, Paul. You and Trudi made plans.' Joe squeezed Paul's shoulder. 'Tessa said you were going to propose to Trudi at the barbeque today. The ring. You're going to give Trudi your grandmother's diamond ring.' Joe tried to keep a calm tone, but knew he was failing. 'Think about Trudi. Your life together. Your future together.'

'I *am* thinking about Trudi. We don't have a future. You know that. You've seen it too many times. What the partners go through. They suffer too. I can't put her through that.'

'You worked through it together before.' Joe felt his heart thudding in his chest. 'And you can do it again.'

'You saw first-hand what your mother went through before your father … before he …'

Joe sat back against the cold wall, felt the sharp edges of the brick like a knife in his back, but ignored the pain. 'Go on, you can say it. Before he shot himself. My mother was happy before. But after … Yes, I saw what my mother went through,

227

year after year. Sad. Abandoned. She suffered after my father killed himself, not before. She'll never, never get over it. Sure, she learned to laugh again. But she never learned how to be happy again. She lost the capacity—the desire to ever be happy again when she lost him. My mother would feel guilt ridden if she ever let herself be happy. Which means she can never be truly happy. Don't do that to Trudi.'

'Admit it, Joe, you've never allowed yourself to commit to a relationship. You know what our life does to our partners. I can't put Trudi through that.'

Joe looked at the black metal in Paul's hand. 'Give it to me, Paul.'

'Every night. The nightmares. Every day. The visions ... the visions. They're imprinted on my eyelids. A permanent reminder. I'm sick to the stomach, always sick.' He pointed the gun at his head. Took it away, pointed it to the ground. 'Do you know what it's like to think—no, not think—know that you'll always be sick to the stomach. That it'll never go away.' His face was covered in tears and snot. He pointed the gun at his head again.

Joe squeezed Paul's shoulder again. He hoped the touch of another human being would help to ease Paul's pain. But deep down, he knew it wouldn't. 'I'm so sorry about what's happened. How it's made you feel. But think about it. Give yourself time. We can get through this together. Think of Trudi. Don't do this to Trudi. You love her. She loves you so much. Remember what you told me. That you want you and Trudi to grow old together. Trudi wants that too.'

Joe released the tight grip on Paul's shoulder. He closed his eyes and rested his head against the wall. 'Think about the Paul in the future. No, don't think. Imagine. Imagine the Paul in the future. The married Paul with a family. Is this what that Paul in the future would want?'

Paul lowered the gun. 'I'm sorry ... I can't ...' He raised the gun and pointed the gun at his head again.

Joe pleaded. 'Put down the gun. I'll take you to hospital. We can work through this. We worked through it before. You worked through it before. We'll do it better this time. Give yourself time ... don't make me lose my best friend. For me, for Trudi, put the gun down, Paul.'

Joe reached over to Paul's arm and gently coaxed it down.

Paul pulled his arm from Joe. 'I can't ... I can't ... everywhere there's horror, cruelty ... there's no end ... there's only one end.'

The howling wind gave way to dark, grey clouds. The night came earlier than it should have, and the lengthening shadows moving across Paul's face grew darker.

Joe put his arm around his friend's shoulder again, pulled him in closer. 'Whatever you do, Johnson is a free man. You can't change that. But you can make a difference. Don't rob the world of that difference, even if it's just one family or just one person. It will be a tragedy to them if you don't make that difference.' Joe pleaded again. 'Don't force me to live with the vision of my best friend dying. It would stay with me for the rest of my life. Think of me.'

Paul looked up into the distance, but not the thousand-yard stare this time. He squinted and nodded, as though seeing something for the first time. He lowered the gun to the ground. 'You're right. You're always right. I love you, Joe.'

36

'Do you have plans for tonight? I mean ... have you got time to come back to the station?' Joe asked Tessa as they left the hospital emergency.

'We should have stayed with Trudi. At least until they get Paul settled into the ward.'

'Paul's in excellent hands. Your aunt, I mean Sister Rose, she'll stay as long as Trudi needs her. We'd just be in the way.' Joe wished he had more words to reassure Tessa that Paul would be okay. *How can I convince Tess if I can't convince myself,* he thought? 'So, can you come back to the station?' Joe asked again.

'Has this got anything to do with why you left the barbeque so early?' Tessa said.

'Yep.'

'Yes, I had plans for tonight. Yes, I can break them. And yes, I can come back to the station. I caught a taxi here, so I'll go back with you.' She caught Joe's glance. 'No, I didn't drink much. All I had was a prosecco and two of Papa's favourite chiantis. And it's been hours since I had the last wine.'

'Where's your car?' Tessa said when they reached the main

door of the hospital.

Joe looked sheepish. 'At the back of the car park.'

'Of course it is. Do you have an umbrella?'

'It wasn't raining when I parked the car. And given the circumstances, I wasn't thinking about the weather forecast.'

'Well, it's pissing down now.'

'You stay here, I'll get the car.'

Joe ran seventy metres to his car. With thoughts of Paul and the case, he dismissed any concerns about getting into his car with wet shoes.

Joe saw Damien talking to Tessa as he drove back towards the hospital entrance. When Joe pulled up next to them, Damien gave Joe the 'ring me sign', opened his umbrella and walked towards the car park.

'Why was Damien here?' Joe said as Tessa climbed into his Monaro. 'What did he want? I thought he had plans tonight. Where's his car?'

'What is this, the twenty-one questions game? My favourite is, if you had a time machine, would you go back in time or visit the future?'

Joe turned to face Tessa. 'What did Damien want?'

'Okay, okay. Papa rang him and told him about Paul. So he came to see him. I told him Paul is in intensive care and maybe come back tomorrow. What's the big deal? He was acting considerate for a change—well, pretending anyway. It's out of character for him to show he cares about anyone but himself. But I guess because Papa rang him, he felt obliged. For whatever reason, he wants to keep in good with my family.'

'What else?'

'What else, what?'

'What else did he say?'

'He told me to get my red gumboots and meet him at his

apartment later tonight, so we can have kinky sex.'

Joe bashed the steering wheel with his palm. 'For Christ's sake Tessa, what did he say?'

'What's the matter with you? What's happened to Mr Iceman?'

'What do you think is the matter with me?' Joe uncharacteristically raised his voice above his normal calming decibel level. 'One of our best friends just tried to commit suicide. And we've got a serial killer on the loose.'

'No need to shout. You're the one always telling me that losing our cool won't help catch the bad guys.'

Joe sat silently for a moment. He took a deep breath and slowly let it out as he started the car. 'I'm sorry. You're right. I told Dean the other night that keeping you under control keeps me under control. Looks like we've reversed roles.' Joe put the car into gear. 'Thanks. Mr Iceman is back. Now tell me, please, what else did Damien say?'

'Nothing much. He said to remind you about catching up with him on Monday night. He asked if I needed a lift home and I told him you were getting the car and we're going to the station to do some more work on the case.' Tessa fastened her seat belt. 'He made a sarcastic comment about me being the ever-conscientious cop. Why?' Tessa shrugged. 'Who cares anyway what Damien said?'

When they pulled out of the hospital car park, Tessa selected favourites on her mobile. 'I'll give Alex a quick call. She'll want an update on how Paul is. And it looks like the rain is easing, so maybe she could drop by with some barbeque leftovers for our dinner. I've got a feeling it's going to be a long night.'

37

Back at the station, Tessa called her parents to update them about Paul's condition. She watched Joe as he positioned a clean whiteboard in front of the existing board covered in multi-coloured sticky notes, photos, and criss-crossing arrows pointing to names, dates, and locations.

'Hang on, Mamma,' Tessa said as she lowered her mobile. 'What are you doing, Joe? If we're going over the case, we'll need our notes.'

'We need a clean slate for this,' Joe said.

Tessa finished the call with her mother and made coffee for them both as Joe prepared the blank whiteboard. He drew a series of vertical lines crossed by horizontal lines on the board. He listed hair, eyes, height, and other characteristics in the first column. He labelled the next columns Yolanda's description, Sanders, Kowalski. He left the last column blank.

'Is the last column for Aaron Thompson?' Tessa leaned against the edge of her desk. 'We've just about ruled him out. But I still think we can't discount him completely.'

'Agree. But we'll put him at the end of the list with a question mark. See if he fits in with the top three.'

'Top three? I've got ten fingers.' Tessa held up two fingers. 'And I only needed two of them to count our top contenders. Kowalski and Sanders.'

'Stay with me, Tess. Let's start with what Yolanda told us. The physical description ...' He paused.

'What's that?'

'What's what?' Tessa asked.

'The envelope on your desk. It looks like Paul's handwriting.'

'I don't know. I guess I was so focussed on you and the board I didn't notice it.' Tessa looked at the envelope, front and back, and frowned. 'It *is* Paul's writing.'

'What is it? Open it, Tess.'

She removed a note from the envelope.

Joe watched as Tessa's eyes moved quickly left to right as she scanned the note. Her lips were moving, but no sound came out. 'Jesus, Tess, what does it say?'

'Paul must have written this before he wrote ... you know, the other note.'

'Tess. What—does—it—say?'

'Sorry.' She read out loud.

We know the killer is male. He's intelligent, exceptionally organised, ruthless. You're looking for a manipulator. He's confident and controlling. He feigns charm, and he gets what he wants at any cost. He's a monster. A highly functional monster who blends in with normal society. He has no empathy for his victims. The motive isn't religious. It's vengeance. He had something taken from him, not material, something more important to him. It's possible he would score high on the traits associated with the dark triad, narcissism, Machiavellianism, and psychopathy. Look for somebody with an exaggerated sense of self-importance, arrogance, a lack of empathy, a need to be admired, who has a sense of entitlement. He has an intense desire to compete and win at all costs. You must rescue society from this beast. You're looking for a narcissist. A highly intelligent, at times charismatic narcissist—one of the most dangerous kinds. He is the worst of what humanity has to offer. His existence is a mask that hides his evil nature behind a false charm.

Tessa handed the note to Joe. He re-read it to himself, twice. Joe stood silently for a moment as images flashed past closed eyes, one after the other like clips from a horror movie—the rose, the note, the victims, Zoe, the transcripts from the dating sites, Sammy. He opened his eyes, and with an almost imperceptible nod, murmured, 'Yep, this is him. This describes him perfectly.'

'Describes who?'

Joe rubbed Sebastian Sanders and Ed Kowalski's names off the board.

'What are you doing now?'

Joe went to his desk. 'It's neither of them, not Kowalski, not Sanders.' He opened Phoebe's file. 'Read the transcript … out loud.'

Tessa sat as she read the transcript from the dating website between Phoebe and PartyGirl.

'Read this line again,' Joe pointed.

Tessa read, *Perfect. See you then. And BTW my name is Zoe. Ciao.*

'And now the last line,'

That's fine. Tessa read. *See you then. Ciao.*

Joe opened Yolanda's file and pointed. 'There, he says it again. "Sounds perfect. See you then. Ciao." The transcripts from Amber's iPad and Issy's laptop. He says *ciao* again.'

'You think he's Italian?'

'What did Damien say before he left the barbeque?'

'I don't know. I wasn't taking much notice of him. To be honest, I was happy he left early. I think I gave him the finger as he was leaving. And we couldn't find the cricket ball he hit over the fence … arsehole.'

'Focus, Tess. Damien said, "It's been fun. Ciao everyone." He said *ciao*.'

'He always says *ciao*. I think he got it …' Tessa trailed off. 'Got it from me,' she said almost to herself. 'You don't think … No, no, no …' She stood. 'Jesus Christ, Joe, it's just a word. Lots of people say it. You can't suspect him because of one stupid word.'

'There's more, Tess. The pieces are falling into place. That was just the catalyst. It was like a magnet drawing all the pieces into position.' Joe stopped talking. *No, it wasn't what Damien said. It was Sammy. Sammy was the catalyst,* Joe thought. 'Do you remember when Sammy growled at Damien? Dean made a joke about Damien being a lawyer. I didn't think about it at the time. But Sammy senses undesirable characters. No, I'm wrong. I *did* think about it, but I didn't dwell on it. I stored it. I stored it with all the other stored pieces that are falling into place.'

'You're rambling. *You* don't ramble. *I* ramble. You're not making sense. You're wrong—way wrong. A growling dog, and Damien said ciao … is that all you've got?'

'There's more—way more. It's coming together.'

Tessa sank into the chair, stared at Joe. She shook her head and mouthed 'No' as though she'd lost her voice.

Joe handed her a bottle of water. 'Here, drink this.'

'Are you trying to tell me I lived with a killer for three years? That I didn't see the signs? No. You're wrong.'

'But …'

'No, Joe. You're not often wrong. But you are this time. I'm better than that. I can read people. I can read their body language. I would have known.'

'Sometimes … often, we miss things in the people we're

closest to. You only see what you want to see.' Joe pulled his chair in front of Tessa and took both her hands in his. 'I didn't see the signs, and I've known him since we were kids. You were in lust with Damien.'

'Maybe. I can't believe I was in lust with somebody of the opposite sex.'

Joe wasn't sure if Tessa was serious or joking, despite the tears rolling down her cheeks. 'Anyway, you picked up on the signals, but you didn't connect the dots. Besides, he wasn't killing when you were living with him. That we know of.'

Mascara stained Tessa's face as she wiped the tears from her eyes. 'No, you're wrong. Why Joe, why would he do this? Are you sure?'

'No. Yes. Well, not one hundred percent. So, let's join the dots.' He kissed her on the cheek. 'You should clean your face before Alex gets here with dinner. We don't want to discuss this with anyone until we're sure.' Joe walked to the board. 'But I am sure. All we have to do is prove it.' As an afterthought, Joe said, 'Alex is coming with dinner, isn't she?'

38

Joe ruled two more columns on the board. He wrote Sebastian Sanders' and Ed Kowalski's names on the board again. 'Let's look at what we've got and match it up with Sanders, Kowalski and Damien.'

'Kowalski and Sanders are still contenders then?' Tessa asked.

'I don't think so. But you're right, we shouldn't rule them out yet. Part of me hopes it *is* Sanders, the arrogant shit. But I doubt it.' Joe said.

'Part of me wishes it was Aaron Thompson. The slime.'

'All of me wishes it was nobody, and it never happened.' Joe pointed to the copy of the note that the killer pinned to the victims' breasts. 'But it did. So, back to the note.'

'It's Calibri font,' Tessa said. 'I don't think we can read anything into that, it's pretty standard, the default Word font. But what's he trying to tell us?'

'We kept asking ourselves—who's the message for?' He stood back and re-read the words. *Trust not too much to appearances. The beauty hides the thorns.* 'The message is for you, Tess. Damien is talking about you.'

'No, no, no … I'm not the reason he killed those women.' Tessa stood, paced. 'No, it can't be my fault.'

'Of course, it's not your fault. It's him. You know what he's like. He can't stand to lose anything. You've said it, I've said it. Remember how you said he reacted when he lost the case defending the drug dealer?'

'Do you mean the time he threw his whisky glass against the wall on his outdoor terrace?'

'That's right,' Joe said. 'And the time he avoided me when I beat him at chess. He can't handle loss. And he lost you. Worse, you were stolen from him.'

'I didn't think he loved me that much.'

'I doubt that he ever loved you at all. I don't think he's capable. But you belonged to him. You were his possession. And Alex stole his possession. He didn't go through a normal grieving process when he lost you. He just went straight to revenge.'

Tessa sat. 'Alex? Do you think …'

'Yes. He plans to kill her—eventually.' Joe put the photos of the victims on the board. 'Look at them. Amber, Isabel, Phoebe, Yolanda—all petite, blonde, pretty … gay. Just like Alex. And you and Zoe. You're Zoe. Beautiful. Long dark hair. It hit me this afternoon at the barbeque. The resemblance between you and Zoe. And Alex and the victims. That's why he chose them.'

'And me? Does he plan to kill me?'

'Probably, but not before he kills Alex. He'd want to see you suffer first. What better way to get his revenge—kill the one you love. Watch you suffer.' Joe raised his eyebrows, shrugged. 'Who knows, I might be a target too. He might plan to kill me before he kills you. Or he might want to watch me suffer and kill you first.'

Tessa sipped her coffee, wrinkled her nose. 'This is cold. Why do our coffees always end up cold? I'll make another one

239

for us both.'

Joe continued making notes on the board and ten minutes had passed before he realised Tessa hadn't returned. He went to the kitchen and got there just as she was coming in the back door. 'Where've you been?'

'I rang Alex. She's fine. She's on her way here. Then I went outside for an emergency cigarette. But I didn't have one. I forgot. I was too focused on recalling the three years I was with Damien. Trying to remember tell-tale signs. I forgot to have a cigarette.' She tossed the emergency packet in the bin. 'If I don't need one now, I never will. If it's true, well … I slept with … had sex with … I had sex with a monster. The eyes. I can see them, just as Yolanda described them. Those cold dark eyes peering at me when we were having sex.' Tessa shivered. 'Even if Damien's not the killer, I'll always remember those eyes now as monster eyes. Killer or not, he's a … What is he? I don't know now. Not sure I ever did.'

They made coffee and went back to the board.

'Are you okay?' Joe asked.

'Sure. When I had my non-ciggy break, I ah … well, as you would say, I rationalised. We don't know for sure it's Damien. It's just supposition. And if it is Damien, you're right. Shit, Joe, it's so annoying.'

'What? What's annoying?'

'That you're always right.'

Joe kissed the top of her head. 'You'll just have to learn to live with it.'

'Even if it *is* Damien, you're right, none of this is my fault. I didn't make Damien a psychopath or narcissist or whatever he is. He always was. He's controlling. He manipulates the situation to get his own way. But ever so, so charming when he needs to be. Jekyll and Hyde. He has no empathy for anyone or anything.'

'True,' Joe agreed. 'Only a callous bastard would joke about a victim being in a coma.'

'You're talking about the day we went to see him about Johnson, aren't you? The comment Damien made about Kaitlin not being a reliable witness because she was in a coma, right? Oh God, what did I see in him? He doesn't have a compassionate bone in his body.'

'Don't forget about wins at any costs,' Joe added.

'Who wins at any costs?' Alex said as she carried in a large red esky. 'I didn't bring wine. Just food and mineral water.'

'Pellegrino, I hope.' Joe winked at Alex. 'We have to keep up the Italian theme. You staying for a bite?'

Alex declined Joe's invitation to eat with them. 'I've got a not so patient, hungry feline at home.'

'Wait, Alex,' Tessa said. 'Before you leave.'

Alex frowned. 'You look worried, Tess. What's wrong?'

'Promise me you'll go straight home. No stops. Go straight inside. Don't open the door. Not to anyone. Ring me as soon as you're safely inside. Or just text. Whatever. Just let us know you're safe. Promise.'

'Sure, promise, but … why?'

'Just promise.'

'Yes, I promise. But what aren't you telling me?'

'We can't tell you everything,' Joe said. 'Because we don't know for sure ourselves. But what we do know, and you know too, there's a killer out there, targeting young, blonde women. Petite. Pretty. Women just like you.'

***

Tessa and Joe ate quickly and in silence. There was no time to savour the food, as delicious as it was. They returned to the murder board with their mineral water within twenty minutes of Alex leaving them.

'I think we agree Damien fits the profile and has a motive,' Joe said. 'But I don't think we can arrest him based on how his eyes looked when you guys were doing the wild thing.'

Tessa rolled her eyes. 'Oh, you mean we need actual evidence.'

Joe ignored Tessa's sarcastic comment. 'And we still have to look at Ed Kowalski and Sebastian Sanders.'

'Agree. I think Sanders could fit the profile. Intelligent, organised, controlling, superficial charm and most definitely an exaggerated sense of self-importance.'

'And Phoebe ended the relationship the same as you ended yours with Damien.'

Tessa looked at the photos of the victims as if seeing them for the first time. 'If he did do this, and I'm why he did this … how can I…?'

'It's not your fault, Tess.' Joe pointed to the photos. 'You didn't do that.'

'Okay. I don't have time to feel sorry for myself. That can come when this is all over.' Tessa looked at Paul's note. 'Not sure about Kowalski. I guess he ticks most of the boxes. But …'

'But he doesn't have any charm, superficial or otherwise. And I don't think he has as strong a motive as Damien or Sebastian.'

Tessa shook her head. 'I must have blind faith in you. You've based all this about Damien on a possible motive, a dog, and the word "ciao." And the victims' resemblance to Alex and Zoe to me. Do you have any evidence at all? I'm still inclined to Sanders.'

'We need to rewind, go back to where I think it all started,' Joe said. 'Go back to when you were living with Damien.'

'What about when he was a kid? And his parents? Isn't that where it usually starts. Was he molested? Did he torture and kill cats?'

Joe looked at Tessa. Said nothing. He picked up the mineral water, put it back without drinking it, and walked to the kitchen. He came back with two coffees. 'I know you were half joking, but you're right.'

'He killed cats?'

'No. About his childhood. His father was, and still is, domineering and controlling. And his mother doted on him. Then his mother died a few days after Christmas, before the new year. And then you left him not long after his mother died. It was the perfect storm. He was abandoned by the woman who doted on him and the other woman who, in his mind, was supposed to idolise him.'

Tessa took her coffee back to her desk. 'Was he ever violent when he was a kid?'

'He didn't kill cats. Not that I know of. But there were many times when he was aggressive, angry.' He told Tessa about the end of semester, friendly touch football game where Damien's competitive, win-at-all-costs nature took over and he put another student in hospital.

'I don't know. I was so, I guess, shocked at first, and I believed you. But there's just not enough to even consider the possibility that Damien might be a suspect. He's in his thirties. Most serial killers start in their early twenties.'

'True, but there are plenty of cases where they didn't start till their thirties or forties or even older. Did you ever read about the married couple, the Copelands, in the United States? They were in their sixties and seventies.'

'You want to believe it's Damien.' Tessa shook her head. 'I don't. Where does that leave us?'

'You're wrong. I don't want to believe the person I've been friends with since we were kids is a serial killer. But ...' Joe hesitated. He felt a knot tightening in his belly. 'But hear me out. Snippets of comments and events are falling into place for me. It's like splicing separate pieces of film to make a movie, a movie that's beginning to make sense.'

'English, Joe,' Tessa said. 'Plain English, please. What are you trying to say?'

'Did Damien ever buy you flowers?'

'Only if friends came for dinner. You know, pretending he was thoughtful.'

'What sort?'

'Of flowers? Roses, he knew they were my favourite.'

'Not anymore.'

'What?'

'That's what you said at the beach when you saw Phoebe's body. You said roses used to be your favourite, but not anymore.'

'How did you remember what I said about roses? We were examining Phoebe's mutilated body, for Christ's sake.'

'I guess it just slipped into my memory bank. You know how stuff does. And sometime between then and now I made a mental note not to buy you roses—that is, if I ever had a reason to buy you flowers.'

'I've got a birthday coming up. I'd prefer chocolate. Dark. You converted me to dark with the ones we had at your place with Paul the other night.'

'Chocolate it is. Back to Damien.' Joe walked to the board. 'What have we got?'

'Chocolate. Paul. Oh God, Paul. He's going to be okay... isn't he?'

'He's in good hands. He'll come back stronger than before.' Joe knew he didn't sound as convincing as he hoped. 'He'll do it for Trudi.'

'I'll take some chocolate to the hospital tomorrow. That

might help to cheer him.'

'We'll cheer him by using his profile to track down this killer,' Joe said.

'Okay, okay. So, we agree Damien fits Paul's profile of the killer, and …' Tessa stood, paced.

'And?'

'Jesus. My stomach just did a backflip. Saying Damien and killer in the same sentence. I'm not sure I can deal with this, Joe.'

'You have to. Time is running out. He, whether it's Damien, Kowalski or Sanders, he'll strike again … soon.' Joe stood in front of her. He held her shoulders and waited till she made eye contact with him. 'It's not about you, Tess. Or me. It's never about us or how we feel. It's about the victim. You know that.'

'I know. And it's about making sure there are no more victims. I know.' She breathed deeply as she ran her fingers through her hair and tightened the band around her ponytail. 'Let's get on with it.'

'Okay, back to what we know.' Joe walked to the board. 'We agree Paul's note describes Damien. He's intelligent, organised, and ruthless, and gets what he wants at any cost. And you've said it yourself. He has no empathy. But he can be charming. Even Yolanda said that he, that is the man who attacked her, seemed sweet at first when he offered her a lift.'

'Yolanda's physical description of her attacker matches Damien. Light brown hair, dark eyes. Similar height, build and age to you. He's right-handed, and he smokes.' Tessa wrinkled her nose. 'Smells like an ashtray. I didn't notice the stink when I was smoking too.'

'Must be unpleasant for his clients,' Joe said.

'Do you mean his scum of the earth, who gives a shit what they think, mostly drug-dealing clients? Most of them smoke too.' Tessa poured two glasses of mineral water, handed one to

Joe. 'The note—*Trust not too much to appearances. The beauty hides the thorns*—you said he was talking to me. About me. Why?'

'You're beautiful, but you deceived him. You weren't what you appeared to be—to him, anyway.' Joe sipped his mineral water. 'You were supposed to be in love with him, under his control. You weren't supposed to leave him. Especially not for a woman.'

Tessa cocked her head and bit her bottom lip.

Joe could see her eyes moving side to side. 'What? What are you thinking?'

Tessa picked up Paul's note from the desk. *His existence is a mask that hides his evil nature behind a false charm.* 'That says a similar thing about Damien as we think the note on the victims says about me. We both hid our true nature.'

'Yep, the same, but different. You didn't hide an evil nature. You just denied a part of yourself until you met Alex.'

'What else do we have? What other piece has fallen into place for you?'

'The scratch on his face. When we went to his office the other day, he had a scratch on his face. You assumed it was from playing rugby. Remember? It hasn't healed. I noticed it today at the barbeque. Yolanda hit her attacker in the face with her shoe.'

Tessa nodded. 'I remember. But it's all conjecture. We need proof. Damien moves heaven and earth to get off a lousy drug dealer. Imagine what he would do if it was him in the firing line. We need undeniable proof.'

'The black-rimmed glasses you hadn't seen before. He said he was waiting on a new prescription. That was just a few days after the killer's glasses were broken when he attacked Yolanda. I'm betting the partial fingerprint the lab found on the lens will match Damien's print.'

Tessa shook her head. 'It's barely a partial. And after all this time, I don't have anything that might have Damien's prints on it to match it with.'

'I do. When he was leaving the barbeque, he left his empty glass on the table.'

'The partial print won't be conclusive. I'm betting on it. We need more.'

Joe raced over to his laptop and opened his emails. 'Look at this email from Damien.'

***

Looking forward to catching up next week.
I've attached the restaurant's website.
Not far from your place.
See you at 7:30
Ciao

***

'What do you notice?' Joe said. 'I don't know why I didn't notice it before.'

Tessa stared at the screen for a moment before she spoke. 'A hard return after every sentence. Just like his messages on the dating sites. And of course, the obvious ciao.'

Joe opened more emails from Damien. They all had the same hard return after every sentence. 'I'm right, Tess. But I wish I wasn't. You're right. All we have is circumstantial—not sure we can even call it evidence. It would be easier to get evidence and prove if it was Sanders or Kowalski. We need rock solid evidence against Damien.'

'And we need it before he kills again.'

39

The wind and the heavy rain had eased to a light drizzle when Alex drove home after dropping off barbeque leftovers to Tessa and Joe at the station. The reflection of the streetlights on the wet roads and the star-patterned glare from oncoming cars reminded Alex of another evening. An evening just like this one.

Relaxed by the rhythmic tick tock of the windshield wipers, Alex reminisced about that evening last year when she and Tessa met. She recalled the awkward first five minutes that morphed effortlessly into comfortable conversation. She smiled when she remembered Tessa's comment, 'Oh, so we're friends now, after five minutes and one sip of wine,' when Alexandra told her, 'My friends call me Alex.'

And the wine Tessa chose. A Western Australian chardonnay. Alex noticed Tessa was careful to choose a quality wine, but not too expensive. It was perfect. But everything about Tessa is perfect. She's smart, beautiful, fiercely loyal. Perfect. Perfect now, that is. Tessa was an honest person. She told the truth, nothing but the truth, but not always the *whole* truth. Alex never hid her sexual preferences from her family. They were a little disconcerted at first, but eventually accepting. Video conferencing was good, but Alex was looking forward to taking Tessa to Perth at Christmas to meet her parents face to face. Tessa had spoken to Alex's parents many times. They were open about their relationship with Alex's parents. But Tessa had refused to reveal her true relationship with Alex to her own family until this afternoon.

Tessa hadn't told Alex what she had planned. Alex had wondered why Tessa had been jittery all morning. She assumed Tessa was nervous and excited, but happy about her father's birthday celebration. When Tessa told her parents and brother at the barbeque and her parents were so accepting of Alex. Well, not immediately, but once their jaws regained the proper position on their faces, Alex knew she and Tessa had cemented their relationship.

The only downside was Tessa's brother. He'd walked off in a sullen huff. Embarrassed, Alex assumed. If only Tessa had told her brother before he'd asked Alex on a dinner date.

Alex's thoughts drifted away from Tessa's brother, back to Tessa. The last few months with her fulfilled every wish that Alex had for a relationship. She'd never been able to commit before now. All the dates she'd been on, the women and men she'd met online. 'Shit.' She bashed the steering wheel with the heel of her hand. She still had her profile on the dating website. She'd been meaning to delete it but hadn't got around to it. *How honest was my profile,* she wondered? The photo was less than two years old. But the description …

Fifteen minutes after she left the station Alex turned left off the highway. The headlights behind her turned left. She drove five hundred metres and turned right. The same headlights behind her turned right. *Odd,* she thought. This was a cul-de-sac, and few cars came this far in. Alex slowed and pulled over to let the car go past. The headlights slowed, then drove past Alex to the end of the cul-de-sac and parked. Alex didn't recognise the car and thought it must belong to a visitor. A visitor with a very nice and very expensive car. Her curiosity got the better of her and she waited to see who got out. Nobody. Alex guessed the driver must have been lost and stopped to check directions. After a moment, the car turned and drove slowly down the street towards her car. Alex lost interest. *Obviously made a wrong turn,* she thought, and turned into her driveway.

Maxi meowed a greeting when Alex opened the front door of the house that she hoped to share with Tessa soon. 'Oh sorry, Maxi, I left your food in the car.' When she turned to go back out to the car, her passage was blocked by a tall figure whose features were obscured by the dark night and rain. Alex took one step back and inhaled sharply as she covered her mouth with her hand.

'I'm sorry. I didn't mean to alarm you. I was just about to ring the doorbell when you opened the door.'

Her hands trembled as she turned on the porch light. The stranger standing in front of her had grey hair and looked to be around sixty.

'I'm sorry,' he said again. 'I'm trying to find Lawson Street.'

Alex felt herself breathe out a sigh of relief and then take what she thought must have been her first breath since she saw the man standing in front of her. A harmless man, lost, just as she initially thought when she first noticed his car. *But I will feel safer when there's two of us living here.*

After giving the man directions and fetching Maxi's food, Alex sent a text *'Home, locked in, all safe. Love you.'* She settled in to visit the online dating site while she ate a dinner made from barbeque leftovers. She read her profile. *'I'm a journalist with interests in all aspects of life, including politics, history, current affairs, human behaviour and diverse viewpoints. I would love to meet somebody who I could share lively conversations and debates with. Somebody who could learn from me and somebody I could learn from. I'm petite, but athletic.'*

Alex had a few dates. But she hadn't visited the site since she met Tessa. There were several new replies that she didn't bother to read. *What a waste of time that was.* She was about to unsubscribe, then changed her mind. Online dating could make for an interesting article. *I can set up interviews with the okay dates I had,* she thought. *The willing ones, that is.*

She opened her 'Ideas' folder on her laptop and began brainstorming themes, questions, and possible contacts for the article. She was ten minutes into the process when her mobile rang.

'That's okay, I'll wait up … Just working on an idea for a new article.'

Alex told Tessa about the man looking for directions. 'I was a little startled at first, but … yes, I've got the deadlock on … no, I won't open the door to anyone.'

Alex changed the subject and told Tessa about the online dating site and the article idea.

'I was going to unsubscribe, but … What, no, I won't unsubscribe … I changed my mind when I had the article idea …'

Tessa's intense reaction about the man who came to the door confused Alex. And the dating site. Was she jealous? Surely not. Their relationship was built on trust and honesty. There was something else. *Surely Tess doesn't really believe I could be a target for the killer.*

40

'First in again,' Tessa said as she handed Joe a coffee.

'We should contact Bathurst ...' Joe stopped mid-sentence when he noticed Tessa's wrinkled shirt and mismatched boots, one brown, the other black. 'You look like you've had a hard day's night.'

'Eight in the morning is a little early to be quoting Lennon and McCartney. And yes, I had a hard day Sunday and Sunday night till about two this morning.'

'Anything to do with why you left here without so much as a goodbye after you called Alex on Saturday night?'

Tessa told Joe about the dating site and the stranger who came to the door. 'It was nothing. The stranger wasn't stranger danger, just somebody asking for directions. Anyway, it was a catalyst for the inevitable—me moving in with Alex, that is. You were right.'

'I...' Joe paused. 'I was right?'

Tessa grinned. 'Do you know—your eyebrows connect when you're confused about something. I meant you were right about telling my family the truth about Alex.'

Joe nodded, shrugged, and then moved on. 'The dating site? I'm assuming nothing came of that, otherwise you would have called me.'

'Nothing that looked like Zoe. Zoe, Damien. Shit, shit, I still can't believe Damien is Zoe.' Tessa toyed with her coffee. 'Alex decided not to delete the site because she wants to write an article about dating sites. And it's probably a good idea to leave it until this is over. If it's ever over.'

'It will be. Soon.' Joe looked directly into Tessa's eyes. 'And then you can put Damien out of your life. Forever.'

'I pray you're right. And before Zoe goes after Alex. I'm going to monitor the dating site.'

'Damien knows Alex won't reply to any communications on the dating site now. Not with you on the scene. He's planning another strategy to get to Alex.' Joe sipped his coffee. 'But she's not his next target.'

'There's no way of knowing that for sure. We don't know what his end game is.'

'Do you remember when you told me about Damien playing computer games and not quitting until he won?' Joe drained his coffee, finishing it while it was still warm this time. 'He was the same at university. He would sit up all night working on assignments. But not to finish them. He always finished his assignments well before the due date. But he would sit up all night fine-tuning them. He was the same with sport. He would keep training for hours after the rest of the team left. Damien is driven. He has to finish what he starts. Anything. Everything. And it has to be perfect.'

'What has all this got to do with him not going after Alex?'

'He won't go after anyone until he's finished with Yolanda. He has to finish what he started.'

'I hope you're right.' Tessa closed her eyes and shook her

253

head. 'No, no. Of course, I don't mean I hope you're right about him going after Yolanda. I mean, I hope you're right about him not going after Alex yet. It's a good thing Yolanda went home to stay with her parents in Bathurst.'

'He's smart,' Joe said. 'He'll know Yolanda won't go back to her unit. It won't take much for him to find where she is.'

'When I first came in you were saying that we should contact Bathurst police. Right? Agree.'

'Such a Mariani thing to do. Ask a question and then continue without waiting for a reply.'

'I've been thinking about …' Tessa stopped, surveyed the office. By eight-thirty the early morning sounds of silence were turning into a cacophony of 'How was the weekend?', 'I need a coffee,' telephones ringing, printers whirring. 'Let's head down to Athena's.'

***

Early mornings at Café Athena mainly catered for those rushing to get to work on time and in need of a quick take-away caffeine fix to kick start the day. When Joe and Tessa arrived, a couple, deep in intimate conversation, occupied a table. And just one other person, reading a newspaper, occupied a second table. Joe and Tessa had their pick, and they made their way to Joe's favourite table at the window.

Nik's morning Greek ballads reminded Joe of the day he had coffee with Olivia. The day that started so well with her when he felt they had connected. And then ended so badly. He wondered if they connected again at Tessa's barbeque. She'd left the table before he had a chance to say goodbye. So probably not.

Joe stirred the froth in his cappuccino. 'What's on your mind?' Joe looked at the table where Olivia had sat when he and

254

Paul had coffee the other day. He'd asked Paul the same thing he'd just asked Tessa. *'What's on your mind?'* He told Paul that only a fool lets happiness slip away. Is that what's happening with Olivia. Is he letting happiness slip away?

'Ground control to Joe.'

'Sorry, I'm back. And I *was* listening. You were saying we have no evidence.'

Tessa leaned across the table with folded arms. 'You said yourself, we have no DNA, no fibre, no murder weapon, and the fingerprints probably won't be conclusive.'

'The fingerprint analysis is a start.'

'But if we know for sure,' Tessa leaned further forward across the table. 'We can forget Kowalski and Sanders and focus all our attention on Damien.'

Joe's eyes narrowed. 'I know you, Tess. What are you planning?'

Tessa bit her bottom lip. Hesitated.

'The clock is ticking. Out with it.'

Tessa breathed deeply. 'Okay, you're not going to like it.' She looked directly at Joe. 'And you're not going to talk me out of it.'

'And?'

'Well ... You're meeting with Damien tonight for dinner. Right?'

'No, I ...'

'Yes, you are. And while you're there.' Tessa cleared her throat. 'I'm going to Damien's apartment and check out his laptop. I know his password—NotGuilty—all one word. How easy is that to crack if you didn't already know it?'

Joe opened his mouth then closed it again.

'Say something, Joe.'

Joe sipped his cappuccino. 'This is no time for joking. We're running out of time.'

'Yes. We're running out of time. And I'm not joking.'

Joe leaned forward shaking his head. 'No. No. It's too risky, Tess. And even if you found something, we wouldn't be able to use it.'

'But we'll know. One way or another, we'll know. Ring him, confirm the time.'

Joe said nothing.

'I've still got a key, so it's not like I'll be breaking in—all above board. I won't touch anything else. I won't remove his laptop. Hell, I won't even move it a centimetre.'

'I don't like it. We should wait for the fingerprint result and then we can get a warrant.'

'Ring him. Make a time to meet him.'

'I don't know if I can pretend …'

'You have to. One way or another, I'm going to his apartment whether you're in this with me or not. I told you. You're not going to talk me out of it.'

'We should follow the process.'

'We can bend the rules. It's not like I'm planting evidence. Do you want to follow the process to the letter and risk Zoe killing and mutilating another innocent victim?'

41

Tessa parked her car in a side street. She walked fifty metres and then turned left into the street where she once lived in a ten-storey apartment complex with Damien. The building loomed like a massive monolith, dwarfing the few remaining structures erected mid last century. Its architect had surrendered to simplicity and sterility in place of aesthetics. Despite the warm evening, Tessa shivered. The building's cement and glass facade reflected Damien's cold, calculating character. A few apartments had vines cascading over their balconies, providing some softness and colour to an otherwise austere exterior. Floor to ceiling windows offered uninterrupted views. Much like Sebastian Sanders' apartment, Tessa thought. And just like Sanders, Damien owned the penthouse. But unlike Sanders, Damien's views were of a bay dotted with sailing boats and cruisers, not a beach congested with surfers and sunbathers.

Tessa looked up towards the penthouse. Lights glowed in most of the apartments, but Damien's was in darkness except for one dim night light that Tessa knew he always left on when he was out. She walked to the glass entry door and swiped her security fob. Still works. She walked the five metres across marble patterned tiles to the elevators. Tessa paced as she waited for the elevator. She checked the time—it was only seven fifteen. Joe had finally agreed to have dinner with Damien. So she knew Damien wouldn't be home for a couple of hours at least—probably ten o'clock at the earliest. But she wanted to get in and out of Damien's apartment as quickly as possible. The lift eventually arrived. Tessa nodded a greeting to the couple who got out. She swiped the fob and pressed the button for the penthouse floor.

Before the doors closed, a man of about sixty entered and pressed the fourth-floor button. He turned and smiled. 'The views from the penthouse are lovely, aren't they?'

Tessa nodded a half smile. A semi-polite smile that said, 'I'm not really interested in talking to you.'

The man didn't take the hint and kept prattling. 'My wife and I looked at the penthouse while they were still building, but' —the doors opened on the fourth floor— 'we decided...'

Tessa nodded towards the open doors. 'I think this is your floor.'

'Oh yes, of course. Lovely chatting with you.'

The elevator whooshed to the penthouse without further interruption. The doors opened onto large rectangular, shiny white tiles. Like the ones in Sanders' penthouse.

Tessa opened the penthouse door. Damien hadn't changed the extra lock he'd installed. She walked through the foyer past the kitchen and dining room on her right and turned left into the hallway that took her past the gym and into the study. She frowned. The laptop wasn't on the desk. It's always on the desk. She went back out into the hallway and into the guest room, the bedroom, back into the dining room. No laptop. Tessa's mobile rang. 'Not now, Joe,' she said under her breath as she declined the call. The phone immediately rang again. She let it ring out. It rang again. She muttered, 'Shit,' and answered it this time. 'I can't find the laptop. I'll ring you back when…What do you mean he's on his way back here? … Why? … How long ago?'

Tessa calculated she had less than fifteen minutes before Damien walked in the front door. She saw his wallet on the kitchen bench. He never forgets his wallet. Why tonight?

Her eyes shifted from the kitchen to the dining room and then to the outdoor terrace where Damien enjoyed sitting with a whisky, contemplating the next move in his current case. Of course. There it was. The laptop was on the granite terrace table. The table that Tessa could never understand why Damien would pay over three thousand dollars for something so tasteless.

Tessa opened the laptop and keyed in Damien's password. She found a dating site he subscribed to. The same one Yolanda subscribed to. She checked the time. She had five minutes at the most—not enough time to dig into the site. She scanned Damien's emails, calendar, notes and Facebook. Nothing. She checked his tasks. Tessa stared open-mouthed at the most recent entry for a full ten seconds. *It's him. It really is him.*

***

Tessa was just closing the door when she heard the elevator ping. She put her knuckles up to the door, pretending to knock, when Damien walked up behind her. He put his arms around her waist and whispered. A whisper that was a scream in her ears. 'Tessa, darling. This is a pleasant surprise.'

Tessa turned to face him. She looked up into his dark, predator eyes. Snake eyes like a viper preparing to strike at any moment. 'I called by on the off chance you were here.' She hesitated. 'I think I left my runners in the shoe box. I'm going to start running again and I can't find them.'

He was smirking. She knew he didn't believe her. 'Surely, you knew I was meeting Joe and I wouldn't be here.'

Tessa shook her head. 'No, I didn't. We don't keep tabs on each other's social life.'

Damien cocked his head and narrowed his eyes. 'You really thought I'd be here?'

Tessa nodded.

'You've got a key—you should have let yourself in.' He smirked again. 'If I can't trust a law enforcement officer in my apartment, who can I trust?'

'I didn't bring the key.' Tessa could feel her heart racing in her chest. 'I wouldn't use it, anyway. Never mind. If you find my runners, just … donate them to charity…whatever… I don't care.'

He grabbed her shoulders and pulled her in closer. 'You've come to make up with me, haven't you? I saw the way you looked at me at the barbeque. You miss me, don't you, my darling Tessa?'

Damien is so arrogant, Tessa thought. *It doesn't occur to him he might be a suspect. That I might be here looking for evidence.*

She squirmed out of his grip. But she was trapped between Damien and the door. Her stomach turned as she looked into his dark, demonic eyes piercing her own, as though reading her thoughts. Her mobile rang. 'That'll be Alex.' She could hear her voice was shrill, higher pitched than normal. She prayed he didn't notice her face was burning. Was it fear? Or anger? Both? 'I have to go. Forget the runners.' She knew Joe would keep ringing. She didn't want Damien to realise it was Joe and hoped he didn't notice her switching her phone to silent.

He pulled her in closer again and nuzzled his chin firmly into her neck and whispered in her ear. 'You miss the feel of a man's arms around you. Strong arms. My arms. Alex doesn't do it for you anymore, does she?' Then he pushed her hard against the door. 'I told you when you left, you'd be back. That you need me.' He pushed her again, glared at her.

Tessa had never seen so much hate in anyone's eyes.

'Well, it's too late, darling Tessa.' He pulled her away from his door and pointed to the elevator. 'Go home to your wee little blonde slut. You might look good on the surface, but you're tarnished goods.'

***

Back at the station later that evening, Joe and Tessa planned their next steps. Tessa yanked the ring pull on a can of soft drink and studied the can without drinking from it. 'I thought he'd be suspicious. But he's so arrogant and self-centred, he really believed that I wanted to go back to him.' She sipped her drink. 'You might look good on the surface, but you're tarnished goods. That's what he said before he went inside and slammed the door in my face.'

'The beauty hides the thorns,' Joe said, more to himself than Tessa.

Tessa had gone straight back to the station after she left Damien's apartment. She filled in the time till Joe arrived by reviewing files, making notes, and studying the murder board. Tessa knew now it was Damien. She didn't doubt it anymore. Damien was the psycho monster, killing and mutilating innocent young women.

She looked at the files now with a fresh perspective, looking for clues. And if there were no clues, looking for where they could retrace their steps to find the clues. It was Damien. They just needed enough evidence to put him away. Put him away for good. And when they do, she can do what Joe said. Put Damien

261

out of her life. Forever.

When Joe arrived, he uncharacteristically threw his keys on the desk and dragged his chair over to sit next to Tessa at her desk. 'Are you alright? Tell me everything. Damien spent the entire time over dinner talking about his latest cases. His new boat. He blabbered all evening. About shit I wasn't interested in.' Joe spoke rapidly, short, sharp sentences. 'And right at the end of the evening. When we were walking to our cars. He told me you were at his apartment. It was like he was waiting till the end of the evening to tell me something that I'd be interested in. Jesus Tess, why didn't you tell me when you called me back? What happened?'

'I didn't want you distracted when you were with Damien. It was going to be hard enough for you. Considering.'

'I've been calling you since I left Damien. Why didn't you answer?'

'You didn't call. I would have … oh shit. My phone's in my bag and it's on silent. Sorry.'

Joe sat back in his chair, visibly relieved that Tessa was safe. 'Okay, did you find his laptop?'

Tessa winked and nodded a slow nod. 'I found a dating site. The same site as Yolanda's.' Then Tessa took a deep breath and bit her bottom lip.

'What's wrong?'

'You were right, Joe. I checked his calendar. Nothing much there. He had the usual court reminders and tonight with you. Then I checked his tasks. One word only. All caps. YOLANDA.'

42

The next morning, Joe opened files, closed files, made coffee, let the coffee go cold, made more coffee. Joe's mind flitted between how to gather evidence against Damien, concerns for Paul. And now Sammy. Dean had called Joe on the weekend to tell him the sad news about Sammy. Sammy's health had rapidly deteriorated. Dean made the tough but kind decision to let Sammy go in peace.

'I'm going with you,' Tessa said.

'Where?'

'To Sammy's memorial. I'm going with you. You need support. And I loved Sammy too.'

'The files …'

'We'll be back in an hour. I can take an hour for Dean—and Sammy.'

***

Joe and Tessa joined Dean's family and friends, mainly police and retired police, for Sammy's memorial. They gathered under a large fig tree in the park where Sammy and Bonnie enjoyed many hours together playing and chasing frisbees. The sun filtered through the gaps in thick cumulus clouds.

Dean's hand shook as he read from his prepared tribute to Sammy. 'Sammy was born in Sydney ...' he stopped. 'I don't need this.' He screwed the paper into a ball and put it in his pocket. He removed his reading glasses, rubbed his eyes, and then looked at the gathering. 'Sammy's in my heart. I ...' He paused and took a deep breath. 'Ol' Sammy was my mate till the end. He was born twelve years ago, next month. Sammy's pedigree was more than impressive. His mum and his dad were police dogs. Sammy's grandmother was a New Zealand police dog.' Dean didn't wipe away the tears that ran down his ruddy cheeks. 'But Sammy was the runt of the litter. And the trainers, well, they didn't hold much faith in him at the start. He was quiet and wasn't as high spirited as his brothers and sisters. The trainers didn't think he was as smart as his siblings. Well, he wasn't the smartest, but he wasn't the dumbest either. But God knows, he was ...' Dean's voice wavered. He hesitated, bit his lower lip, and then composed himself. '... he was loyal, he was conscientious, he was a worker. And he was a true hero. The bond between us was instant, and it was strong. Together we grew, and we learned from each other. Mostly I learned from him. I learned to trust him—always. When we were tracking, and logic told me we were going in the wrong direction, we weren't. My logic was wrong. Sammy was always right. He was never wrong—never. We know nothing can replace a dog's nose for finding people, and Sammy was one of the best at searching and tracking. During his career he found toddlers lost in the bush, even a neighbour's missing dog.' Dean smiled at the memory. 'And he was responsible for over a hundred arrests. He was happiest when he was working. But gentle as a kitten at home when he was off duty. If I were to put all my feelings on paper, I could write volumes about Sammy, and yet there are not enough adjectives in the dictionary to describe the beauty of his nature and the unconditional love he showed me. Nobody had a better friend. Deciding that Monday ...' The words caught in his throat. He paused, closed his eyes, and breathed deeply. 'Deciding that Monday was Sammy's last day on earth was the second most painful thing I've ever done.' Dean's voice broke. He sobbed. 'Watching him suffer was the most painful. I miss you, Sammy.' Dean paused again and composed himself. 'Dr Seuss said, "Don't cry because it's over. Smile because it happened." ... My eyes are crying, but my heart is smiling with the memory of Sammy's love. God rest you, Sammy, my best mate.'

At the end of the memorial, Tessa watched Joe take Dean's hand in his and put an arm around his shoulder as he whispered in his ear. Dean hugged Joe and kissed him on the side of his face.

When they got in the car to head back to the station, Tessa asked Joe what he said to Dean. 'Tell me it's none of my business if it's private.'

'I told him ...' Joe put the key in the ignition just as his mobile rang. 'When? We're on our way, be there in twenty.'

'Who was that? What's wrong?'

'Trudi. She's at the station. She'd been out in the morning and when she got home, Paul's car was gone. He must have caught a taxi home from the hospital. He left without being discharged.'

43

Paul parked his car outside the dilapidated single-storey red brick house. The gathering clouds turned the afternoon sky grey, reflecting his mood. He looked at his watch. It was still early, ten minutes to one. The gloom of the afternoon made it feel much later. *It is late,* Paul thought. *Too late for me.*

His hand shook as he reached into the glove box for his Glock. A kookaburra laughed at Paul from a distance. He held the gun in his hand, felt the smooth, cold black metal, and contemplated what he was about to do. Despite the cool afternoon, perspiration dripped from his brow. He placed the gun on the seat next to him and grabbed his water bottle instead. Water splashed down his chin as he gulped from the bottle. He put the bottle against his forehead, rolling it from side to side, trying to massage away the heat and the building tension. Five minutes passed, then ten. He re-read his note to Trudi and Joe. *I have to do this,* he told himself. But the pain in his pulsating temples and nausea in the pit of his stomach overtook his resolve. He put his foot on the brake. Started the engine. Put the car in drive. And without checking for other cars left a trail of black rubber as he screeched a U-turn.

I have to do this, he told himself again. His resolve returned. Paul won the battle against the nausea and the headache before he reached the next intersection. He made another U-turn and pulled up again in front of the sixties' red-brick house. He put his car in park and turned off the engine. Before he changed his mind, he put the note in his pocket, grabbed the gun, got out of the car, and slammed the door behind him. He opened the squeaky front gate and strode up the footpath overrun by weeds growing through the cracked concrete.

Paul banged on the faded green front door with a clenched fist. He waited ten seconds. No answer. He peered inside the cobweb-covered window. Saw no movement inside. He banged on the door again with more force this time.

Moments later, a gravelly voice yawned from inside. 'Who is it?'

'The police. Detective Paul Shipway. Open the door. Now.'

Johnson opened the door. He wore only underpants, and a singlet stained with what appeared to be a red spaghetti sauce. His face, covered in black stubble, looked like it hadn't seen a razor for over a week. His singlet looked and smelled as though he'd taken it out of the dirty linen basket instead of putting it in the washing machine. A black serpent tattoo slithered up his right bicep and shoulder. The serpent's red forked tongue kissed his neck.

'Do you dress like that when you're cooking at your parents' restaurant?'

'I'm on leave—stress leave, after what you guys put me through. What are you doing here, anyway? You shithead, poor excuse for a cop.'

'Stress leave? Is that what they call it when even your own parents don't want you working for them?' Paul sneered. 'You'll be on permanent leave when I'm finished with you.'

'What are you talking about? Piss off.' Johnson spat through tobacco-stained teeth. 'I don't have to talk to you anymore.' He started to close the door. Paul stopped the door with his foot.

'What are you doing? Piss off you bag of shit.'

'Aren't you going to invite me in?' Paul said as he pushed past Johnson into the house. The house stunk of cigarettes and stale beer. Blow flies buzzed over empty pizza cartons on the coffee table.

'What do you think you're doing?' Johnson reached for his mobile. 'I'm calling the police.'

Paul pointed his gun towards Johnson. 'Did you forget? I *am* the police.'

'What do you want? Put the gun away, you crazy shit.' Johnson's voice was a high shrill. 'What're you doing?'

'Julie Porter. You threatened her. That's why she didn't testify.'

'I don't know what you're talking about.'

'You raped and bashed her. You and your sleazy mate.' Paul took a step closer, raised the gun, pointed it at Johnson's chest. 'And later you threatened her. You told her that her little sister was next if she told anyone.'

'You don't know what you're talking about. I was found not guilty.' Rancid-smelling sweat slithered, like his serpent tattoo, from his armpit to his already filthy singlet.

'A not guilty verdict doesn't mean shit.' Paul pointed the gun at Johnson's head. 'Not guilty doesn't mean innocent.'

'Put the gun down. What do you want?' He backed away and bumped into the coffee table, upsetting the pizza cartons, beer cans, overflowing ashtrays and tattered pornographic magazines.

Paul pointed the gun at Johnson's mobile. 'Pick it up. Ring Julie. She's expecting your call. You've got her number. Apologise to her. Tell her you will never threaten her again. Tell her what

268

you did to her was evil. But she's safe now and so is her sister.'

Tears ran down Johnson's grimy face. 'Will you leave if I call her?' Spittle dripped from his mouth to his chin.

Paul pointed the gun at Johnson's head again. 'Call her, you cowardly excuse for a human being.'

Johnson picked up his mobile, and after two shaky attempts that resulted in two wrong numbers, called Julie. 'Sss … sorry. What I did … it was bad. Your sister … I won't touch her. I promise …You're both safe. I …' Paul grabbed the mobile from him, threw it on the floor and crushed it with his feet.

'What are you doing? I did what you told me.'

'Yes, you did. But you didn't mean it.' Paul raised his gun again, pointed it at Johnson's forehead. 'I'm going to make sure you're sorry—really sorry.'

'I am. I am sorry. Leave me alone,' Johnson pleaded.

'I'll leave you alone. I'll leave you alone when I'm done.' Paul readjusted his aim to Johnson's chest, then back to his forehead. 'Where do you want it?'

Johnson covered his face with his hands, fell to his knees. 'No, no …you don't want to do this,' he howled through his tears.

'You're wrong. I do want to do this.' Paul realigned his aim. 'And I'm going to do this.' He jolted backwards when he heard a car backfiring. Then he realised what he'd done. *No, not a car backfiring. It was my gun. I did it.* He looked at Johnson. Saw the shock on his face. Saw the blood radiating from the area where Johnson's testicles used to be.

'You might need a doctor to check that out for you. By the way, your raping days are over.' Paul rang an ambulance and left.

Paul felt a calm come over him he hadn't felt since he first solo sailed on Lake Macquarie. He drove to his next destination, ignoring the incessant ringing of his mobile phone.

44

Trudi was pacing in the reception area when Joe and Tessa arrived back at the station from Sammy's memorial. She ran over to them, clutching her mobile. 'He's not answering. Something's wrong.'

Tessa put an arm around Trudi's shoulder and led her into their office.

Joe kept ringing Paul's mobile while Tessa tried to reassure Trudi that Paul would be okay. After a few minutes, Tessa looked past Trudi towards Joe. He could see the concern and the questioning in her eyes. He shook his head and tried Paul's mobile again.

Trudi stood. 'I can't sit here doing nothing. I'm going to the hospital. Find out what happened.'

'Paul is fine,' Tessa said. 'He's probably questioning a witness or a suspect and doesn't want to stop the interview. You should stay here and wait for him. Paul wouldn't want you driving while you're worried about him.'

Trudi fumbled in her bag for her car keys. 'I have to do something. I can drive. I'll be okay.'

Joe knew Tessa's reassuring words didn't convince Trudi. They didn't convince him, either. He could feel his heart thumping and his stomach starting to churn. 'I could do with some air. If you're sure you can drive, I'll walk you to your car.'

Joe took Trudi by the elbow when they reached her car. 'Paul is okay. He's going to be fine.' He kissed her on the cheek and opened her door. 'I'll call you.'

When he returned, Joe took his mobile out of his pocket to try Paul again. It rang just as he selected Paul's name from his favourites. He answered, frowned, and mouthed 'Damien' to Tessa.

He could hear Damien shouting on the other end of the phone. He could hear him but couldn't comprehend, or didn't want to comprehend, what Damien was saying. Joe couldn't move, couldn't speak.

Tessa picked up snippets of what Damien was saying. 'Police … Paul …Get over here … Now.'

Joe dropped his mobile and slumped in the chair. 'Paul, no… what have you done?'

Tessa picked up the mobile. 'What is it? What's wrong, Damien?' Silence, then, 'No, shit no, holy mother of God, no.'

Tessa's voice reached Joe's ears from a faraway tunnel. 'C'mon Joe. We've got to get over there.'

She rang Olivia as they ran to the car. 'We need you. Joe needs you—now. Meet us at the car. Hurry, Olivia.'

***

Tessa double parked outside Damien's office building thirty-five minutes after the call. Joe jumped out of the car and ran two steps at a time up the two flights to Damien's office. Sarah, the receptionist, sat behind the counter, dabbing her eyes with a tissue. Damien stood next to the receptionist counter, talking to the police. Joe pushed his way past the police, grabbed Damien, and shook him. 'Where's Paul?'

Damien pushed Joe away. 'What are you doing? No need to shove. Have you gone crazy too? He's in my office.'

Tessa and Olivia arrived at the reception area just as Joe raced towards Damien's office.

Joe opened the door and started to walk in. When he saw his friend lying dead on the floor, his head in a pool of blood, he froze and took a step back. He swayed and leaned against the door frame for support.

'Joe.' Olivia tugged at his elbow. 'C'mon, Joe. Look away. Come out of there.'

Joe heard Olivia's voice, but her words didn't register. He couldn't move. He didn't want to look. But he didn't want to not look.

He stood motionless for a full minute. His mouth opened, but he couldn't speak. Then he felt the heat rising through his body as shock and dismay turned to anger. He bashed his fist against the door. He turned and marched over to Damien. 'What happened—every detail? You son of a bitch. What did you do?'

'Take it easy. I did nothing. It's not my fault.'

'Sure it is,' Joe shouted. 'Everything…' He didn't wipe the spit that ran down his chin. 'Everything is your fault. What happened, Damien? Tell me what happened.'

'Okay. Just calm down.' Damien put both hands up in a surrender gesture. 'Paul told Sarah he had an appointment with me. He didn't. I was in my office, I heard him shout at her. "I've got an appointment with him, Sarah, I'm going in." I stood just as he slammed open my office door.' Damien walked over to examine the door. 'At least it doesn't look damaged.' He frowned. 'Actually, there's a small dent where you just punched it.'

Joe sensed Tessa move towards Damien. He put an arm out to stop her. Through clenched teeth, he articulated each word slowly. 'How did it happen? What did Paul do?'

Damien walked back to the reception area. 'He implied I'm a narcissist. No, he didn't imply. Paul accused me of being a narcissist. He said, "This vision is for you. I hope it haunts you for the rest of your narcissistic life." And then he put the gun to his head and shot himself. Shit, the blood. What a mess. I'll need to replace the carpet. I'll make sure the department pays for the clean-up.'

Joe stared at Damien. His heart pounded. His nostrils flared. His breathing was rapid and shallow. Then, as the adrenalin rush became too much for him, Joe threw a right hook that landed Damien on the floor, smashing the glass coffee table as he fell backward. Blood spurted from Damien's skull, streaking the broken shards of glass, and staining the grey carpet red. Joe didn't hear Sarah's ear-splitting scream. He ignored Olivia pleading with him to stop. He straddled Damien. 'You'll rot in hell for what you've done. Everything you've done,' he said as he pummelled Damien with continuous right hooks until the police grabbed him and dragged him away.

'What's got into you?' Damien said, as Sarah helped him to his feet. 'I thought we were friends.'

Joe glared at Damien. 'Don't talk to me about friendship. You are a narcissistic ...' Joe stopped himself before he called Damien a murderer. He turned to Sarah, who was staring at him, her face stained with mascara and smudged lipstick. 'You have no idea who your boss is, do you?'

Damien shouted after him as the officers motioned Joe towards the door. 'You and the department are going to pay for this. Pay big time.'

Joe shrugged off the officers and turned to reply to Damien.

'You …' He stopped when he saw Olivia walking out of Damien's office, holding an envelope. She handed it to him. It was addressed to Joe.

One of the officers reached out for the envelope. 'I'll take that. It's evidence.'

Joe looked at him with a raised eyebrow as he took the note out of the envelope. The officer dropped his arm.

Joe read the note from Paul.

You're my best friend Joe. You were right. At the station, when you asked me not to force you to live with the vision of me dying. I understood. You were right. You don't deserve it. So, I saved it for Damien. He deserves the vision.

The world is in despair. I'm in despair. I can't do it anymore.

I love you, Joe. Don't cry for me.

Don't cry for me, Trudi. I love you with all my heart. Goodbye, my love.

Joe put the note back in the envelope and handed it to the officer. 'Read my lips, Damien. *You* will pay.'

45

The fingerprints comparing the pair of broken glasses left at the scene of Yolanda's attack with the empty glass Damien left behind at the barbeque came back inconclusive. Not conclusive enough to convince the magistrate there were reasonable grounds for a search warrant for Damien's apartment.

'We're back to square one.' Joe paced. 'With a warrant, Damien's laptop would have come into play. His location data on his mobile and the GPS in his car. Proof where he's been and when. Exact time and place. We just need to …' He walked to the window.

Tessa followed him to the window. 'Do you think you're telling me something I don't know?'

'I know. I'm sorry. I just need to … I'm rambling.' Joe walked back to his desk. 'I just can't focus. I keep seeing Paul, the blood … I …'

'We *have* to focus.' Tessa sat. 'We can't let anything happen to Yolanda.'

Joe sighed as he closed his eyes and clasped his hands behind his head, his elbows cradling his face. After a moment, he looked over at Tessa. 'We have to go to Bathurst. Talk to Yolanda. Show her Damien's photo.'

'Damien has similar physical features to Kowalski and Sanders. And to you. Do you remember when we showed her Sanders and Kowalski's photos?'

'She said it could have been either of them,' Joe conceded. 'But Yolanda is our best chance. Damien's photo might jog her memory about some other detail.'

Tessa sprang from her chair. 'Shit, shit, holy shit.' She waved her mobile in Joe's face. 'He'll know now where she is and what she's doing. Look at this. I'm sure we told her to delete her Facebook account.'

Joe looked at a photo of Yolanda with two other women. The caption read, 'Welcome home, Yolanda. So happy you're back teaching with us.'

'She didn't post it.' Joe said. 'Her friend obviously tagged her. But you're right. We did tell her to delete her account. All the more reason to go to Bathurst. If we leave now, we can be there by five, five-thirty at the latest.'

'I'll call her. Tell her we're on our way and delete her Facebook account immediately.' Tessa looked at her watch. 'She's probably in class. I'll leave a message.'

***

'Take a right here, then a left.' Tessa checked Google maps on her mobile. 'And another left. Over there. There's a McCafé. You get the coffees. I'll call Yolanda, let her know we're only fifteen minutes away.'

Joe had just ordered the coffee when Tessa ran up behind him. 'We have to go. She's not there. He must have her.' Tessa continued as they ran back to the car, 'She didn't answer her mobile. I rang her parents. She didn't come home from school. They'd rung her mobile, school, her friends. Nobody has seen or heard from her since school finished this afternoon. They contacted Bathurst police. The police are looking for her now. Her car is still in the school yard.'

Joe stopped to check his mobile before getting in the car.

'What are you doing?' Tessa shouted. 'We're running out of time. Just get in the car and drive.'

Joe exited the McDonald's car park and headed south.

Tessa pointed. 'No, you're going the wrong way. We should be heading north.'

'He's taking her somewhere near the river. And he's heading south.'

'What? Why?'

'That's why I was checking my mobile. Hold on ...' Joe checked over his right shoulder, accelerated and overtook an old slow-moving VW. 'I'm tracking him.'

'Joe? You're what?'

Joe heard the disbelief in Tessa's voice. 'Remember what you said. We can bend the rules if it means stopping Damien. When I had dinner with him, he went to the gents. And he was gone long enough for me to set it up.'

'How did you get into his mobile?

'Easy. His password was only going to be one of two. It wasn't NotGuilty, the password you said he uses for his laptop. So, it had to be his mother's birth year. He uses that for most things. You know that.'

'Right. Pray it works and we get there in time. So, why didn't you check sooner?

'I did. This morning. He was still at home. And later he was at the office.' Joe accelerated a few kilometres beyond the speed limit. 'He was following his normal weekday routine.'

They drove for twenty minutes. The trees and landscape were a green blur as they sped along the highway.

'We're too late,' Tessa said. 'He's had her too long.'

Joe slowed as a kangaroo hopped on the road and then back into the bush. 'Do we know what time Yolanda left the classroom?'

'No. She told her parents in the morning that she would be staying back after school for a while to prepare lessons for the next day. That's why they weren't initially concerned when she didn't get home at the normal time.'

'So we don't know how long he's had her.' Joe overtook a semi-trailer. 'He might not be far ahead.'

They drove another ten minutes. 'Over there.' Tessa pointed. 'His car. Over there, behind the trees. Near the river.'

Tessa threw open her door and jumped out of the car before Joe had fully stopped.

He put the car in park and raced after her to the riverbank.

'They're not here,' Tessa shouted. 'They're not here. It's going to be dark soon. We'll never find them.'

Joe turned three sixty degrees, looking up and down the riverbank, into the bush leading back to Damien's car. Then he stopped and pointed to the water's edge. 'There's footprints. In the sand.' He ran over to study the prints closer. 'They went north.'

They ran two hundred metres along the riverbank. Tessa caught up with Joe when he stopped suddenly. He pointed towards the bush. 'Over there. I heard something.'

A piercing scream from the direction Joe was pointing was followed a split second later by a flock of shrieking lorikeets protesting the sudden noise and abandoning their evening resting place.

More screams.

It took Joe and Tessa less than fifteen seconds to find the source of the screams.

Damien had Yolanda pushed up against a tree. His hands around her throat.

Joe fired a warning shot in the air. 'It's over, Damien,' he shouted. 'Let her go.'

Damien wrenched Yolanda in front of him and held her by the throat as he reached for his gun.

'Put your gun down,' Joe shouted. 'It's over.'

'You put yours down, or she's dead.' Damien pushed his gun into the side of Yolanda's head.

'You've got the shot … kill him, kill him.' Tessa's screams were silenced in Joe's head by Amber's mother's words … *don't kill him … death is too good for him … death is too good for him …* Echoes in Joe's head … *death is too good for him. Don't kill him.*

'Jesus, Joe. Take the shot. Kill him.'

'Drop the gun, Joe.' Damien pushed his gun into Yolanda's head with more force. 'Drop it. Or she's dead. Then you and your slutty lesbian friend will be next.'

Joe was less than five metres from Damien. He looked into Damien's eyes and for the first time since he'd met Damien more than twenty-five years ago, he saw the real Damien. He saw satanic darkness and hate oozing from his eyes.

Yolanda struggled to free herself from Damien's grip. 'Please, please … let me go.' Mud and tears streaked her face. Her long hair was matted with leaves and twigs from either falling or being dragged by Damien through the dense bush.

Damien aimed his gun at Joe. 'Drop your gun'

'It's no use Damien,' Joe yelled. 'You're outnumbered. Let Yolanda go. And drop your gun or you're a dead man.'

'Maybe. But I'll take at least one of you with me,' Damien yelled back.

Joe looked from the monster's eyes to Yolanda's terrified and pleading eyes.

What followed unfolded in slow motion for Joe, but only took seconds in real time.

Joe lowered his gaze towards Damien's left ankle. 'Tess, how deadly are Eastern browns?'

Damien took his eyes off Joe for a split second. He looked down in the direction of Joe's gaze, causing his gun hand to move centimetres away from Yolanda's head. A split second was long enough for Joe to take aim and shoot the gun out of Damien's hand. Blood spurted from his wrist. He shrieked in pain. Despite the pain Damien managed to wrap his injured arm around Yolanda. He pulled a large double-edged knife with his uninjured hand from the leather knife pouch around his waist. He plunged it towards Yolanda. Tessa reached him in time to kickbox the knife from his hands. Damien raised his hands in surrender and dropped to his knees. Suddenly he grabbed the gun still lying on the ground. He aimed at Joe, fired, and missed as Tessa dislodged the gun from his hand with another kickbox. 'Not so good with your left hand, are you?'

Joe stood over Damien. 'Stand. By the way. There was no snake.'

Damien didn't move. His eyes darted from Tessa to Damien, back to Tessa.

Joe saw confusion in Damien's eyes. 'It's over Damien. Stand. I've won this contest. Our last contest.'

Damien looked towards the river as he slowly stood.

'There's no escape for you. It's over,' Joe said as he walked towards Damien, still aiming the gun at him. 'I said it's over.' He stared into Damien's dark eyes. 'But it's not quite over. This one is for Paul.' The bullet from Joe's gun shattered Damien's kneecap.

Damien screamed obscenities at Joe that a Hells Angels bikie would be proud of.

Tessa grimaced. 'I imagine that hurts.'

Joe looked at Tessa. 'I guess ... I guess ... I shouldn't have ...but ...'

'He shouldn't have tried to run,' Tessa said with a wry smile. 'You had no choice.' She looked at Damien's mangled and bloodied knee. 'I guess there won't be any rugby for you in prison.'

46

Joe stood, leaning his arms on the wide timber railing of his deck, deep in thought. A cup of lukewarm coffee sat untouched on the railing next to his elbow. He watched the sun turn the drifting clouds red and pink as it slowly sank towards the tree-lined horizon.

Joe closed his eyes and inhaled the soft scent of his flowering gardenias. His thoughts drifted like the clouds in the sky, with nowhere in particular to go and in no particular time.

He thought about Paul's memorial service the day before. Why did the sun still shine? What right did the birds have—to still sing, as though the world hadn't changed? The world *has* changed. Paul isn't in it anymore. But the world hasn't changed. It was Joe's world that changed—again. His mother's words came back to him. *You didn't cry when your father died.* He didn't cry when Paul died, either.

Joe's thoughts drifted again. He thought about Dean. Thought about how Dean allows himself to let go and isn't afraid to show emotion or shed a tear, even in public. Letting go is Dean's survival mechanism. Not afraid to share his emotions with Lorna. Accept her support. When Dean was in the department, it was how he overcame the physical and emotional stress of police work. But Dean's a professional. He's always in control when the situation calls for control. He thought of how Dean's belief that one person can make a difference, gave him the strength to go on when he was in the force. It was why he pleaded with Joe to stay. *Whoever saves one life saves the world.*

Joe thought of Sammy's reaction to Damien at the barbeque, and then of Tessa's question in the car, 'What did you say to Dean at the end of Sammy's memorial?'

I told him that Sammy was a police dog to the end. He helped us track down a killer.

Joe thought about Tessa—thought about how often he had to remind her to take control. And recently, how the tables have turned, and Tessa has had to remind him to take control. Was he losing his self-control? Or was he, like Dean, starting to allow himself to show his emotions. Tess is never afraid to show her emotions. Often anger at the atrocities that people inflict on each other. But not only on other human beings ... also the pain and cruelty they inflict on animals. He looked over at Bonnie—safe now from that pain and cruelty.

He thought about Alex's question at the beach the morning the surfer and his dog found Phoebe's body. 'How do you sleep at night ... facing horror and tragedy every day?'

'Sleep? It doesn't come easy, Alex. A lot of nights I don't.'

Then Joe's thoughts turned back to Paul. Paul cried, showed his emotions, and he tried to bury his emotions in alcohol. Nothing helped Paul cope. Dean copes. Tessa copes. Paul couldn't. Then Joe thought of his father. Like Paul, his father turned to alcohol. And like Dean, his father wasn't afraid to show his emotions. But he still didn't cope. Why? There's no answer. How could he survive if his father couldn't survive? This job. No. It's not a job. It's his life. He lives it with every breath he takes. He couldn't imagine any other life. But was this life destroying him?

Was he heading in the same direction as his father ... and Paul? Joe didn't want to think about Paul or his father that way. He wanted to remember only the gentleness he often saw in Paul's eyes that reminded him of the same gentleness in his father's eyes. Two wonderful people who were here for a short time. But while they were here, they made a difference. Joe thought of Dean's Dr Seuss quote at Sammy's memorial. 'Don't cry because it's over. Smile because it happened.' *Dad and Paul. Imagine what the world would be like if everyone were like them, if ...* Joe shrugged. *Stop dreaming,* he told himself. *People are what they are.*

Joe's guitar rested on the table next to him. He considered it, picked it up, sat and strummed a few chords with unpractised fingers. Then a few more chords, until his strumming morphed into John Lennon's 'Imagine'. Bonnie inched closer to Joe. Lost in thought now about his father and Paul, Joe didn't notice Bonnie. Still not aware of Bonnie, Joe's eyes watered. His throat constricted with the effort of holding back the tears that stung his eyes. Then, no longer able to hold back those tears, he wept. Joe cried like he'd never cried in his life. The release was a long time coming. Too long—fifteen years. Fifteen years, almost to the day since his father committed suicide. Bonnie rested her paw on his leg and looked up at him. Joe, surprised at Bonnie's touch, the gentle pressure of her paw on his leg, looked into her brown eyes. Those gentle eyes that touched his soul. He saw love, and he saw complete trust at last in the depths of those eyes. Joe stopped sobbing, put down his guitar and hugged Bonnie. The bond he and Bonnie formed at that moment was the start of their healing journey they would travel together.

After a moment, Joe reached for his mobile and called Olivia. 'Bonnie and I are going for a moonlight stroll along the beach. Would you like to join us?'

A few seconds later, Joe smiled and ended the call.

A Note from the Author

If you enjoyed this book, I would be very grateful if you could write a review and publish it at your point of purchase. Your review, even a brief one, will help other readers to decide if they'll enjoy my work.

If you want to be notified of new releases from myself and other AIA Publishing authors, please **sign up to the AIA Publishing email list**. You'll find the sign-up button on the right-hand side under the photo at **www.aiapublishing.com**. Of course, your information will never be shared, and the publisher won't inundate you with emails, just let you know of new releases.

Acknowledgments

I would like to thank my editors Tahlia Newland, Alida Sewell and Barbara Scott Emmett for their assistance in refining my work, and a big thanks to the AIA Publishing team for bringing this story to publication.

9 781922 329288